Last Orders
and Other Stories

Brian W. Aldiss

JONATHAN CAPE
THIRTY BEDFORD SQUARE LONDON

First published 1977
Jonathan Cape Ltd, 30 Bedford Square, London WC1

Individual stories © Brian W. Aldiss 1973, 1974, 1975, 1976
and © Southmoor Serendipity Ltd 1977
This collection © Southmoor Serendipity Ltd 1977

British Library Cataloguing in Publication Data

Aldiss, Brian Wilson
Last orders, and other stories.
I. Title
823'.9'1FS   PR6051.L3

ISBN 0 224 01487 0

Printed in Great Britain by The Anchor Press Ltd,
Tiptree, Essex

For Philip, Jane, & Co.
with love

Contents

Acknowledgments

'Last Orders' was published in *S.F. Digest No. 1*, 1976. 'Diagrams for Three Stories' was published originally as 'Diagrams for Three Enigmatic Stories' in *Final Stages*, 1974. 'Live? Our Computers Will Do That For Us', was published in *Orbit 15*, 1974. 'Monster of Ingratitude IV', was published in *Nova 4*, 1974. 'The Aperture Moment' was published in *Epoch*, 1976. 'The Expensive Delicate Ship' was published in *Nova 3*, 1973. 'An Appearance of Life' was published in *Andromeda 1*, 1976. 'Wired for Sound' was published as 'Listen with Big Brother' in *Punch*, 1974. 'Journey to the Heartland' was published in *Universe 6*, 1976. 'The Eternal Theme of Exile', 'Three Coins in Clockwork Fountains' (as 'Three Coins in Enigmatic Fountains'), 'Year By Year the Evil Gains', and 'Creatures of Apogee' were published in *New Writings in Science Fiction*, Nos 23, 26, 27, and 31 respectively, in 1973, 1975, 1976, and 1977 respectively.

My thanks go to the editors, in most cases my friends (how else ... ?), of these excellent publications.

The excerpt from W. H. Auden's poem 'Musée des Beaux Arts' comes from *Collected Shorter Poems 1927–57* by W. H. Auden, and is quoted by kind permission of Faber and Faber Ltd.

Author's Note

So this man in the sharp suit pushed his way through the crowd of people.

And at the far end of the smoke-filled room was a guy leaning over a typewriter as big as an upright piano. He just sprawled there, taking no notice of anyone, tapping out a few sentences on the keys. And the man in the sharp suit said, 'What you turn out that fantasy stuff for? Play something happy, something familiar.'

And the guy looked up from his typewriter and kind of smiled, and replied like this:

'I believe in what I do. This is where I sing the science fiction blues. This is my kind of music. I work in an underprivileged, underrated medium, sure, and even within that medium my style offends a whole lot of people. See, I don't mind that antagonism any more. Maybe it powers my typewriter. You have to have something to create *against*, right?'

And the man in the sharp suit said, 'People want to be cheered up. They want to hear about real things.'

'One or the other you can have. Not both. See, my stories are about human woes, non-communication, disappointment, endurance, acceptance, love. Aren't those things real enough? Nobody's fool enough to imagine that any near-future developments will obliterate them. Change there will be ... But the new old blues sing on for ever ... '

The man in the sharp suit said, 'You should use your talent, such as it is, on something positive.'

He pushed his way through the crowd as the other guy

began again to pick a tune from his typewriter. Everyone in the crowd was drinking fast, laughing and gesticulating. They knew the world was going to end next week.

B.W.A.

Last Orders

The alphameter indicated that two people, perhaps more, were somewhere in the block. The Captain took his ACV slowly down the street. There was a canal to his left; its waters churned as if they were living.

He kept the vehicle window open. Gusts of rain, by turns icy and hot, beat against the narrow battlements of his face. They helped him stay awake. His was one of the last rescue parties and he had gone without sleep for over three days.

At the end of the foul little street, a light showed. Oil, probably: electric power had failed long before the city emptied. He sounded his hooter, peering through the murk, through a bar window. A small figure gesticulated in shadow.

The Captain stopped his engine; the craft sank on to cobbles. He waited. The man inside was still talking, or whatever the thing was he was doing. The Captain felt for a pill in his oilskin jacket and squirted it down his throat with a spray from the drink-tube on his dash. Then he climbed out and made his way to the bar. His movements were stiff with controlled weariness. A slate whirled past his head and dashed itself to bits against a bollard by the canal-side. He did not blink.

Pushing the bar door open, he went in. A dim light on a counter revealed the outlines of shambles. The last earth tremor had broken most of the furniture and the bottles behind the bar. Mirrors were cracked. He picked his way forward between shattered floorboards.

At the bar stood a stocky man of indeterminate age, dressed with incongruous neatness in an old-fashioned suit. His round head was covered in a fuzz of colourless hair. Oyster eyes sat in his round face. He was talking with a jovial animation to a thin old lady dressed in black who perched on a high stool, her hands folded together on her lap. A beer stood by her elbow, half finished. The man had a neat little liqueur by him which he had not touched.

Taking all this in at a glance, the Captain said, 'You're supposed to have been out of here hours ago. How come the patrols missed you? In a very few minutes – '

'Yes, yes,' said the stocky man, 'we're just drinking up, we're fully aware of the seriousness of the situation. You look a bit tired – have one with us while we're finishing ours. We'll go together.'

'Leave your drinks. We've got to get to Reijkskeller Field. The last ferry is almost due to leave.' The Captain took the stocky man by the elbow.

'Just a moment. Have a beer. This lady here says it's very good. No, no trouble, won't take a minute. We'll all travel better for another drink.'

He ducked behind the bar and came up smiling with a foaming glass.

'I've got to get you out of here, both of you,' the Captain said. 'Our lives are in danger. You don't seem to realize. The Moon, as you must know, is about to – '

'My dear man,' said the stocky man, coming back round the bar and striking a positive attitude before his untouched liqueur, 'you need not remind us of the gravity of the situation. I was telling this lady here that I was right there on the Moon, in Armstrong, when the first fissure began. I saw it with my own eyes. It was a funny thing, really – you see, I'm a xenobalneologist, specializing in off-Earth swimming pools with all their attendant problems, and you'd never believe how many! – Do you know that there are – or were, I suppose I should say – more swimming pools on Luna than in the

U.S.A.? And I'd just been over to see Wally Kingsmill, who owns – well, his family owns – one of the biggest and most splendid pools in Armstrong, and as I was pavrunning down Ordinary, I could hear people shouting and screaming. First thing you think of on Luna is always that the dome might be damaged. As it happened, I had all my breathing equipment by me – I'd used them in Wally Kingsmill's pool, you see – and I said to myself, "Right," but it wasn't the dome at all – though that went a couple of hours later and it was curious how that happened, but this time it was the crack, it came snaking along, travelling fast in erratic fashion, and zip, it ran under the pavrunner, which stopped. Just stopped dead, just like that – '

'The Moon has been evacuated. Now it's our turn. Now we've got to go. At once,' said the Captain. He felt mist gathering in his brain. 'At once,' he repeated. He took up his beer and sipped it.

'It's a lovely beer,' said the old lady. 'Seems such a shame to waste it.' Her gaze returned to the stocky man on whose every word she fastened avidly.

The stocky man poised himself before his daintily shaped liqueur glass, lifted it, drank it off at a gulp, poured himself another from a green bottle, and resumed his vigil over the glass, all in one movement.

'So of course I climbed off, and it's a curious thing, but that crack reminded me of one on the ceiling of the Sistine Chapel, you know, where Michelangelo painted his – of course, it's in Houston now, and I've studied it many times, being interested in art – in fact, about five years ago, about the time that the President visited Venusberg, I was commissioned – '

'That was seven years ago next month,' said the Captain. 'The President visiting Venusberg. I know because I was on Venus at the time, on a posting to the Space Police. Anyhow, that's immaterial, sir. I must insist you come along now.'

'Immediately.' He trotted behind the counter and poured the old lady another beer. 'You're right, it was seven years ago, because at that time I was under contract to the planetoids. Funnily enough, I was just saying about Michelangelo and, in fact, the grandest pool we put in at the planetoids was finished with a mosaic, consisting of almost a million separate pieces, of Michelangelo's 'Creation', with God reaching out his finger to Adam, you know, covering the entire bottom of the pool. Beautiful. You should go and see it. At least the planetoids will be unaffected by all the gravitational disturbances, or so one hopes.'

Having finished his beer, the Captain could not tell whether he felt worse or better for it. 'Not only are we all three in grave danger, sir, but you and this lady are contravening martial law established ten days ago. I shall be fully within my rights to shoot you down unless you accompany me to my vehicle immediately.'

The stocky man laughed. 'Don't worry, I'm a strong supporter of martial law in the circumstances. What else can you do? I think it's marvellous – a credit to all concerned – the way the evacuation of Earth has gone so smoothly. I just wish that more attention could have been paid to the art treasures; not that I'm criticizing, because I know how little warning we've had, but all the same … You can build more swimming pools, but you can't resurrect Michelangelo from the dead to paint his masterpieces again, can you?'

As he spoke, he stared more and more fixedly at his liqueur glass, which gleamed in the yellow glow of the oil lamp. Suddenly, he pounced on it and drained its contents as swiftly as before, immediately pouring himself another tot. The old lady, meanwhile, climbed down from her stool and was threading her way through debris over to the window.

'Where are you going, ma'am?' the Captain asked, following her. 'I told you to leave.'

'Oh, I won't go away, officer,' she said, laughing at the thought. 'I am as upset about it all as you are. Poor old Earth, after all these millions of years. It's Earth I worry about, not the Moon. The Moon was never much use to us in the first place. I just wanted to see if I could see it out of the window.'

Her words were drowned by a tremendous buffet of wind which shook the whole building and set doors banging and weakened walls collapsing. The window shattered as she reached it; luckily, the shards of glass were swept outwards.

'Oh dear, it's dreadful, what are we coming to? Anyone would think it was the end of the world.'

'It is the fucking end of the world, ma'am,' the Captain said. 'Are you coming, or do I have to carry you?'

'Of course you don't have to carry me. I'm not drunk, if that's what you suspect. You look absolutely worn out. Look, there it is! How I hate it!'

She pointed into the darkness and the Captain stared where she pointed. Furious winds had blown away the cloud. In the night sky, fuming in silver and crimson, was the biggest mountain ever invented, one side of it curved, the other ragged, looming almost to the zenith of the heavens. Gutted lunar cities could clearly be seen across its shattered face. They wondered that it did not fall down upon them as they looked.

Grasping the old lady roughly by the elbow, the Captain said, 'You're getting out of here at once. That's an order. Do you know this guy? Is he your husband?'

When she looked up at him, smiling ruefully, he could trace faded youth among the lines and blemishes of her skin.

'My husband? I only met him today – or yesterday, I suppose. What time is it? Though I wouldn't mind a husband like that, old as I am. I mean, he's so fascinating to talk to. We have a lot in common, despite a few years' difference in age. A very sympathetic man. Do you know, officer, he was telling me a few hours ago, before we came in here – '

'Never mind what he was telling you, we've got to get him out of here. This is a rescue operation, understand? It's urgent, understand? Look at the damned thing out there, arriving fast. What's his name?'

She laughed nervously and looked down at her neat little feet. 'You're going to think this is plain crazy after what I said just now, but I've never married. Not legally married, you understand. My life really hasn't been – this may sound as if I'm terribly sorry for myself, still, you have to face facts – but it hasn't been fortunate as far as the other sex is concerned. Goodness knows what his name is. When I was younger, I was often in despair. Very often. After almost every man left – despair again. Yet I wasn't ugly, you know, or possessive . . . I'm sorry, officer, I realize this heart-searching may not interest you – I'm not a particularly introspective person – '

'Lady, it's not a question of interest, it's a question of desperation. We're going to get ourselves killed if we aren't away from Earth within the next hour – '

'Oh, I know, officer, but that's exactly what I'm complaining about. Don't think I don't feel as bad as you do. As I was saying, I never had luck – you know what I mean? – with men. I was telling our friend here, and he was so sympathetic, that my flat was partially destroyed in the first of the earth tremors, when they first told us that Earth might have to be evacuated. And I couldn't bear to think that my little home, and my garden, and the town where I've lived for over forty years, should have to be left behind. I wept, I'm not ashamed to say it, and I wasn't the only one to weep, by any means – '

'We've all wept, lady, every one of us. This was the planet we were born on, and this is the planet we are going to die on, unless we move fast. Now, come on, for the last time – out!'

The stocky man had put down another dose of liqueur. He came across the broken floor, carrying two beers, his plain face wrinkled in a smile.

'Have a quick one, both of you, before we go. It'll only be wasted. I shouldn't stand by that broken window, it isn't safe. Come back to the bar.'

'Nowhere's safe. Everywhere's doomed. That's why – '

The old lady said, 'I was telling this officer how my flat was partially destroyed and – '

'It'll be totally flattened, with every other building on Earth, in a short while. Now, I appeal to you both for the last time – all right, I'll just drink this beer, all right – look, I'm exhausted, and I know your flat was ruined, but I'm appealing to you both – '

'You know my flat was ruined!' the old lady exclaimed with anger. 'What do you care about my flat? You just don't listen to what I'm trying to say. I told you about this first earth tremor, when my chest-of-drawers fell over, flat on its face. I was in bed at the time – '

The Captain, with a certain weary sense of unreality, drew his gun, stepping back a pace to cover them both. He clutched his half-finished beer in his other hand.

'That's enough. Silence, both of you. Vehicle outside. Out of here, move!'

'You've got a funny way of going about things, I must say,' the stocky man said, shaking his head in regret. 'What's the point of violence at a time like this? At any time, really, but particularly at a time like this, when the whole world is about to be crushed out of existence?'

In his stance and gestures, he presented a vitality which the Captain experienced as an assault on his own depleted resources. He found himself saying apologetically, 'I don't want violence, I'm just trying to do my duty and –'

'We've heard that one before, haven't we?' said the stocky man to the old lady, but in such a jovial way that even the Captain could not take offence. 'Duty, indeed! You ought to hear this lady's story, it's an extremely nice little anecdote – far more than an anecdote, really, a – what's the word?'

'An epic?' the Captain suggested. 'No time left for epics.'

'Not an epic, man – a vignette, that's the word, a vignette of a life. You see, when her chest-of-drawers crashed over, the lady was in bed, as she has related –'

'It was two o'clock in the morning – of course I was in bed,' said the old lady, as if something improper had been suggested.

'And this chest-of-drawers had belonged to her mother.' As he talked, the stocky man led the way back to the bar, giving the old lady a chance to say to the Captain, *sotto voce*, 'In fact, it's been in the family for several generations. It was a very valuable piece, dating from the mid-nineteenth century.'

The stocky man lifted a full liqueur glass from the counter, drained it swiftly, refilled it instantly from the bottle, standing with his plump hands palm-down on the bar, one on either side of the brimming glass, and managed to complete these manoeuvres almost without a break in his speech.

'So she put on the light – still working fortunately because, if you remember, the first tremor was not severe – in fact a good many people, myself included, I might add, slept right through it. In fact, I'd only just gone to bed, being a bit of a night bird – it was early for me – and she climbed out to see what damage had been done and bless me if the chest hadn't split right down the back, revealing a secret drawer. She had known about the secret drawer but she had forgotten it, the way you do, quite unpredictably, just as you can unpredictably remember something. You see how this ceiling is cracked? We were talking about the cracks in the Sistine Chapel ceiling, but you notice on this ceiling that the cracks mostly run in pretty straight lines. When I was telling you both about the Michelangelo painting, I happened to notice these cracks here, and even as I was speaking I saw that they form a perfect map of a sector of this city which I used to live in when I was an engineering student, and that's going back some thirty years.'

At this point, he made a swoop on his liqueur glass and downed its contents. Seizing her opportunity, the old lady said smoothly, 'And it must have been thirty years since I had used that secret drawer. I put something in that drawer thirty years ago and some trick of the mind – as you say, it's quite unpredictable what you forget and what you remember, particularly when you're getting on in years – some trick of the mind made me forget it entirely until the tremor. And what do you think I'd put in there?'

The Captain went behind the bar and helped himself to another beer.

'I'll put it to you another way,' he said. 'If you aren't out of here by the time I've finished this beer, I'm going to shoot myself.' He set the service revolver down solemnly on the counter and raised the glass to his lips.

'Cheers! I hid a secret diary in that drawer. Mind you, I was no chicken, even then. It dated from my late thirties … ' She paused to sob.

'Don't fret,' the stocky man said, passing her another beer. 'I used to keep a diary for years, and much good it did me. One day, I said to my brother, "Look at all these dreary old – " Ah, wait, yes – there you are, another instance of how memory is unpredictable! I believe I've got an engagement diary in my pocket which contains a map – yes, here we are!'

He brought a little diary out and began thumbing his way towards the back of it.

'I've nearly finished this beer – ' cautioned the Captain.

'Let me get you another,' said the old lady, coming round behind the counter with him, 'because I would like to tell you this rather romantic story before you go.'

'I say, isn't this pleasant?' exclaimed the stocky man, spreading open his diary with a heavy hand and looking up with a smile as he did so. 'You'd never think this was the end of the world, would you? I can't see myself being happy on any other world – not really happy, I mean. Anyhow, here you are, here's the map. I thought I'd find it. Better get my reading spectacles ... ' He began a search of his pockets and then, catching sight of the liqueur glass with a meniscus of drink crowning it, seized that instead, to pause with it half way to his lips. He pressed his lips with the fingers of his other hand and set the glass down on the counter again. 'You know, I believe I'll join you in a glass of beer,' he said, amazed at his own whim.

'Coming up,' said the old lady. 'You know, I think you're right. It *is* nice here. I haven't been up so late in years – well, not since I was in Norfolk, staying with my cousin Beth last May – and I don't feel a bit tired. You don't happen to have a cigarette, do you?'

'There are some packets on this shelf,' said the Captain, reaching for them. 'I'd just spotted them myself. Let's all light up! I'm not supposed to smoke on duty but, after all, these are rather special circumstances ... '

They all laughed, suddenly happy, lighting up cigarettes, puffing away, pulling at their beers, instinctively moving closer in the warm light of the oil lamp. Wind whistled outside. Somewhere nearby there was the escalating rumble of a building collapsing under the weight in the sky.

'It's moments like this that make life, don't you agree?' said the stocky man. 'Far too few of them, that must be admitted. Poor old Earth, I wonder if it'll miss mankind, just a little bit?'

' 'Course it won't,' said the Captain, drinking deeply. 'Mankind has just been a sort of parasite on the face of the Earth, despoiling it, ravishing its fair face. Those stupid gravity experiments on the Moon – they've brought us to this miserable pass, but we're only leaving a world we've ruined steadily, century by century – '

'Oh, I'm afraid I can't agree with that at all, really I can't,' said the old lady, puffing at her cigarette. 'I have a lovely garden at my flat – I wish you could see it – it'll be spoilt, of course, when the Moon crashes – though the roses are very hardy – I've got a lovely show of Queen Elizabeths, I wonder if perhaps they won't survive? And just opposite, there's the park – '

'Quite agree,' said the stocky man. He patted her arm. 'I think we improved the place. It was nothing but jungle till mankind got going. I love cities, theatres, music – swimming pools, naturally, but you'd expect me to say that – and all these snug little bars where you can get together with a few kindred spirits and talk. Take this dear old city – well, here's a map, very small scale, but let me show you where the roads take on the exact configuration of the cracks over our heads ... It's not a very good diary.'

'I was saying about my old diary,' said the old lady. 'Actually, I didn't find it till the morning after the tremor, and there it was, exactly where I'd left it thirty years earlier. And I opened it, and on the last page, after December 31st – just fancy, no more December 31sts ... you can hardly imagine it, can you?'

'That's one day I can do without,' said the Captain, and laughed.

'Ah, but it's the day before New Year's Day,' said the stocky man, 'when everyone makes merry! I've seen some New Year's Days, believe me – '

'What I'd written where New Year's Day should have been was rather a desolate little sentence. I hope you won't laugh when I tell you, officer.'

'Jim,' said the Captain. 'My friends call me Jim.'

'Jim, then.' She fluttered her eyelids, and lifted her glass to him before drinking. 'Don't laugh – I was thirty-eight when I wrote it – I put "My long quest for love – I realize now that it will never be fulfilled" … ' She began to weep.

Both the stocky man and the Captain put their arms round her. 'Don't cry, love,' they said. 'Have another drink.'

'While there's life there's hope,' said the Captain.

'We all have our disappointments,' said the stocky man. 'You have to laugh them off … I know when I was twenty-five I was all ready to throw myself in that canal out there – no, I'm wrong, it wasn't that canal. It was – well, look, it's the spur of the canal that ends at Fisher's Wharf, where Kayle Bridge Street comes in. Let me show you on the map, or you can see it in these cracks on the ceiling. See? There's the end of the canal, at Fisher's Wharf, just by the old chapel, and Kayle Bridge Street comes in here, and on this corner there used to be an old man with a stall selling hot dogs, year in, year out – '

'I'm weeping now,' said the old lady, laughing. 'And I wept when I read what I'd written in the diary, and I remember that I wept when I was thirty-eight and wrote the words down, and yet within a week – well, I'd hidden the diary by then – I met a man called – what was his name? I remembered it not a week ago – '

'The old man with the hot dogs was at the other end of Kayle Bridge Street, where the railway station used to be,' said the Captain. 'Had a big walrus moustache. On the corner you're speaking of, there was – '

A resounding crash made him stop. Part of the ceiling, including the interesting cracks, collapsed, showering them with flakes which fell in their beers. The building next door collapsed. Dust and grit billowed in through the open window.

'The vehicle!' exclaimed the Captain in horror. He set his glass down, removed his other hand from the old lady's clutches and staggered across to the door. Outside, the A C V had half disappeared under rubble which still slid and bounced across the road into the boiling canal.

'Come and look at this!' he called. They joined him at the door.

'We'll have to walk to Reijkskeller Field,' he said. He looked at his watch. 'We'd better get going.'

'It's raining. I'm not going out in that,' said the old lady. 'What time is it?'

'Look at that horrible thing in the sky. Makes you shudder,' said the stocky man. 'What are the chances that it will miss Earth and just swan off into space?'

'Nil, absolutely nil,' said the Captain. 'Let me just fetch my gun and we'd better get going, rain or no rain. The last ferry's waiting for us. Once we hear the siren, we've got five minutes and then they blast off, and we'll be stuck here, alone on Earth. Better hurry.'

He turned back, muttering, into the bar. The stocky man went with him, brushing white dust from his suit. 'I suppose you're right. Let's just have a last drink. One for the road. But you know you're wrong about that hot-dog stall. I was so poor when I was a student that I used to live off hot dogs, so I went to that stall just about every evening for two or more years, so I ought to know, and I remember – '

'All round the wharf was part of my patrol area when I first joined the force, so I ought to remember. The canal finished – hey, where's my gun? I left it on the bar.'

'Perhaps it fell down behind. Look behind.'

'You haven't got it, have you?'

'I loathe guns. Fist fights, no guns. You wouldn't really have shot yourself, would you?'

'Look, it's not here. Are you sure you didn't take it? You could be jailed for that, I'm warning you. God, I feel so exhausted.'

'I told you, I have not touched your gun. The last people left on Earth and you think I'd steal your gun!'

'Don't you two quarrel, just when we're having a nice time,' said the old lady brightly, bustling behind the bar and bringing out three new glasses. 'I always fancied myself as a barmaid. What'll it be, gentlemen?'

'That's the stuff, love,' said the stocky man, rubbing his

hands in delight. 'You're a woman after my own heart. I wish I'd bumped into you thirty years ago, that's all I can say. I'll have another beer and perhaps I'll just have a quick liqueur too while you're pouring it. Keeps the cold out.'

'Mind if I try that stuff?' asked the Captain.

'Help yourself.' He pushed the liqueur bottle over. 'On the house.'

'Your bonny blue eyes, lady!' said the Captain, lifting his drink with trembling hands.

'You're darlings, both of you,' she said, adding, as she lifted her own glass, 'and here's to Earth, the best planet in the whole universe!'

They all three drank. Distantly, a siren wailed.

They winked at each other. 'Time for one more,' said the Captain.

'*His* name was Jim too,' said the old lady, 'and it was really funny how I bumped into him.'

As she lit another cigarette and passed the packet round, the stocky man said, 'We'll go and inspect Fisher's Wharf in the morning and you'll see that I'm right. I can remember exactly the very pattern of the cobbles. Anyhow, as I was saying, Michelangelo – '

The siren died away. A new and more insistent wind sprang up outside.

'I know,' said the Captain, 'let's take our drinks and go into the back parlour. There's bound to be a back parlour, and we'll be cosier in there. Bring the lamp.'

'Good idea, Jim,' said the stocky man. 'These little back parlours take some beating. I know once – '

Creatures of Apogee

From a distance, the one-storey palace appeared to float on the ocean like a wafer.

Three beings came springing out of the lighted rooms of the palace behind the long colonnade, he, She, and she. They ran over the flagstones, laughing. Night crackled overhead in tones of deep blue and sherbet. Joy flared like lightning across two opposed points.

From the chambers behind them, music overflowed. In that music moved nothing but harmony itself, complete in its own cadences, yet the key in which it was pitched carried an oblique reference to the particular loaded time changes of this world. Things grew, eyes sparkled, joints were as nimble; yet this was this fateful planet and no other in the universe.

Take that great terrace, paved with flagstones in which mica emicated beneath advancing feet: across its expanse, illumination played with as many variations as the music. The night itself was a great source of light and, like an upturned cauldron, the sky spilled its nourishments over the intricacies of the building. Into the vaulted ceiling behind the colonnades, the sea smuggled its own messages of light, for oceans have better memories for heat and day than does air. The glaciers, too, and seven tiny moons, all contributed their share of luminance.

And yet those three who ran laughing – they rejoiced in

night, he, She, and she, rejoiced and lived for its qualities. Now they had reached the very end of the terrace, and rested against the last slender column, with its faded paintings of sorcerers and cephalopods. Their regard went first, instinctively, to the lapping waves, as if to penetrate beneath them and view the creatures who lay waiting in the depths, waiting for the appropriate season. They smiled wryly. They raised their heads. Together, they gazed across the auroral sea, watching great glaciers floating on pillows of their own cool breath. Dawn was coming. Dawn, without responding pallor in the sky.

Dawn, the magnet of life. Take their great eyes, set in faces pale, evanescent, baroque; inescapably, the gaze of those eyes was drawn to an iceberg that floated in the east. It lay on the deeps like a memorial to time itself. Its cliffs were of a remembered grey, sombre, stony ... until the moment of dawn. Then the ice lit like a distant signal.

As a flower unfolds from its bud, revealing its voluptuous couchy pinks, the iceberg changed inward colour. The grey became dove-grey. The dove-grey turned chalk, turned to a tender pink wash, all promise.

Between day and night was no severance: their embrace was not to be prised apart by dawns such as this. As the sun rose further, as the iceberg, forgotten by its lamp-bearer, sank back into gloom, it was not radiance which changed but sound. The music ceased. Stale inside their satins, the musicians were stealing home.

The sun was just a point of pleading light, too far from anywhere to prevail. A pearl tossed into the sky would have cast more lustre.

The three turned away, he, She, and she. Very calm, they walked hand in hand upon the edge of the terrace, where the deep ammonias of the sea cast reflections like passing thought upon their countenances.

'Is it brighter?' she asked, referring to the Sun.

'Brighter than in our childhood,' he replied.

'Brighter than yesterday, even,' She said.

Now that the music of the night was hushed, the sussurus

of ocean and air moved closer, speaking to them of the whole poignant fulcrum of existence. Overhead, a seabird sped between the high arches, coming from nothingness momentarily into the orbit of civilization before it disappeared again into the void. At their feet, a concatenation of waves tossed spume on to the terrace, where it soon evaporated into space.

In the three of them moved an intense love for one another, so that they drew closer and walked like one. Not only was life short: far more touchingly, it was cyclic. The leaves that turned brown and died would spring up verdant again in many generations' time.

He said, 'We are now so far from apogee.'

She said, 'The sun grows nearer, and nearer to the Time of Change.'

And she said, 'Our world has its set course – without a course there is no world.'

Their silence was assent; but inside them, where things tangible met things intangible, was a great sense of awe, transcending joy or sorrow, as they considered the planetary motions within which their delicate part was cast. They were the life of their world; but on this world, all life was a mirror image. Two types of life – as different, as dependent, as yin and yang – existed … yet never met, yet never held converse, yet could not even breathe the other's atmosphere. Each type of life existed only in the death of the other. At the Time of Change, the centuries of being changed sentries.

So She said, 'As a creature of apogee, I fear … '

To which she added, ' … yet also perforce love, the creatures of perihelion.'

Which he finished as, 'For they and we together must form the sleeping and the waking of one Spirit.'

They paused to look again across the rolling liquids, as if hoping for sight of that Spirit, before they made the decision to go inside their palace. In turning, they cast their united gaze upon a broad flight of steps which led down from the terrace into the ocean. That was not their way to go. Other feet, of different shape and intent, would walk those steps, when the terrible Time of Change was past.

The steps were worn, their very grain obnubilated, as much by centuries as by tread. Many atmospheres, many oceans, had washed over them, as the world moved on its attenuated elliptical course. Small the world was, and a slave to its lethargic orbit; for in the course of one year, from the heats of perihelion to the cools of apogee and back again, not only lives but generations and whole civilizations underwent the cycle of birth and decay, birth and decay.

As the three looked at those broad steps leading down into the opaque fluids of the ocean, they held inside them the knowledge of what would happen in the spring of the year, when the sun showed a disc again and Change overthrew their kind.

Then the oceans would boil away in fury.

The tides would withdraw.

The steps would dry.

The palace – their palace – would be transformed, would stand revealed as merely the top floor of a mighty pyramid with many floors. The steps would lead down to the distant ground. That ground, no longer an ocean bed, lay over ten kilometres below.

All would be hushed after the storms of Change, except for the wail of atmosphere with its new winds.

Then the creatures of perihelion would muster themselves, and would begin to ascend the stairs. Under the blaze of the swollen sun, they would march up to this topmost place. In their own tongues, with their own gestures, they would obey their own deities.

Until the autumn came round again.

The three beings took firmer hold of each other and retired into the palace, to rest, to sleep, to dream.

Enigma 1:
Year By Year the Evil Gains

Within the Black Circle
Killing off the Big Animals
What are you Doing? Why are you Doing it?

Within the Black Circle

Every year of her life, she had invented something. The first invention she could remember was the separated-vision experience, conducted in bed with one eye above the blanket and one below. She had been four then.

Although she recalled that there had been inventions even before that age, the separated-vision experience had been so seminal that it obliterated its feebler forerunners. Most of the later inventions owed something to the separated-vision experience, which had revealed to her – and still continued to reveal – that if you took up certain positions you could receive dual and conflicting impressions of the universe.

For instance, I used to read a novel, *The Green Hat* by Michael Arlen, over and over again. It was the novel my mother was reading when she died. I came to associate the colour green with sickness and death – not with the colours of nature but with all that is unnatural. Gradually I came to formulate a colour-emotion code; that was another of my inventions.

Some of those inventions were harmful to my psychic

development, I believe, however much the inventiveness itself succoured me. I was very much an isolated child. My father did not live in the Kremlin with me.

Not to be tedious, I will instance only one more of my inventions, and that the greatest of them. It was of a profoundly religious nature.

So many of our family, my uncles and aunts and cousins, disappeared before I reached the age of puberty. People vanished from round me like shadows. I never understood what happened to them until much later. So it came about that I was in an isolated position by the war years, bereft of friends of my own age or of senior years. Only my old nurse was close to me. I used to stare for hours out of my window, over the crenellated walls of the Kremlin, gazing on the great world outside and wondering if it was all as boring there as here. Finally, my breath would mist the pane; the outside world would disappear.

In Moscow during the war years, there was a popular perfume available called Svetlana's Breath, to flatter my father. I used to laugh at that – what could be less effective, or more pathetic, more solitary?

Gazing from my little window, I formulated my religious theory. Stated briefly, it was that nobody ever died and no new people were ever born. Bodies decayed and had to be done away with, to be replenished by new babies, but the vital part, the soul (by which I meant the whole personality), lived on, translated into a fresh body.

Perhaps I was trying to console myself. When my older stepbrother Yakov disappeared in the war, my religious theory came to my aid. I imagined him living elsewhere. The same with old friends, and with my aunts and grandparents, all of whom had disappeared from our gloomy little scene. They were elsewhere, happy.

As I imagined the process when I had perfected it, what happened was that the personality of someone loved would move to another body, perhaps a small child's, living in another part of the country, possibly even in a completely different part of the world. There, the personality would gradually shape the appearance and circumstances of the new life until it came to resemble as closely as possible the old one.

For instance, Sergei Kirov, whom even my father loved, and who had been shot in 1934, was still alive in a new body, somewhere where we should never see him again, but still enjoying life, still remembering me and my dear mother, in Sverdlovsk, or Irkutsk, or even Kazan or Khabarovsk.

Perhaps my mother was still alive, still young in a new body, looking just as I remembered her when I was a small girl, thinking of me yet in Paris, or even Rio de Janeiro or Buenos Aires.

You see how this belief was a development of the separated-vision theory, in a way. Given the right way of looking, you might get an entirely different view of the universe from every-one else. The things everyone regarded as real might be just illusions. I strove to perfect a way of viewing the real reality.

Maybe this all sounds preposterous; but my life-style con-tributed to such alienation. I live one way outwardly, another inwardly. Our 'home' in the Kremlin was miserable, so that I was forced to recall happier times.

Ugh! That Kremlin apartment! My father rarely visited there. I was left alone with my faithful old nurse and the hor-rible domestic retinue, all of course in the employ of the OGPU or KGB. We were housed in the old Senate building, on the first floor, where a wide corridor had been converted into separate rooms. Those rooms still had sections of high vaulted ceiling, which plainly didn't belong. The interior walls were flimsy, the outer ones nearly five feet thick.

Father generally worked on the floor above; there were the offices of the Chairman of the Council of Ministers and First Secretary of the Communist Party and other well-placed bureaucrats. I never went up there, except on one occasion in 1942, when Winston Churchill came to talk with my father. The truth was, I loathed the building and all the people in it.

Small wonder I tried to live back in the times when I was a little girl and things had been happy. When my mother was alive, we used to go down to the Caucasus in the summer, when we'd all drive into the wilds and have great splendid picnics, often with Mikoyan, Voroshilov and Molotov, and all their wives and children. Little we thought then of the terrible times that were to overtake us! My father would sometimes go shooting – mainly hares or hawks – quick, small things – but he was not a great hunter of animals.

He was surrounded by happy people in those days, people he trusted. All of that vanished when mother shot herself. He became colder and harder, year by year, and year by year the evil gained over him, while more treacherous and bestial people surrounded him, notably Lavrentiy Pavlovich Beria. Towards the end of my father's life, say from the war years onwards, I felt that to be near him was like being on the slopes of a high mountain; the atmosphere was so chill, so sparse, that you had to fight for breath. The human spirit expired in his presence.

Once I had discovered how he drove my mother to suicide, relations between my father and me could never be cordial again. Nevertheless, something of that old Georgian warmth remained, even in wartime, even within that terrible black circle he had drawn round himself. We still used to see films together.

Right at the other end of the Kremlin was a small theatre, situated in what had once been the Winter Garden. My father and I would go there late at night, he muffled in his greatcoat, saying not a word, walking very slowly with me through the deserted courts. Sometimes, we heard the rumble of tanks in Red Square beyond the walls.

We never visited the cinema without an escort, even in the heavily defended Kremlin. We were accompanied by many members of my father's bodyguard, all well-armed, of course, and by two armoured cars, which growled along behind us in low gear, following us on our way to see something very frivolous, perhaps.

Inside the cinema, it was generally cold. We kept our coats on. My father and I sat at the front, in comfortable chairs which had survived from Tsarina Alexandra's time. The body·

guard sat at the back of the hall. All watched the screen with equal attention.

There we saw all the best Soviet films, including some with a rather dull propagandist motivation. But what my father and I most enjoyed were the American films, which of course could not be shown to the people of Moscow. When they were too decadent, my father sent the bodyguard to wait outside; but he never sent me away.

My favourite films were musicals. My favourite singing stars were Betty Grable, Alice Faye, and Judy Garland. Sitting there in the Kremlin, we saw *Strike Up the Band*, *Springtime in the Rockies*, *Down Argentina Way*, and other cheerful films. My father did not enjoy all the nudity, but nevertheless the music seemed to relax him.

I used to sing to my nurse, 'You'll find your life will begin/ The very moment you're in – Argentina,' but she would wisely hush me. The words were poignant; I half believed that my mother might be alive in another incarnation in Buenos Aires.

Despite this film-going, I grew to dread my father as I came to understand all he stood for. Yet I wept when finally he died of his stroke. Bulganin, Voroshilov and Khrushchev were there at the last, and they all wept too. After all, they had truly loved him and believed in the common cause. When finally I left the dacha, and we climbed into the car, Bulganin put his arms round me and we wept together.

Somehow, somewhere, there may have been another world where it all turned out otherwise. Maybe we should just have seen things differently and it would really have been different.

Killing off the Big Animals

The ocean was shaped like a body, the Bay of Zubariski like a head. A narrow neck divided bay from sea, where a geological noose had been drawn tight about the throat. On the rocky peninsula at that point, cascading down into the waters, stood the town-heap of Zubariski. Behind it sat the uncompromising shape of the Seventh Exploration Team's starship.

Towards sunset, the five members of the team surfaced almost in unison and climbed out of the darkening water to lie and gasp on the rocks. They pulled off their masks and snorkels, automatically looking back at the ocean.

'It's really great sport,' exclaimed Hamura Redon. 'Like nothing you ever met on Earth.' He wiped the sweat from his face and spat on to the rocks.

'I guess I killed twenty of the bastards,' said Nothing Chaundy, unzipping his plastic suit and laughing. 'Maybe twenty-four, twenty-five, who knows? You lose count ... '

'Oh, why bother to count?' Nils Martenson said. 'There are millions of them in the ocean, just waiting to be exterminated, waiting to die, glad to die! Wow, that socko effect of *feeling* them die! It's incredible. This must be the greatest hunting place in the whole galaxy. Look out there – more coming!'

He pointed out to sea. Peculiar rock formations lent the Great Silarian Ocean a striped effect, where deep water alternated with ridges of rock, heavily fringed with crimson kelp, rising to just below the surface. The ocean was red here, not only with the reflection of the kelp, but with the blood of the slaughtered leviathans, some of the carcasses of which still thrashed feebly near shore. Among them, new shapes moved.

'It's like the last few evenings,' Nothing Chaundy said. 'They're coming in to cart away their dead. Then the dumb goons will be back tomorrow to get themselves killed. They can't get enough of it.'

'Guess we can oblige them,' Joe Carnate said, and they all laughed.

They picked up their gear and trudged through the cancerous spikes of the town-heap, companionably chatting together as they made their way uphill between walls of pitted alleyways. The dark was coming on. They'd had a fantastic day's sport. An evening's drinking lay ahead. And of course there were the girls, waiting for them, chained, in the ship.

'Just one fly in the ointment,' David Schmidt said. 'The

B

Sector Adjudicator is due to arrive tomorrow. He's going to raise hell when he finds how we've been breaking Galactic Law, slaughtering an Inferior Species.'

'We can fix the Sector Adjudicator,' Nothing Chaundy said grimly.

The Sector Adjudicator arrived as expected. His slim vessel put down neatly a few metres away from the Exploration ship, and the Adjudicator himself emerged, when the dust had subsided, accompanied by two law-enforcement robots.

The Adjudicator was a young man, rather delicate to look at, with fair hair and stern grey eyes. His clothes were neat, his gestures likewise. Without hesitation, he marched towards the starship, where the five team-members were lounging, and introduced himself as Judge Jack Paramour. They eyed him with contempt, staring at his lips rather than his eyes as he spoke.

'I received a scatter saying you have made contact with a sentient marine life-form here on Silaria. Is that correct?'

'Correct,' agreed Nothing Chaundy. 'And "established contact" just about sums it up. To put it bluntly, Judge, we been having the time of our lives shooting the aforesaid damned marine life-form to all hell and back, haven't we, boys?'

Laughingly, the others agreed.

'That is a contravention of Galactic Law and carries the extreme penalty, if you have been doing as you say.'

'What do you mean, *if*? Are you doubting our word, Judge?' Hamura Redon roared, in genial fashion. 'Let's take you down to the shore and show you! You'd accept two hundred carcasses as evidence, wouldn't you?'

Paramour drew himself up and said, 'Your attitude is one of extreme irresponsibility. It is my duty to warn you that my robots here are recording everything you say, and that the judiciary computer may use the recording in evidence. If you wait here, I will equip myself for a visit to these marine creatures.' He nodded grimly, turned, and walked back to his ship, the robots marching in step with him. Both robots had eyes in the back of their heads.

'To hell with him,' said Joe Carnate. 'Let's get our gear and go down to the juice. That soft little Earthman can join us if he feels like it.'

He said it loud enough for Paramour to hear.

Paramour did not turn. Entering his ship, he quickly stripped down and dressed himself in a frog-suit. If the marine life-form had developed some primitive kind of communication, as the scatter had suggested, then he hoped to be able to meet them in their own element. He had no need to make a preliminary report; the robots had it all on record.

'This team has entirely forgotten the Exploration Charter,' he observed to his attendants. 'Some force has been at work on them and we must find what it is. It could be dangerous – an airborne spore, for instance, which renders people reckless and uninhibited, and so easy prey to predators. They behave almost like drunks. Could be something water-borne, if they've been much in the water ... '

He returned outside. The magnificent oblate sun floated over a range of hills, its edges ragged, its core streaked with orange furies. It shone on the starship. The team had gone.

Paramour started towards the ruinous pile of town-heap. Soon, he was among its winding alleys. The buildings were all of pebble, bound together with something that could have been mud or pulverized rock. It gave the place a leprous effect. He scratched at a wall and found it uncrumbling. There were doorways, but no doors. After only a moment's hesitation, he entered one of the buildings.

The room was irregularly formed. It might have been a cave. It contained no artefacts. At the back of the room was a slope with crudely formed and irregular steps cut in it. He climbed them cautiously, to find himself on the next floor. He called to the robots to stay below and guard.

This room was dark, lit only by a window no bigger than a hand. Paramour went to it and stared out. Through the shafts of other buildings he could see the distant glitter of oceans. He moved to another room on the same level. That also was empty. The floors were uneven. There was a stale damp smell everywhere. He stood silently, his hand on one pitted wall, thinking, wondering. The empty space of universe came down and touched him.

He climbed up two more storeys. That was as high as he could go. Where there were windows, they were small and irregular; all looked towards the ocean. Paramour extended his senses, trying to comprehend what sort of life had filled the building, the town. All that came back to him was a faint sound of waves.

Something made him reluctant to leave.

Finally, he retraced his steps, emerging into the shadowed street. Without a word, he motioned to the robots to follow him. He walked down an incline, over irregularly placed stones. No weeds grew between stones, not a blade of grass. He came to the rocks.

Various items of undersea equipment lay scattered by the water's edge. He noticed spare oxy-helium cylinders, flippers, two magnificent harpoon guns, before he turned his attention to the waters.

To his right side was the sweep of the Bay of Zubariski. Although the water looked still, except where it lapped against the land, it was dark and uninviting. He observed that the sand which fringed it was black and of volcanic origin. To his left lay the expanse of ocean. He sent one of the robots down into the water to collect a sample and make an analysis. While that was happening, he stood with arms folded and eyes narrowed, looking about at the land, the coastline with its distant bays, the ocean, the orangey sky with its freight of cloud.

The robot read off its analysis. The ocean was the usual vat of salts, cast up from the early days of the planet, constantly replenished by the elements, constantly yielding itself.

A shape came rolling up the water, thrashing with a clumsy arm. It rotated as it did so, and a spiral swathe of crimson poured from a breach in its vivid yellow body. Paramour looked down at it with interest, adopting a professional stance which concealed both pity and distaste. An arm was flung from the ocean and struck rock. For a moment, it seemed as if the creature was going to heave itself from the water, and Paramour stared into a horizontal face – at least, there were two wide-spaced eyes, with lids that blinked and pupils that appeared to weep. Then the thing fell back into the water.

Another creature blundered to the surface beside it and died. This one had a harpoon right through one of its eyes.

'Photograph them,' Paramour ordered the robots. 'I'm going to stop those men. The entire Exploration Team must have gone mad. This situation is about to turn into a massacre, and I can't let it happen.'

His face went pale with rage. The act of summary execution lay within his powers as Adjudicator, and he was prepared to use it rather than stand by and see wild life so casually wiped out. He zipped up his suit, snapped down the face-plate, and prepared to enter the water. At the last moment, it occurred to him that he was about to face five irresponsible men; he turned and snatched a harpoon-gun from the rock, charging it as he kicked himself below the surface.

The water was murky with blood from dying animals. He switched on his beam. All about him were slowly thrashing limbs. He realized that the current was bringing the maimed creatures in towards the neck of the bay, and that the trigger-happy members of the Exploration Team were possibly some way out to sea.

The marine creatures had six legs, two pairs at one end of their pod-like bodies, one pair at the other. The long legs were distinctly four-sided and covered with markings which might be scales. The underside of their bellies was a sombre green, in contrast to the bright yellow of their backs. Large mouths were set in these bellies. The mouths were open as if in pain, but Paramour saw no teeth there. He did not believe that the creatures were or could be dangerous. They looked as helpless as babies.

As he dived under another great carcass, a human figure swam to meet him and clutched his arm.

'I order you to stop this insane killing,' Paramour shouted.

The other man pressed his face-plate to Paramour's and said, 'Glad you could join us. You investigated that town-heap? It's used by the land-going phase of these beasties. Isn't that crazy? But it's light-years more fun to slaughter them down here!'

He broke away and was gone. Alone again, Paramour kicked out for deeper water.

The ocean floor fell away below in a startlingly steep descent. The water was clear of blood, so Paramour switched off his beam. As he did so, a new sensation came over him.

He began wishing he could meet an unwounded creature face-to-face. He felt he could … he felt he could put it right. In some way, these silly creatures had gone wrong. They had become too big and too clumsy. They were also – no doubt of that – too damned trusting. So damned trusting that you could not in part help realizing that they deserved all they got.

These reflections were slightly feverish. Afterwards, Paramour could never recall how exactly he experienced them. He only knew that he was overwhelmed by a lust to sort these great innocent boobies out.

At which point, one of the creatures rose from somewhere below him, materializing out of the thick fathoms of green. He watched it coming, with only its rear legs kicking, its front pairs raised as if in some idiot form of greeting. Its body was rocking, so that he saw the eyes and the open mouth in turn, on either side of the pod-shaped body. It looked rather as if the creature was making a foolish grinning face at him. He blasted off with the harpoon-gun almost without realizing what he did.

To his delight, the bolt caught the creature in the corner of its mouth. It went into immediate contortions of pain, crumpling up most satisfyingly, trying to wrap all its limbs round the point from which death was pouring into it. Paramour seemed almost to catch some of its agony, and sweet was the taste of it. He deliberately flipped through the curtains of its blood as he went in search of another target.

There were many more creatures around. They were flocking in, almost as if asking to be killed. He longed to slay every one of them, to make them die lingering deaths, to suffer and sink and suppurate in blood. A great pair of eyes turned on him from the depths. This creature, he saw, was monstrous the biggest yet, and had two small creatures at its side. By the gravities, it was a mother, suckling two infants as it went along. The demand to kill *her*, and to blow the infants apart, was irresistible. He loaded up, letting her see what he was doing — just in case, as he hoped, she was intelligent enough to understand his action. Then he blasted her between the eyes. The little ones clung to her twitching carcass until he shot them just as anticipated, limbs drifting slowly apart, curtains of guts disentangling.

The human figure was back again, pulling at his arm. They touched face-plates.

'You're doing good, Judge. There's masses more of the bastards out where we are. Come on!'

'I'm coming,' Paramour said. 'Did you see the way I blew those babies apart! Jesus, what terrific sport!'

Together, they kicked out for deeper water.

What are you Doing? Why are you Doing it?

While Jack Paramour was enjoying a sporting holiday on the planet Silaria, he had a strange dream. It came and went, and was like no ordinary dream. When the gravo-neuronic rhythms of the body are disturbed by a strange planet, dreams are never ordinary, their architecture indicates a cellular awareness of planetary differences.

Jackson Paramour, Jack's father, had been a brilliantly successful costume-jewellery designer in his time. He had been single-minded in his profession, always working, always travelling — either to acquire exotic stones or to sell his creations — and had had little time for his wife and three sons. 'Let's face it,' the eldest son, Roy, once said to Jack, 'Father's as vulgar at heart as his gawds. He's got nothing to offer us but tinsel.'

Jackson Paramour, who drove himself too hard, died when

the boys were young. It was a sunny day early in May, when the blossom was on the bough, and Paramour had cornered the zircon market. His sons were poured into suits and ties and taken to a dreadful mausoleum modelled on the Hagia Sofia in Istanbul (but five times bigger), where the tarted-up remains of Dad were ceremonially enclosed in a coffin of white marble. They went back home laughing to their private hot-cat track. Tea was served at 4.30 as usual.

The exploration starship *Hamura Redon* had discovered a G-type sun with nine planets. Captain Nothing Gabitas checked with Shipmind.

'It is Sol, The Sun,' said Shipmind, when it had munched up spectrographic and other data.

'Hey, we've found The Sun, boys,' Gabitas said into his chair-mike. 'Pure accident. All this while, everyone thought it was over in Galaxy Six – just shows how wrong you can be.'

'Say, Cap, why don't we just tiptoe on past it and leave it among the lost?' Conroy said. 'I'm for heading for home and a change of women.'

Some agreed with Conroy, some disagreed.

'I think we ought to look in on it while we're in the vicinity,' Gabitas said. 'Considering people have been searching for it for centuries. Wasn't it supposed to have a couple of inhabited planets or something?'

'To hell with mythology, I'm with Conroy – let's get home,' said Pete Ulysses, who had a wife waiting for him, he hoped.

'Let's put it to the vote,' Gabitas said.

Three were for heading straight on and forgetting all about it. Four were for taking a quick look while they had the chance.

Gabitas spoke to Shipmind.

'Take us in,' he said. 'And start waking up our bodies, will you?'

Jack Paramour was a grown man now. He wore the insignia of his clan. He was walking through a museum with a friend when they came on the Books section. Looking idly about him as they strolled past the crowded shelves, he caught sight of his own name on a faded cloth spine and went closer.

You Get More By Being Nice. By Jackson Paramour.

'My father wrote that Book!' Jack said, and burst out laughing. 'Sorry, what were you saying about interplanetary subterfuge as applicable under the law of tort?'

They strolled on.

Later, he thought about the Book. The trajectory of his father's life had evidently not been the straight brutal rise from infancy to millionairedom to coronary as hitherto believed. Somewhere, there had been other impulses in the man. Jack Paramour was not imaginative – at one time, he had been a passionate stamp-collector – but he suddenly realized that the costume-jewellery which was his father's trade might have begun as more than just an immensely profitable line; it might even have originated in a real creative spark. He decided he must acquire a copy of his father's Book.

He advertised for *You Get More By Being Nice.* Since money was no object, he soon had a copy in his hands. The leaves seemed to tremble as he opened it.

They were bellowing with laughter on the *Hamura Redon.* The sun The Sun was close now; the crew were all back in their bodies, exercising and exhibiting them like new suits. But Shipmind was assuring them that the sun ahead had only eight attendant planets, and not nine.

'Then you've ballsed things up again, Shipmind, sorry,' said Gabitas. 'You say yourself there should be nine planets. You've got your readings all wrong.'

They loved it when they thought they had caught Shipmind in error, like children rebelling against parental stupidity.

'The readings all point to my initial assumptions being one hundred per cent correct,' said Shipmind. 'Luminosity, composition, rotation, magnetics, ventality – all the figures check out. The sun's The Sun okay. What's happened is that, over the ages, one of its planets has disappeared, or blown up, or gone chasing a tramp sun, or *something*. Funnier things have happened.'

B*

'Let's go and have a shufty, then,' Mark Polo said. 'Which planet is missing?'

'Third from The Sun,' said Shipmind.

'Third was always a tricky position,' Gabitas said.

Jackson Paramour's third son, Jack, closed *You Get More By Being Nice* and put it down in front of him. He had enjoyed it. He found it a touching story. It told him much about his mother, whom he did not remember as vividly as his father. At least, the two main characters were Johnny and Sheila, and he assumed they were really his parents in literary disguise, since Johnny was a sculptor who had never made good because of his artistic integrity and Sheila was the most beautiful girl in the world. For the first time, Jack found himself wishing he had known his parents – 'really known them', as he phrased it – before the world closed over their heads and their hopes.

Not a great deal happened in the novel. Most of it was set on Shrivdale Farm, an idyllic place practising old-fashioned dirt agriculture for the sake of tourists. Shrivdale was situated on the outskirts of Stringhove. Johnny and Sheila met and fell in love on the farm. Later, when Johnny, on the verge of suicide, unexpectedly inherited a fortune, he and Sheila bought the farm and lived very happily there. They reared lots of cows and three daughters.

Stringhove actually existed. Jack Paramour bought large-scale maps of the area. Sure enough, the name Shrivdale appeared there.

Jack resolved on a sentimental pilgrimage.

The crew had a ringside seat at one of the most amazing views in the universe. The *Hamura Redon* sailed in orbit about The Sun's biggest planet, the fourth from primary; the ship had surrounded itself with a strong magnetic field as protection against the blasts of radiation coming from the planet.

At the present moment, the gas giant appeared in half-phase. Its great streaked face loomed beyond the ports, mantled with bands of grey, orange, and salmon-pink. To the south of the planetary equator was a curiously enigmatic feature, an oblong expanse of an angry brick-red hue some forty thousand kilometres long.

Shipmind was busy rattling off endless series of figures which flashed across the read-screens over the control panels.

So much chemical fury boiling away outside kept the men silent in awe. Finally, Gabitas said, 'It seems we have arrived just in time, according to Shipmind's reading. This planet, Sol IV, is mostly composed of hydrogen. The spectroscope tells us that the cloud-belts we're looking at consist of hydrogen, deuterium, helium, methane and ammonia. The planet's meteorology is internally powered – it is radiating three point nine times more heat than it receives from The Sun, and that figure is building up, as is the emission of protons and high-energy electrons.'

'Then the sooner we get clear the better,' Pete Ulysses said. 'The implication is clear – this planet is unstable and is about to transform into a miniature sun.'

' "About to" is a relative term,' Gabitas said. 'Certainly a pseudo-nova condition is imminent, but that means, at the least, some ten thousand years ahead of relative stability.'

Shipmind said, 'A curious anomaly exists as regards the great red spot. In its centre is a circular dark patch, sometimes obscured. You see it?'

'I see it,' Gabitas said. 'I thought at first it was an optical illusion.'

'My readings show that the red spot itself is a column of heated gas blowing from the planetary interior. The black patch is comprised of solid matter, and exists at a much lower temperature. It would be possible for you, and not especially dangerous, to fly the ferry down and land on the black patch.'

'Now why in hell's name should we want to do a crazy thing like that?' Polo asked.

'Because my readings suggest that the black patch is our missing third planet, embedded in the face of the gas giant.'

Heavy rain had fallen the previous evening. This morning it was misty and dull. The ground was waterlogged. Within five minutes of leaving his car, Jack Paramour was wading across boggy ground, with peaty water pouring into his shoes.

Nevertheless, this was Shrivdale Farm, or what was left of it. He had his large-scale map in his hand, and the precious copy of *You Get More By Being Nice* in his raincoat pocket. Although he knew where he was, it was still difficult to orientate himself. The original drive-way had gone, wiped out by a small packaging factory. He had approached obliquely, climbing through barbed wire, past a barking dog. What had been remote countryside in his father's day was now a glum stretch of non-country on the outskirts of Stringhove, with thistle-choked fields and polluted streams. No doubt the developers of Stringhove had already parcelled up the rest of the open land with their fat red grease-pencils.

There were suburban homes all round, fenced, patched with pretty strips of garden, the odd tennis court, the odd swimming pool. Little girls sat on ponies. Lawn mowers purred. Milkmen chuntered from door to door in square vehicles.

All the same, the morning's fog did much to counteract this lapse into genteel mediocrity. It lent mystery and a vanishing perspective. Mist was indigenous here, like nothing else.

He squelched over to a rank copse, consisting mainly of beech and silver birch trees. He jumped a ditch, climbed over more wire, and was among the trees. He saw a small hut ahead, very tumbledown. As he worked his way round to the front of it, he found that an old car had been driven into the hut for shelter. The wheels of the car had gone long ago, and its every window was broken. This was a miserable spot where journeys died for lack of destination.

Paramour coughed a little. The noise reminded him to light a cigarette. He smoked and thought, and listened to the solitude. Despite the muffling effect of the fog, he could hear traffic moving on two nearby roads. He had no sense of escape, or of being back in the past, or of finding his roots, or indeed of any vaguely hoped-for discovery.

Only then did the make of car register on him. It was a Ford. He turned to the novel, pulling it from his raincoat pocket, riffling carefully through its pages. Johnny had driven a Ford.

At one crucial point in the story, Johnny had driven into the market town of Stringhove to meet Doreen and had chanced on her sister, Sheila, instead. That was when the romance between Johnny and Sheila began. Of course, it might not be the same car at all. The model was not specified.

And the shed. The trees had grown up round it since. He went out and looked more carefully at the ground. A track had once run this way, fringed with a laurel hedge. Then he identified the shed; it was the apple store which featured in Chapter Six. He was standing here, alone, smoking his cigarette, at the very place where his parents had had that monumental quarrel and then made love. If the sketchily fictionalized account was to be trusted, it was on precisely this waterlogged spot that he had been conceived, long ago.

He leaned against the ancient wood of the doorpost, smoking his cigarette and trying to feel something profound. The noise of the traffic bothered him.

Five suited figures climbed from the ferry into a landscape that possessed the extreme beauty of ruination. Grey smoke and drifting orange mist enshrouded them, while the sky all round flickered with the poisons of the gas giant's atmosphere. Only a few miles to the north of them were clusters of raging volcanoes, where the third planet's core was boiling itself off, donating its petty furies to the birth of a new sun. But they trod relatively safe ground, protected from the furious heart of the giant by the planetary bulk on which they walked. That planet bobbed high in the gas giant's atmosphere, buoyed by geysers of semi-liquid gas under pressure.

Through their suit radios, Shipmind said casually, 'My readings suggest that the foreign body is sinking slowly towards the core of the gas-giant. It will ultimately trigger off a nova condition.'

'Like a snowball sinking into a pot of treacle,' Polo said.

There was little to be seen through the dense atmosphere. They straggled out over the uneven ground, instinctively looking for a focal point. In their helmets was the tremendous roar of static, which no rectification system could phase out.

Underfoot, burnt-out stumps of trees. Smoke still drifting from some of the stumps.

It was slow going over the treacly ground. Gabitas stumbled across a low charred thing. He fumbled at it, walked round it, shining his beam. His slow nightmare movements almost persuaded him he was underwater.

He had happened on a machine of some sort. Part of the metal had been molten, and was now cool again, its original shape bleared and distorted. He heaved at the whole thing, but it did not budge. He stooped, examining one end. There was an emblem of some sort, still reasonably intact because it lay against the ground. Activating the manual servo-mechanism, Gabitas wrenched at the emblem and got it free. It said FORD. It must have meant something to someone. The third planet had probably been inhabited. He stuffed the artefact into a pocket of his suit and straightened up.

The orange mists seemed to be closing in. Overhead, there was flame in the sky.

'Better get back to the ferry,' he said. 'There's nothing here.'

A friendly asexual being was saying, with its arm round Jack Paramour's shoulders, something he could not understand.

'What did you say?'

It sounded like, 'Searching for roots may be necessary, but remember that flowers do not blossom underground.' Paramour was confused and woke resentfully. He tried to struggle back to that mysterious conversation. It had fled.

Eventually he sat up and found himself refreshed. Climbing out of bed he yawned and went across to the window.

The sun shone outside. There lay Silaria, like a dream.

Enigma 2:
Diagrams for Three Stories

The Girl in the Tau-Dream
The Immobility Crew
A Cultural Side-Effect

Each of these three stories deals with a confusion of identity. The theory behind the subject is that when an age has no firm identity, then the players strutting on the stage at the time are unable to be certain of their identity. How can they be certain when the cultural matrix about them is in a state of flux? So these were designed to be stories for our Grand Post-Renaissance Age.

The first story was supposed to show people under stress, the second people and cultural matrix under stress, the third the cultural matrix itself under stress.

I don't think I shall ever write them out properly. Or maybe they already are 'written out properly'. I have worked them up in places from the original notes. Since this is also an age of incomplete art, producing sketches not finished paintings, cartoons not tapestries, questions not answers, it may be that each story can go no further towards completion.

The Girl in the Tau-Dream

This first story was planned as a love story; the second, as an adventure; the third, as a wry comedy.

The love story. It was to have been about Olga. A girl who liked the age she lived in. After getting to know her better, I could see why. Both physically and mentally, she was equipped to be ambiguous. If I had completed the story, it would have centred on her mental ambiguities, which caused me to confuse her, in my life first and then in my dreams, with the writer, Anna Kavan.

As to her physical ambiguities, the robes and shoes she wore gave one an impression of height. One thought of her as a tall and slender girl. As for her lovers, who were not many – she was like Anna in being attractive to but rarely attracted by both sexes – they came to realize that she was in reality a short and rather plump girl.

I say 'in reality', but it is a meaningless phrase. There may possibly be a common reality, but we all have our personal versions of it which we carry about like an identity card. Olga's physical appearance may have been somewhat below the average in height and pleasantly chubby; but her preference for being tall and slender was rooted – I thought – in sound metaphysical reasons. Spiritually, she was a tall and slender girl.

She was also beautiful. She seemed, let's put it, extremely beautiful to me; though I also saw her looking downright plain. The hair she piled upon her head to increase her stature was black. 'In reality', she was blonde. Her origins being what they were, blondeness was a contradiction; her personality, as Olga divined, was that of a dark girl. Her artifice was truth.

The story would have been taken up with a lot of surface detail. The eternal fascination of meeting a new woman. Of seeing her when she meant nothing. Of her gaze meeting yours (is it all decided then?). Of speaking, seeking similar topics.

Of first touching her. Of realizing that the currents of your two lives were flowing together. Such details, as with every new love affair, seem to offer vital keys to the mystery and excitement of the new being who has entered one's life. In Olga's case, these details were elaborate enough.

In brief, I had taken Anna with me to look at a small country cottage. We hoped she might like to live there, despite her heroin dependency which kept her oriented towards London and her kindly doctor. The cottage belonged to a Mr Marchmain. Anna was withdrawn and did not care for the place or the situation. It was set by a little stream and looked towards the Berkshire Downs.

We drove away after our inspection of the cottage, stopping a mile down the road to buy petrol at a crossroads filling-station. I got out of the car to avoid Anna's silence. With a tremendous crash, two cars met at the crossroads. I was in time to see one come spinning towards us. It struck a lamp standard and ground to a halt on its side. The other car, a white Mini, was turned right round in the road, extensively damaged.

I ran to the overturned car and looked in. A young dark woman was strapped in the front seat. In the back was a child, strapped into a kiddie seat. Both were conscious. In a moment, the child began to cry. I climbed in and helped the girl out, after which I went back and got the child. It was a boy of about three; he put his arms tightly round my neck and stopped crying. I helped the girl into the filling-station office.

That was Olga. She was badly shaken and not coherent, but the garage mechanic recognized her and said she knew a guy called Marchmain who lived in a cottage a mile away. The cottage we had just left.

I took her there. Marchmain rallied round, plainly embarrassed. Child not Olga's. Whose? He phoned somewhere. Olga lived in a country town some miles away. It turned out that she had been collecting a Mrs Somebody's small boy from play-school.

Despite Anna's protests, I volunteered to take the boy back to his mother, and to deliver Olga to the nearest hospital for examination. Marchmain saw us off with relief. As we were leaving, he took me to one side and said, 'Look, I'm sorry about this – you shouldn't have brought Miss Illes here. We were intimate friends once, but last week we parted for good. Which is why I wish to sell up my house and leave entirely this district.'

Miss Illes. Marchmain, I realized for the first time, was foreign.

So I delivered the boy, who never cried again, back to his mother, and I took Miss Illes to the hospital. By the time I left, she seemed perfectly all right; I gave her my card. Then I drove Anna back home.

An incident. Part of life. I was deeply involved with a new project at the university at this time; my reputation was somewhat at stake, so I prepared myself to think no more of what had happened.

The next morning, I received a letter of thanks from the boy's mother and some flowers – daffodils and yellow tulips mixed – with a note signed 'Olga Illes'. I was amused. It is rare for a woman to send a man flowers.

There was to be a good deal in the story about my work at the university. We were testing out a synthesis/atomization theory of dreams. We had already identified three different types of dreams, which we designated sigma, tau, and epsilon; my reputation was involved with this system of identification. We were now specializing in the tau-type dream, which is a phenomenon of median second-quarter sleep. The special function of a tau-type dream seems to be to explore above and below the conscious meaning of everyday events. That is, to relate an everyday event to greater spheres of meaning up to the cosmic level and to dissect its meaning to more minute fragments of being which in themselves relate to the total individual personality.

Although we had plenty of student volunteers in the laboratory, I often used myself as a guinea-pig since, for some reason, my own tau-type dreams seemed particularly vivid.

Thus, to cite two examples, I dreamed I was one of a team of four men who were trained in extreme anomic conditions to relate to the extra-sensory manifestations of their own personalities. They spent many weeks watching television pictures of empty rooms. Eventually, they hunted down a small fast-moving thing which was so inimical to them that they beat it to death. As a result, one of the men died. They learnt that the fast-moving things were projections of themselves.

The second example was similarly a synthesis/atomization. I dreamed that aliens were living among men in cordial conditions, enriching human life on the cultural plane. They were visually indistinguishable from men; only their striking power of charisma made it plain that they were something entirely distinct from human. Their admiration for the most minor figures in Earth's cultural history was flattering, fascinating and enjoyable. And infectious. Everyone on Earth became interested in the arts. It gradually became apparent to the 'I' figure in the dream, a character who visited one of the 'aliens' at home, that they were in fact utterly changing the nature of what they admired and reshaping it – although perfectly innocently and unknowingly, because art had previously been outside their experience. So their mere admiration changed everything, as translation changes a poem. One instance: 'my' alien greatly admired Robert Louis Stevenson, a nineteenth-century Scottish writer, and he and his family played me recordings of a Stevenson opera based on the legend of Robin Hood, and a tone poem which sounded to my ears like a poor mixture of Mozart and Offenbach.

Both these tau-dreams related to elements in my own personality but also to the state of the world – what I have termed the confusions of identity of the Post-Renaissance Age in which we live.

My next tau-dream, two days after I had taken Olga to the hospital, was about Olga. It contained all the richness and double-layering of the typical tau-dream.

I dreamed that I was going to see her in a cottage in the country. She was wishing to sell her cottage. I presented her with an armful of flowers, which she accepted in payment. She showed me how terribly injured was her right leg. I was sorry for her. Anna was there, but Anna left. Olga and I went

upstairs together. We could see a millstream from the bedroom window. We lay on the bed and now I noticed that she
had been deceiving me; her right leg was uninjured; the wounds
were painted on. I took her into my arms. Her clothes fell away,
and I saw that her left leg had been practically amputated in
the crash.

After this disturbing dream, I had to see Olga again.

I phoned Marchmain. No, he still had not sold his cottage.
I said I would buy it. I went immediately to the university
printer, presented my card, and got him to print me a new one.
Then I drove to Marchmain's cottage.

He was amused at my precipitance. Yet I could see he was
in some way frightened too. To cover his feelings, he told
me something about himself. He was a Hungarian, a refugee.
He had been brought to England as a baby in 1938, after his
family, one of the great landed Hungarian families, had had
trouble with Admiral Horthy. They had changed their name
to an English form. At the same time, cousins of his had also
left Hungary and settled in Brazil. Olga Illes was remotely of
the Brazilian branch of the family.

The news caused me some excitement, for I too, although of
Scottish stock, had been born in Brazil, in the Consulate in
Santos.

We settled the deal. He even agreed to be out of the cottage
by the end of the week. Various details here.

I send Olga my new card with the cottage address. I ask her
to visit me. She will not come. I realize that the tau-dream
experiment has confused my thinking, and I am in real life
playing role-reversal with Marchmain (asking to be rejected?)
just as I did in my dream about Olga, where I sent her the
flowers.

This makes me stubborn. I must have her. I believe myself
in love with her. It is easy to quarrel with Anna. Anna is always
in flight. Sometimes one may hold her in one's arms and she
is not there. She retreats far beyond the snow, elusive even
to herself. She retreats once again and I am free to pursue the
new woman.

Details of my first visit to Olga's house in the country town.

Her book-lined room. Her appearance and voice. How her accent became gradually more and more 'foreign' – and so more familiar to me – when she realized that I had been born in Brazil, just as she had.

Notes on our conversation about the English climate. The day was dull, misty, with that light rain the British call 'mizzle'. Ambiguity of landscape forms. English watercolour painting. All so different from the brash certainties of sun in São Paolo or California.

More research. Working to all hours of the night. Fresh difficulties with Anna. Difficulty in seeing Olga. Trying to settle into cottage. Trying to persuade Olga to visit cottage. Conversations with her over the phone. Taking her to London to see Luis Buñuel's *The Discreet Charm of the Bourgeoisie*, a film we both enjoyed. Trying to seduce her.

Synthesis/atomization theory challenged by Dr Rudesci's group in St Louis. Anxieties. Another attempt to seduce Olga in my room in college. This time, we are both naked when she refuses me; Olga's saying, 'When we know one another better.' Respect for this unfashionable morality, even when it goes against me, even when I know the refusal goes deeper than morality.

Taking her to meet friends in Oxford – dancing with her until the small hours. How happy we were.

Dramatic intervention of Koestler into dream-theory debate. Unexpected relevance of our findings to his own work on random elements in cerebral evolution. Some fame for me.

A film being made of our department and our researches. Some dreams being dramatized, including my Olga dream. Olga has played small parts in several films. I persuade her to play herself in my dream.

She is delighted by the proposal. I make the suggestion in her little house, which she shares with a girl friend; so we have to be careful. But clearly the prospect of acting excites her. She dances about her living-room in her loose flowing dress. Give readers glimpse of innocent-seeming but erotic caper. I grasp her. We trip and fall on to sofa. This time, she does let

me make love to her. We do it although the door into the hall
is open and the friend is about.

Great pleasure and excitement, better than first times often
are. Her sweet cries. A stocky girl, not tall, with fair pubic hair.
We both laugh a good deal and really love each other. She
declares I have tau-screwed her, at once drawing her together
and disintegrating her. She says, 'I'm sorry I couldn't admit
you before.' We try to speak in Portuguese to each other.

She agrees to spend the next weekend with me in my cottage.
Somehow, it seems that I have exorcized the ghost of Marchmain. Olga clearly regards the chance of play-acting herself
as liberating. She says, 'Since I am always self-conscious in
my role in life, a role in a film as myself will free me from such
restraints. I shall be able to under-act my own over-acting.'

Olga has a strange sense of humour.

I am so excited that she will come that, on the Saturday, I
walk up the road to the crossroads to meet her. Everything
is dripping wet, as Arrhenius supposed that Venus would be.
Shapes of woods and hedgerows all vague! Fields, ploughed
and still empty, fade into infinity. I hear the crash before I
have reached the crossroads, and cover the last one hundred
yards at a run.

Her car has collided with an oil tanker emerging from the
side road. She turns her gaze to me once before dying. Her
hand makes a theatrical gesture. She utters something which
I turn over and over and over afterwards in my mind. What I
believe she said was, 'I'm sorry I couldn't − '

Try to make all this credible to the readers.

The Immobility Crew

This would have been the adventure story.

You may not think that the adventure element is very strong,
but that takes us back to the confusion of identity theme again.
One theory has it that adventure itself has changed, become
much more inward. The biggest adventures so far this cen-

tury – the journeys to the Moon and Mars – were undertaken practically in the foetal position. Never did man get so far just by sitting on his ass. There's a lesson there for all of us.

You can see why the first story did not work out. This one did not work out for a different reason. It was too impossible, just flatly impossible. I planned it originally for a science fiction magazine; the editor bounced the synopsis with a flat little message saying 'This could never happen.'

That's the sort of story I like. If the events in it are impossible the chances are that the truth will shine out more brightly. Readers must judge for themselves from what exists of the story in its present state.

The first section is fairly complete. It is about a four-man team which is trained in extreme anomic conditions to relate to extra-sensory manifestations of their own psyches.

The facts in the case may be stated briefly.

Four human beings had been selected to tolerate high immobility levels. Their training took place over two years. At first, they were trained as a group; after six months, they were trained in isolation, to maximize nul-stimulus conditions.

The men were chosen initially for age and fitness. Three of them were in their sixties; the oldest was seventy-one. When a human being's reproductive years are behind him, or almost so, he is freed from biological directives and open to less mundane impressions.

The surnames of the men were Jones, Burratti, Cardesh, and Effunkle. They had all led active lives before volunteering for the project. Jones and Burratti had served in the Armed Forces. Jones had written two novels in his twenties, one of which had been made into a television play. Burratti held religious convictions. Cardesh had lived in the wilds of Colorado for many years; he had worked manually for most of his life. His hobby was taxidermy. Effunkle was a rich man. He was an architect who had spent many years moving around the globe. He had designed an entire city in a small Arab kingdom in the Middle East; he volunteered for the project because his wife died and he had lost interest in the outside world.

During the last eighteen months of their training, the four men lived separated from one another, with no human company. They were situated in isolated places, Jones in a deserted chemical factory in Seattle, Burratti in an abandoned ranch house in Oklahoma, Cardesh on the unoccupied fourteenth floor of a big office block in Chicago, Effunkle in a deserted naval arms depot in Imperial Valley, close to the Mexican border. To each trainee, a crew of ten or twelve operators was assigned, but the crews remained concealed from the trainees at all times.

In order to achieve most effective deprivation of stimuli, the trainees were conditioned under three heads: Immobility, Environmental Stasis, Reality Disinvolvement.

Immobility. The trainees wore immobility suits. These suits were padded to isolate their wearers from any tactile environment, and controlled at several points in order to undermine muscular autonomy. Thus, the five fingers of the gloves of each hand extended into cables which could be activated from a distant control board when desired, causing the trainee to raise or lower his arms or perform gyrations. Similar cable extensions enabled the distant controllers to make the trainee stand or sit as required without any other form of command.

During training hours, the trainees were generally placed on a circular platform. The platform could be revolved if desired.

Environmental Stasis. The four areas of containment for the four men were large, in order to obviate the intimacies of four walls, and in order to bring the weight of long perspectives to bear. Walls were soundproofed and painted white. Lighting was uniform (darkness was avoided because of its tendency to induce sleep or hallucination). Acoustic systems were introduced in three of the four training areas, so that the trainees could be fed back their own intimate body noises, rustling of garments against skin, etc. Use of television screens for heightening of isolation was sparing, except in leisure periods. The operators remained always out of sight, in both training and leisure periods.

Reality Disinvolvement. This formed another aspect of the weaning from normality implicit under the previous two heads. Tuning of trainees' metabolism was to be achieved without use of drugs; but foodstuffs were carefully controlled with regard to protein- and carbohydrate-content, flavourlessness, viscosity, temperature, and colour. During the isolation training, the normal twenty-four-hour-day cycle was modified into a nineteen point five (19.5) hour day, so as to adjust circadian responses to a more rapid rhythm. Training areas were designed so as to be adjustable with regard to size and shape. Infra-sound was used during the first periods of isolation training, but was abandoned when signs of discomfort were detected.

Notes for continuation of story

Emphasize increasing confusion of identity in each case. Follow with detailed account of the men's leisure time, most of which is spent gazing at static views through television screens. Make it clear indirectly to reader that no sexual activity is permitted/possible (fornication, masturbation, wet dreams, erections, etc.). Psychic damming. TV screens working to same end.

After two years, all four men are passed as fit for operations and are 'landed' in an alien environment. (An old airport has been 'converted' – describe tantalizingly to reader, so that nothing is entirely clear. Large adjustable partitions; baffles; extra corridors; some ninety-degree corners obviated. Considerable blank areas everywhere. Vistas through plate-glass windows always hazy – 'English type' misty day being artificially generated. Or set in Newfoundland.)

Four-man team has to spend twelve hours every day patrolling environment and mapping it. Parameters of territory changed by operators moving partitions at intervals. Lighting changes. Rest periods include individual isolation and four full hours TV-screen watching.

Sample viewing programme

Sentence-viewing:

> The trainees wore immobility suits. These suits were
>   padded
> wearers from any tactile environment,
> and controlled at several points to undermine
> The five fingers of the gloves of each hand
> cables which could be activated from a distance
> When desired causing the trainee to raise
> Gyrations similar cable extensions
> the distant controllers to make the trainee
> Without any other form of command

> Shuffle every thirty seconds, and so on.
> Animal-viewing:
> Three TV cameras have been established in an okapi enclosure containing two female okapi. One camera is self-mobile, two are fixed. Temperature kept low to ensure maximum inactivity from okapi. Viewers watch three monitor screens. Screens will remain empty for most of the time. Occasionally, parts of okapi will be seen. Describe in detail.
> And other viewing programmes, to be made credible to reader.

Work into this intransigent material vivid but brief notes of the men's dreams, sigma and epsilon, stressing gradual disappearance of tau-type dreams. Possible cause: a build-up of the integrative-disintegrative faculty elsewhere *outside the psyche*.

Reader is thus prepared for gradual emergence of adventure

element. The four-man team in its cartographic excursions has been mapping 'emotional force' lines they detect in airport. Reader believes this to be delusion, gradually realizes it is happening. At which point, preliminary sign of APL (Alien Psychic Life) is revealed.

Men first see (visually) manifestation of APL in narrow square room with high walls. APL indicates its presence in ratty way. Old newspaper blows (*Daily Telegraph?*). Their apparent inability to feel excitement. No certainties exist for a long while – do they see a figure running outside the airport, dashing at full tilt into a concrete wall and disintegrating? – do they see Jones falling down an escalator, being strangled? (Strange old clothes? An armchair smouldering in an extinct office? *Mottled* quality of light? Insert Olga's car-crash dream here.) They have been so sensitized by training that most things are viewed anew (i.e. as if alien). Their dialogue. Antiseptic.

Climax

Maybe it would make a better film than story. The people who filmed *Probability A* would do a good job. Music would help. Maybe a little Erik Satie and Poulenc. Nothing more frightening or soothing than the ghost of a piano.

The men have been calm all the while until now. Subdued, seemingly timid. We never see inside them, except through their dreams. Then during one patrol – when they have received plenty of indicators – they catch 'sight' of one of the entities. Immediately, they become brutal and depraved with the idea of the hunt. One whiff of violence depraves them. They all seize weapons, cudgels, truncheons, and so on – for the presence of which no explanation is given in text. A tremendous hunt is on. Outside, more APLs are self-destructing against walls and locked doors.

Violence of hunt. Much glass broken, partitions torn through, doors broken in, desks overturned.

By accident, Burratti leads them through into a control point, from which a crew of two operators have been recording the proceedings. Both operators are hauled down, trailing cable, and sadistically put to death, after which the corpses are hurled out of the windows. Some of the interior lighting fails during this escapade.

Effunkle is badly injured. He falls two storeys down an elevator shaft and is left on a weighing machine. The white stubble on his jaw and cheeks. The other three succeed in hunting down one of the entities.

Great care needed here with description. Just so much and no more. The APL is dressed in human-type clothes (it is hinted, of odd, old-fashioned kind). Its size is 'hard to judge'. It is very active. It shouts in an obscene (absurd?) voice. They hit it. It cries. It is so repulsive that they cannot resist beating it up. They mash and dismember it before themselves collapsing.

When they rouse, Effunkle is dead and the remains of the APLS they killed have gone. They are zombie-like again. As when animal- and sentence-viewing. Jones, Burratti, Cardesh.

Perhaps some more material needed here. Anyhow, they then retreat through the wreckage (smoke drifting in the airport?); each goes separately into catalepsy, or at least manifests severe withdrawal symptoms. Okapi non-movements. (Reindeer?)

Other manifestations – or just broken glass dropping from shattered windows?

One certain manifestation. Glimpse of old coat-collar turned up, funny old hat. Cardesh aroused to action. Seeks out Burratti and Jones. They begin the hunt again. Slow at first. Murderous. Then violent, almost mechanical, action. Glimpses of the little whirling thing, coat-tails flying, half-clown, half-horror. Glimpse of Cardesh's face, possessed by this being. It shouts as Cardesh pursues.

A snatch of communication. What did it mean? What did it say? A command?

They halt. Have they understood the APL 'language' all along? Who is the hunter, who the hunted? They are powerless in their roles. They break through a screen. There the thing is, with a girl smiling in furs as it – he – holds the reins of the reindeer and they move to kiss ... then the flash is gone, and there is just the scurrying APL and three men in violent pursuit. They are powerless not to kill. They have it in a corner, all three piling on to the frantic form.

But is – is it not beautiful? Is it not naked and pure and intact – and all the things they believe it could never be? Cardesh slams it across the face. It is the village idiot, the criminal, the moron outsider. It shines like a star. Innocent as an animal.

It smiles brokenly, bloodily, and says, 'You and I are one person.'

Cardesh knows what he confronts. As the other two kill it, he dies.

Just as in my dreams.

If ever I wrote it, I would want to make the ending less like the ending of the previous story.

A Cultural Side-Effect

This is the most impossible of the three stories. The events are plausible enough – in a sense they have already happened – but to tell them in the old story-book way, with beginning, middle, end, and lots of character by-play between times (the way they liked it back before the Post-Renaissance Age!) seems to me beyond the bounds of the possible. Or the decent. Anyhow, this is as far as I got.

Aliens were living among men in cordial conditions, enriching human life on the cultural plane. Culture was their devouring interest. They were physically indistinguishable from men and women (?); only by an overpowering element in their charisma was it plain that they were something entirely different from human. Appearances were misleading, just as they are traditionally supposed to be.

I was invited to the home of one of the aliens. Despite pressure of work at the university, I decided to take a day off and visit him. I had been all too involved in the laboratory since Olga Illes and my friend Cardesh died. (Cardesh, I found later, was Olga's brother; they died on the same day; but this note is only for those who enjoy the curlicues of nineteenth-century-heyday fiction.)

The aliens have fantastic houses, although they live by preference in the middle of terrestrial cities. A certain ritual approach through three dimensions must be made before one can enter the core of their homes. The intricacy of this ritual approach – which includes participation in the four elements, air, earth, fire and water – has a strange but beautiful effect even on an ordinary human being. Upon arrival at the core, there's a sense of – something – a sense of *uprrdesh*. There's no native word for it.

This alien's name was Ben Avangle. His wife's name was Hetty. I say wife, but that is just terrestrial shorthand for their relationship. They had two teenage children, Josie and Herman. They received me cordially, but their mere presence was like a blow to the heart. All four of them, as Ben mentioned casually to me as we climbed to the core, were absolutely fascinated by Robert Louis Stevenson.

'Stevenson, eh?' I said, jovially. 'Old Tusitala, the Teller of Tales? Fine stylist the man was!'

'A fine stylist,' Ben agreed.

I knew that that was to be only the beginning of the conversation; yet I felt fairly confident that I could continue and even enjoy it. Literature had been one of my passions in student days, even before I had begun to note how writers of a certain type of fiction – I could instance Horace Walpole, Ann Radcliffe, Mary Shelley and Stevenson himself – had relied on dreams for the sources of their conscious creative work. More than that; after Olga's death, I inherited her library; in altering her will to my advantage, she must have been very prompt to attempt to gratify the mind of the man who gratified her body; and among sundry works in Portuguese, including more editions of Camoens than I really required, were some British novelists, prominent among whom – none other than the great R.L.S., in the guise of that monstrously long Tusitala edition, edited by Lloyd Osbourne. I had (I was now happy to recollect) dipped into it here and there.

'And more than a fine stylist,' Hetty said. 'Style can cloak meaning as well as revealing it. At his best, R.L.S. uses style to do both, so that one perpetually hovers between mystery and revelation.'

'You can't discuss style as if it were equivalent to function, mother,' Herman said, laughing.

Ben smiled at me. 'I'm afraid that Herman's the moron of the family.'

'I may be the moron of the family,' Herman said, 'but I still say that style is form rather than function. Once you get style usurping function, as for instance in the words of William Locke (1863 to 1935 – no, sorry, 1930), then you see a certain non-functionalism in the content – '

'Yeah, yeah, but we're talking about R.L.S., big mouth, not Locke,' Josie said, making faces at her brother.

'I am talking about R.L.S., too,' Herman said. 'There's nothing non-functional about R.L.S.'s content, and that's precisely my point – '

'Why don't you two go into the games room and continue to discuss that aspect of Stevenson among yourselves?' Ben suggested.

Etc., etc. Give the reader as much of this sort of literary horse-play as he can take. Eventually Ben and I will settle down for conversation, two characters being easier to manage than five.

Notes on aliens. Make it clear somewhere that these aliens are not from another planet; that notion has whiskers on it. Make these aliens a sudden surge from the human race in one generation, just as there was a generation of great engineers towards the end of the eighteenth century. But these have been generated by a pharmaceutical error, like the Thalidomide children of the nineteen fifties and nineteen sixties. In this case, the error was a new tranquillizer administered to mothers during early pregnancy. Since it alters only cultural attitudes, the strange side-effect was never detected on research animals.

The cultural gene has now shown itself to be inheritable. Aliens are everywhere. Culture-obsessed.

Ben and I settle down to talk about Robert Louis Stevenson. I struggle to keep my ego intact in his presence.

'You aren't embarrassed by my talking frankly about his writings?' Ben asks.

'Heavens, no. Why do you ask?'

'You're a civilized man. Some people are frightfully embarrassed. The way an earlier generation of you humans was embarrassed to talk about sex. But it's such a fascinating subject! Why be ashamed? When I think above all of Stevenson's *Robin Hood* – superb marriage of form and content ... '

'Do you mean *The Black Arrow*?' I asked.

'No, no, no. It was published the same year as *The Black Arrow* – 1888. Perhaps that's why you are confusing the two novels. The full title is *Mebuck Tea and Robin Hood*. It is *the* great book in world literature, I'd say, which dramatizes the plight of a man having to play two roles, neither of which he understands fully – although of course he comes in the *end* to appreciate both – he of course being R.L.S.'s great legendary hero, Robin Hood, whom he makes into a sort of tragic Faust figure. A greenwood Faust. You don't know the book?'

I looked confused. He pulled a copy down from his shelves and placed it in my hands.

'The 1891 reprint,' he said. 'The edition with the Frank Papé illustrations.'

It was bound in black buckram, a fine royal octavo, with lettering in red on spine and front boards: *Mebuck Tea and Robin Hood*. I could not recall seeing the title in my Tusitala edition. I observed that this copy was dedicated to Sir Edward Elgar in R.L.S.'s handwriting.

'I've been reading *Catriona*,' I said.

This absurd dialogue should be broken up. Perhaps 'I' should visit the Avangles more than once. Is more social background necessary? (Huge riotous poetry readings and mass-exegeses of Arnold Bennett's works ousting more traditional sports like football.)

Describe Ben Avangle. Bald, chubby, no-nonsense, yet impressive. Blue-skinned. Rub it in that the aliens are blue-skinned. Emphasize charisma to make final surprise slightly more credible (projection of personality like physical object). Avangle more forceful, 'I' more ineffectual?

'*Catriona* hardly compares with *Mebuck Tea and Robin Hood*,' Ben said forcefully.

'Still, I enjoyed it … '

'Oh, you can't have too much Stevenson. It's a pity that some of his writings sometimes go out of print. You may know that I'm trying to get a law through Congress, making it illegal for any publisher not to have at least three R.L.S. titles on his list and in print. Unfortunately, I'm being very greatly hindered by that maniac Bergsteinskowski, whose partisanship of Maria Edgeworth strikes me as just a little unbalanced.'

'I don't care greatly for Maria Edgeworth's novels myself.'

He brought himself up and looked incredulously at me. 'But wouldn't you say that *Castle Rackrent* is a magnificent piece of work? Grant Bergsteinskowski that! How can one read James Joyce – or Beckett for that matter – without a sound appreciation of *Castle Rackrent*?'

'Well … '

'But I would agree that her two symphonies are probably the works by which posterity will best remember Maria. What a miracle it was, when they turned up behind the wainscotting in Malahide Castle, the year before last! '

I hadn't heard.

'To get back to Stevenson,' I said.

'Of course. I'm sorry. Stevenson. Yes, you were saying how much you'd enjoyed *Catriona*. Now you must go on, if you haven't already done so, to read its sequel, *Morings Id*. That unforgettable opening line: "The deplorable littoral of our island kingdom is part of our life on the ocean, and the know-

c

ledge should help you in coming to a decision the next time you see a friendless and bestial sailorman." Only the master of prose can begin so boldly and so baldly.'

'*Morings Id*, eh? Must get round to it.' The title meant nothing to me.

'You'll fall under its spell immediately. It's a veritable tone poem. Talking of which ... You recognize the music, don't you?' He smiled teasingly. The effect was overwhelming.

I had been aware of music in the room. Now when I bent my attention to it, I realized that I had already judged and dismissed it.

'I don't quite place it,' I said. In fact, it sounded like a mixture of Mozart and Offenbach, collaborating on an off-day. 'Nineteenth century, is it?'

Ben almost clapped his hands. 'Right! Right! It is, of course, the tone poem "Red Igloos" by R.L.S. himself. That distinctive melodic line ... '

It still sounded like Mozart and Offenbach. Made unwary by annoyance, I said, 'I had no idea that Stevenson wrote music.'

He was trying not to look shocked. He gazed at me long and searchingly.

'Not only composed but performed. Close friend of Elgar's. Introduced to him by W. E. Henley, himself no mean performer on the violin. Henley had a chamber quartet with Wells, Whistler, and – what's his name? – Campbell-Bannerman. Oh yes. Stevenson's music is well known and loved, always has been. His symphonic poem "Renickled" had its influence on Debussy. I fancy we aliens have been instrumental – if you pardon the pun – in bringing his music a little further towards the public ear ... '

More of this kind of thing. As much as readers' nerves will bear.

The aliens are so full of creative appreciation that they are undermining the fabric of culture. Culture thrives on a certain minimum attention. Later in the story, I decide to investigate the alien unconscious; persuade Ben Avangle to come to the laboratory by emphasizing the cultural significance of our dream research.

Late at night, before I put Ben to sleep, we are talking together in the lab, and I ask him some searching questions about Stevenson's other works.

'You probably know that Hetty and I went out to Samoa, where Stevenson died,' Ben said. 'There I found the manuscript of his greatest prose work *My Unasyns*. It was being offered for sale in a downtown bazaar. I brought it back and had it published. As you'll recall, it was the sensation of the literary season three years ago.'

I did not recall, and I thought the title sounded highly unlikely.

'How did you make a literary discovery of that magnitude, Ben?'

Again his searching look. Such charisma! He removed an electrode from his left temple and reached for a pencil.

'I'll be frank with you. I played a hunch first of all. I detected a pattern in R.L.S.'s titles. You know the novel he never finished? — *Hermiston*, or *The Weir of Hermiston*, as it is often called?'

He drew a diagram on a sheet of filter paper, thus:

HERMISTON —

'Imagine a ten-space letter dice — or nine dice, each of which will throw six letters, with a gap to be inserted where you will. O.K.? Then you ask yourself what other titles of R.L.S.'s would fit into that same diagram.'

Without my even consulting my mind, it came up with an answer:

'KIDNAPPED —'

'Very good. Quick thinking!' he said.

'Why on earth should Stevenson want to fit his titles into such a pattern?'

'His inspiration must have come from his own name, also nine letters:

'STEVENSON—'

'What other titles of his fit the pattern?' I asked, wondering what I was getting into.

For answer, he smiled and wrote:

ROBIN—HOOD.

'But that wasn't the complete title,' I protested. 'The complete title was *Mebuck Tea and Robin Hood*.'

In cool triumph, he wrote:

MEBUCK—TEA.

'There's all his wonderful music, too!' Ben cried:

'RENICKLED
NO—SCALTER
RED—IGLOOS.

'And of course the sequel to *Catriona* about which we were conversing so interestingly and rewardingly the other day:

'MORINGS—ID.

'And what about his epic poem to illness? —

'MENINGITIS.

'Now do you see what I'm getting at? It was a simple matter for me to compute the letters on each of Stevenson's dice, once I had a few guide-lines. The permutations are many, but not infinite. It began to look more and more as if there existed, or had existed, a work from his mighty pen entitled

'MY—UNASYNS.

'Sure enough, there it was, awaiting discovery in Samoa. Hetty and I found some of his sculpture, too.'

The story ends, or will if I ever see my way clear, with our laboratory test of Ben's dreams, when we proved conclusively that the epsilon dreams of aliens are capable of materializing in concrete form under certain circumstances. Happily, the alien mentality seems entirely harmless, so that these materializations should never prove dangerous.

The concluding paragraphs relate how sorry I am that Ben Avangle was able to stay and sleep in the laboratory for only one night. How, the next morning, I stride moodily about the room. How I discover, beside the sink in the lecture room, a novel bound in limp leather. How I pick it up and look at it. How it is called *Ken's Stone*, by R. L. Stevenson. How this copy is signed in R.L.S.'s own hand, and dedicated to his friend and fellow-violinist, W. E. Henley.

Story must be more than a joke. The aliens alienate us from our own culture.

These psychic projections made tangible are quantitatively but hardly qualitatively different from the fictions of Walpole, Radcliffe, Shelley, already mentioned, which came from the dreaming self; the alien mentality, owing to some by-pass in the brain, simply generates enough energy to produce the finished product direct, during sleep. Introduce other passages to make notion plausible.

At this time, Anna was living with me again, and we contrived some happiness between us. There were days, weeks even, when I could pretend to myself that she was no longer on the drug. One evening, we had some Brazilian friends with us, and were sitting round a log fire discussing the recent sensational haul of Samuel Johnson's oil paintings.

No, that's too much.

Try to show how difficult life is for people, even for aliens.

How difficult art is. How it dies when reduced to a formula.

How art perhaps *should* be difficult and not have wide appeal. Even how enigmatic the universe is, full of paradoxes and unpredictable side-effects.

How *arbitrary* everything is ...

How the aliens are undermining and devaluing what little culture we have, simply by cherishing it too much.

That's why I could never finish the story. I don't agree with the inescapable moral.

Live? Our Computers Will Do That For Us

Colding Marchmain held out his hand to Gloria Blake, but she elevated and turned away, shielding her sympathetic nervous system from his learned scrutiny.

'I don't want you to leave for Earth just now,' she said. 'I keep getting glimpses of other rooms. Bare rooms, with people weeping.'

'You've experienced it all before,' he said reasonably. 'You've had it explained to you. You're a Sensitive of the Unrealized Multi-Schizophrenic Type B. It's nothing to worry about.'

'Oh, you have it all memorized.' She turned back to him, so that he could see fully that clear luminous face of hers, with the long nose, well-chiselled lips, and lucid blue eyes, framed in coils of her gretchen-green hair. He gauged the degree of contraction of her pupils. 'You have lived with me on Turpitude for five years, yet how much do you understand about responding to me?' she said.

'This is an au revoir, Gloria, not a first-class row!'

'There are times when I don't want you, times when I do. I want you now, and you insist on going back to Earth, not caring at all if you shatter the composure of my mood.'

Studying her kinesics, he saw she was not as concerned as she pretended.

'Haven't we had this conversation before? I know how you modulate your sensory input, Gloria, my love, and I remain fascinated because there's not another woman like you, not anywhere on the Zodiacal Planets. You can use heat and thirst, social isolation, and dance, to induce your deliriums. By your breathing and your fasting and your sleeplessness, you alter your body chemistry. Your very gestures and words are so rhythmic that one conversation puts you in a trance. That's why you are too subliminally aware for your own good. And for mine.'

She moved towards him in a serpentine way and positioned her mouth some fifty centimetres from his, as she breathed, 'I didn't say you didn't understand me; I said you didn't understand how to respond to me. To go to Earth is such a crude thing.'

'My father is dying.'

'Fuck him, let him die! And I suppose you will see your ex-wife while you're there?'

He laid his fingers across her left palm, measuring her psychogalvanic response. 'I want you to miss me, but you aren't going to miss me greatly – your whole body image says as much. Gloria, you always escape me; this whole big act we play out on Turpitude consists of your being elusive. Now I have to go and see my father, and elude you for a change. So you feel obliged to be angry.'

'All right.' She draped her arms loosely round his neck. 'I elude you, Colding, and you regard that – if not as deliberate on my part – at least as a piece of my character composition. Suppose you are wrong? Have you ever in your life enjoyed a satisfactory relationship with anyone, man or woman, in which you weren't feeling they eluded you?'

At considerable expense, Colding had had their egg-shaped eight-room transferred to a high point high up the cliff of the outer urbstak of Turpitude 1, to a socket in the sunward face. His firm, Gondwana Inc., had financed the move, anxious to keep so talented a predestinographologist happy. Unable to bear Gloria's probing – she was sweet as pie until threatened by any kind of parting, however temporary – Colding retreated to his rec room.

For a moment he stood looking out the noctures at the view,

consoled by the immense concave chip of a world in which he made his way, and by the view of many other Zeepees, glinting out in space like malformed sequins, all basking in the giveaway energies of the sun. It was a fine sight, although Colding knew that less successful men, with apts embedded deep in the urbstak, had falsies which showed scenes even more striking than this, with whole mantillas of Zodiacals riding round Earth. Well, his view was real and theirs wasn't, whichever looked better. As befitted the brains behind the new destimeter.

One of the prototypes of the Gondwana destimeter stood in a corner of the rec room. Colding went over to it, sat down, removed his socks, and placed his bare feet on the lower screens. His hands he placed, flat-palmed, on the middle screens, juxtaposing his face against the lines etched on the upper screen. A pressure with the right elbow, and the machine was working. His astrological and biophysical data were already recorded. Now the machine was merely updating dermatoglyphic, chirological, physiognomical and secretional readings against previous data, and formulating them out against Colding's projected Earth trip.

It had long been recognized that the hand – and the foot to a lesser degree – mirrored the internal condition, physical and mental, of its owner. The destimeter was a sophisticated way of tallying all information groups and producing an extrapolative graph. Eventually, Colding knew, later models of his machine would come to rule the everyday life of men and women; they should prove more trustworthy than oneself.

Gloria entered as he sat there. She was slightly in awe of the destimeter.

'Sorry I was bitchy, darling. I do realize that you must see your father.'

'*And* that I shall go nowhere near my ex-wife?'

She hesitated. 'You'll go and see your daughter?'

'Of course I'll flaming well go and see Rosey – what do you think I am? Don't I neglect her enough as it is, poor kid? But that doesn't mean to say I have to see her mother – Rosey lives alone, as well you know. Christ knows where Phyllis is.'

c*

'I'm sorry, Relax!'

He couldn't. The destimeter computer had switched to Readout, and was giving him the likely action (86–87.5 per cent probability) on his Earth trip. He clutched at it, reading sickly. As usual these readouts, or Pre-Destinations as they were called by the media, seemed to be talking nonsense; and as usual their veiled terms produced queasiness in Colding.

Space-passage Discomfort-rating 3. No incidents. Blonde smiling. No overtures intended. Item misplaced. Ramp stumble. Disorientation. First Aid station relief. Injection. Random images. Gravity Traffic High-rise increase.

Hospitalization surprise with parent vocal. Noncommunication. Days in Santos. Time confusion Senile incest obsession causes pain. Memory of other parent weeping in Santas boudoir Nausea of Regret. Argumentation Avoid. Promises Keep now later. Visionary horse.

Random accommodation Tension. Encounter with Death. Previous encounter trigger Fresh onslaught Paranoia Type Lyra 2. Green suit assault. Palms a blank. Superior position. Trinket deserted ...

So it went, growing ever more threatening and less comprehensible. His thinking brain was coolly deciding that the delphic element in these predictions would have to be eradicated before the model went commercial, while another and more basic part of his metabolism was whipped into terror by the menacing phraseology. Before he could read to the end of the recital, he sensed Gloria looking at him intently (it *was* Gloria?); he was unaware of what she was saying until she repeated it.

'Will you look up Anna Kavan?' The very question seemed to echo implications in his readout.

He swung round. 'Damn it, Anna's dead. You know she died in the Alaska Trophy. Must you keep resurrecting her?'

She took in his anxiety, came nearer, and said gently, 'Bad prognosis, I take it?'

He screwed up the readout, would not speak. *Pain, Weeping, Regret, Encounter with Death* ... Yet he was destined to go to

Earth; otherwise the readout would have been blank. She read his expression.

'Oh, sweetie, I'm so sorry,' she said. 'Why can't things seem to hold together? Why can't you ever grasp anything? Why does it all slide away? What have you got to go through while you're Earthside? Tell me, at least let me smell your palm.'

Colding pulled his hand away from her and stroked her cheek with it. 'It can't happen as the machine says. It's not always right. I told you the other day it was playing up ... I'll just see Father and Rosey, then I'll be back. I'll go straight to the hospital. Nothing will happen.'

'*What* won't happen?'

'Nothing,' he said. What the hell good was communication, anyway?

As it happened, Colding saw his father first from the other end of the hospital corridor. The old man was walking slowly, but with a stiff upright carriage Colding remembered; people walked like that only on Earth. Colding himself proceeded slowly, uncomfortably aware of the thickness of the great natural globe revolving beneath his feet. He hoped he would never reach his father. Yet with every step the old man became clearer, with every step some piece of the past, long rejected, returned. An intricate relationship formed in the mild autumn air between them. The old man wore old clothes now. There had been a time when he had been younger, had driven planes and ridden horses, and had swum in the ocean off Santos, where they were both born.

Colding remembered Santos, where the lorry drivers slept under their vehicles in string hammocks to escape the Brazilian sun. He remembered the failing coffee plantation, the farm where he helped raise Zebu-type cattle. The seasons of love. Lights and singing among the trees, the well-maintained church. Cars smashing off the *autopista*. A dead snake. His wife, the arrival of his children, the ranch hands gripped by *macumba*, floating little lights out across the flood of the placid river, chanting as they did so. *Days in Santos.*

This sick old man with the goat's face brought it all back, a whole lifetime and more, structures of hope and failure, and love read in a snake's entrails.

'Hello, Father. I didn't expect to find you walking about.'

'If you're coming to see Phyllis, my boy, I must warn you that she's really upset about you. She will wear black. I told her the other day, I said, "It's not becoming. Only old ladies and horses wear black." ' He laughed. There was a stale smell about him, Colding found, as he took his father's arm.

'Phyllis and I were divorced five years ago, Father. I came back to Earth to see you. Is this your room in here?'

'Well, it's nice to see you again. You aren't wearing black, are you? You're certainly looking older. You look more like your grandfather every time I see you. There must be something in predestination ... According to the palm of my hand, I shan't die till next year. How long's that? What month is this?'

'We have a different dating system on the Zeepees.'

'It seems all wrong to me ... Doesn't make sense. I said to Phyllis the other day, "To think that a son of ours should be forced to live on a man-made chunk of plastic out there in space ... " '

'Father, Phyllis is my ex-wife, not my damned mother.' *Senile incest obsession.* One hundred per cent – God, the machine was good!

'Yes, yes, of course, I'm sorry. I didn't mean Phyllis, I meant Pauline. No, let's see, Pauline's dead too, isn't she? It's sometimes difficult to keep track of who's alive and who's dead ... People keep coming and going ... Anyhow, this is my room. Come in, son.'

They went into it, father and son, linked by more than arms. A wide white room with eight sides, auburn light filtering through a large falsie. A bed, tables, lamps, a cabinet, the big mediscanner, various old-fashioned books and static pictures littering tables and walls. Colding received a distinct glimpse of someone weeping in a black-and-gold boudoir, weeping because she was haunted by other rooms. Then the vision was gone, forgotten, irrecoverable. One more damned unwanted image. Beyond every room lay others, onwards and onwards,

like some complex and old-fashioned astronomic clock repre-
senting an unworkable theory of the universe. He went and
sat down in a white voluptuous chair, sickened.

'This is home, son. We live in petty times. As Kronshaw
says, we're all inmates of the same astro-organic house. The
world's grown too small ... All this predestination. A petty
time to die in.' He stood alone in the middle of his room, looking at the palm of his right hand, leaning slightly on his stick,
nodding his sick old goat head at the incoherent thoughts that
filled it.

'Predestination's been round a long time. I must go and see
Rosey while I'm here.'

'Of course. Your daughter's more important ... I suppose
you're still living on What's-It with that woman Gloria.'

'Turpitude. We live on Turpitude. One of the outer and
cheaper Zeepees.'

'That's where predestination came from. Pernicious theory
... ' The old man sat on the side of the bed and looked across
at Colding. 'All those little ticky-tacky planetoids or whatever
you call 'em – they're all limited environments. Of course they
limit thinking. You need a big world to grow up in, to live in,
to think big.Turpitude ... Predestination is a typical product
of the Zodiacal Planets. A tiny thing. Now you've exported it
back to Earth, the way we used to buy U.S. instant coffee
in Santos made from beans grown in our own good alluvial
soil. Why, that soil was so rich ... Before you were born ... '

Colding stirred impatiently. There was a whispering in the
room.

'Predestination is a science now, Father,' he said. 'An
exact science. The most complex science ever devised, and still
evolving. When it is fully developed, it will embrace all knowledge. It represents the marriage of the human metabolism
back into its local and cosmic environment.'

'Marriage? I don't understand you.' The sick man went
and sat down in a chair, saying resignedly, 'You never worked
out your life, did you? How old are you now? Rosey understands more than you do – or me, come to that. Why don't
you marry Rosey?'

'You're senile, Dad! Rosey's my daughter, you keep forgetting.'

'Oh, yes, I keep forgetting. She's a good girl, though, is Rosey. Time means nothing to me now. What about that artist woman you used to knock about with? Anna?'

'Anna Kavan? She died on the Skidmore Glacier in a car race, if you remember.'

The remark appeared to focus the old man's attention. For the first time he lifted his head to look straight at Colding.

'I'll tell you something, Colding. I know you were making love to her during your first marriage, when we were all living in Alaska. Well, *I* made love to her once, when the two of us were alone in the house. I must have been sixty then.'

'You're lying, Father. You told me that before. You're lying.'

His father's voice took on a womanish note. 'You've experienced it all before – you've had it explained to you. You're a Sensitive of the Unrealized Multi-Schizo Type C. It's nothing to worry about. I'm not a child anymore.'

'You have it all memorized, I know. You keep repeating yourself.'

'Why not? It's a petty world ... '

Colding, in a fit of energy, shook the newsfax lying on the arm of his chair and took it across to the old man. 'Petty? Look at this. Read the headlines. Ingratitude is at war with Ecstasy and Knowledge II. The Third Planet Philosophical Lever has been found at last. The abeings of Saturn are reproducing in the Moscow Exohouse. The shapes of five thousand notable smells have been identified; scentologists are now investigating the shapes of consciousness. It has just been proved on a statistical basis that rigorous application of the three laws of immobility can overcome malnutrition. Holman Hunt's "The Awakening Conscience" has been animated. Antarctic icebergs five miles long and more are being sold to United Mars and shipped entire to the Red Planet. Spontaneous generation is now known to be as much a reality as the luminiferous ether. Isn't all that important?'

'Petty,' the old man said, turning his head away in disgust.

'Petty. People don't have command of their lives any more. That's a fact. Petty ... '

As Colding went towards the door, he said, 'I shall look in again tomorrow, Father.'

'I dreamed about a horse last night,' his father said. 'Or I think it was last night. Is that good or bad, do you believe?'

Not without misgivings. Colding decided that he would visit his daughter Rosey on the following day. He became lost when he left the hospital, failing to recognize a single item in the immense urban landscape which stretched across a continent; in their profusion, in their determination to reach their target, the covered ways had obliterated any true destination. Life here was a temporary shift between mobility and mobility. A trajaxi carried him to a five-star Belvedere Hotel, where he hired an interior room, ate a modest meal, and settled on the bed to sleep.

The doorbell rang.

He went to answer it, and stood there blinking.

The woman was small and dark and something less than pretty. She wore some sort of a green suit and smiled at him with a nervous familiarity. What was that hateful phrase in the readout? *Green suit assault ... ?*

'I saw you come in. I just happened to be stopping by the hotel to bring a picture to a client. Colding, my pet, how are you?'

He backed away. 'Hello, Anna,' he said. She had been dead five years. He could hear the traffic outside and wondered where everyone was endlessly going. The readout from his own machine had specified that Anna would reappear – his own machine, yet he had refused to believe. And the destimeter could not distinguish between objective and subjective experience ...

She came towards him. 'It was always you, Colding. I know I made things difficult for you. But you were the one man with meaning for me. I've had time to think it over. I want to come back to you.'

But he had seen her on the slab after the car crash. She

had been dead five years – or had the crash been a paranoid hallucination? He stood against a wall. Always he lived totally enclosed. No wonder people chose to die in space these days.

'I've got a wife, Anna. And an ex-wife. And a mistress. My life – the surface of it has closed over. There isn't any room in it for you.' He could hardly speak for trembling.

She smiled. The teeth were loose. 'Always your excuses, Colding. And mine, of course … But I've come to the end of mine. We can pick up where we left off – '

'You mean, at the bottom of an abyss on the Skidmore Freeway? That's where we left off, lady. Come on, get – '

'Don't live in the past! Touch me, feel me, put your hands on my breasts – I won't mind any more. What are you doing here, anyway? You're staring at me as if I was a ghost. Do you like my wig? Are you sick?'

'Look, I'm – yes, I'm sick. Anna – you're … you aren't here, or I'm not – '

'I'm off drugs, I swear, right off them. Mix me a drink. This swine Currey, I want to escape him, he has a power over me. He won't let me alone. You know how doctors are. I'm prepared to leave everything with him and start again, take up where we left off. Currey is a hateful man, we'll have to hide, leave Earth – '

She had touched him, put her delicate hands on his chest. He recognized her pressure, could feel her, smell her perfume. *Green suit assault.* He was in terror. He ran, jumped over the bed, said, 'Anna, go away, I want no part of it – '

'You know Currey, don't you? He's the secretary of Wombud – you must know him. Why be silly? Are you drunk?'

He knew Wombud, the new sect believing that life after death was available to all, because real life took place in the nine months from conception to birth; expulsion from the womb was death, into a less real world, into a disembodied world after an intense tactual-sensual one. Human beings were living an afterlife, according to Wombud. And Anna …

'You swallow that Wombud nonsense, Anna? Currey's a madman, a menace just as great as the leader, Mister Queen Elizabeth – '

'So you *do* know him! First you say you don't, then you do! You're not in league with him, are you? I'm going to get all the things from you that you refused me before, Colding ... '

She was coming round the bed.

'I refused you nothing. You sucked from me all I had, over and over again, and you kept coming back for more. No more, Anna, no more – you're dead, shit you, you're bastarding dead!'

'We're all dead, darling – '

He was screaming as he flung the bedding, mattress and all, at her, over her, and threw himself on top of it. They went down with noise and hell and hatred and confusion. Under him, under the muddled pile, she struggled, goading him to shout more.

Then he rolled off on to the carpeting, burying his face, saying over and over, 'The bloody wreckage of my life, the bloody wreckage of my life ... '

'*Life, life, you're always mouthing that stupid word ...*' Who had said that to him recently?

Pulling himself on to his knees, he wiped his sodden hair from his eyes and looked at the muddle of sheets. One of Anna's hands lay exposed, its fingers half curled, the nails carmine with her old paint. The palm was innocent of all lines. No readout.

'Oh, Anna, darling, you'd understand. I kill everyone I meet ... '

That damned night, he slept on top of her, leaving the body where it lay under the sheets.

There were a few late flies in the room next morning. Earth's last wildlife.

The cleaning robots were purging the apartments comment-lessly as he grabbed up his suitcase and left.

With misgivings, he decided he would go and visit his daughter Rosey after seeing his father again. He was lost again when he left the hospital, failing to recognize one single item in the immense urban landscape which stretched across the whole continent. The covered ways, in their riotous proliferation, their madness to reach target, had obliterated any real destination. Life – life – had to fit where it could between interstices of mobility and mobility. Maybe Wombud had something.

A trajaxi fled miles with him, depositing him in Trinket Gardens.

Trinket Gardens was a gigantic pyramid, windowless on the outside. Vegetation perched here and there on ledges and levels. Trinket Gardens had been left in a parched desert of urbanization, a Yucatan Peninsula of modernity. The gate that slid open for him had lost its glass. Ninety thousand people had lived here once, packed in their octagonal boxes. Before he was on the first climbing walk, he knew that little was left but boxes.

At 15,492, his daughter opened the door to him and smiled.

She took him in and put her arms around him, whereupon he began to weep. The same old robot, Motown, was there, but Rosey pushed it aside and mixed him a strange drink that he took down in gulps.

'Oh, Rosey, my little pet, it's good to see you. I'm sick, sick or something.'

'Daddy, you always live in the past. Come on, it's not so bad. You're upset. What are you doing here anyway? You're staring at me as if I was a ghost.'

He shook his head. 'Your granddad's dying. I had to come back to see him. It's like getting stuck in the past. And I think I'm undergoing a Lyra-2-type paranoia onslaught, but I'll be okay again in a minute.'

As he went on talking to her, gradually getting his feelings in order, he tried to absorb her through his gaze. She was a big girl for twelve, well built, self-possessed, with a fine neat crop of mousy-yellow hair cut short about her ears and long at the back. She stood before him, smiling with a gentle friendliness. It occurred to Colding that she probably looked a lot like him.

'I'm sorry I had to leave you here, Rosey. You should have stayed with your mother. Are you making out okay, with just Motown to look after you?'

She glanced away momentarily. 'I see Mother about once a month, Earthtime. There are times when I don't want you, times when I do. My existence has to belong to me sometime, doesn't it? Come and see my secret garden – if you're well enough.'

'I'm okay. I'm overwrought.'

'How's Gloria?' Rosey asked, shifting her weight from one foot to the other.

'Gloria? Oh, she's fine … ' He stood up. 'I must find you a nicer place to live in. It's terrible being a failure of a parent – one of the terrible things about it is that although you know you're a failure, it seems impossible to change. Well, that's what predestination's all about.'

'I don't agree with that viewpoint, but let's not argue. Come and see my secret garden. Motown, you stay here.'

'Take care,' Motown said.

She led him out of the apartment and along the passage, down to another passage where all the doors were shut up with metal sheeting and litter lay thick about their feet.

'It's all broken down.'

'People have moved out of Trinket. I like it better without them. There used to be awful fights and I was scared. I'm not scared any more.'

Down other corridors where desolation and perspective reigned.

At a corner suite, they came to a broken door.

'You have to push it a bit,' she said, leading the way. They stood in a wrecked apartment. Some furniture was left, all ruined. Someone had had a fire in the room and one wall was burned.

'I'll find you a better place to live, Rosey, my darling. I know I've said it before, but this time I will. You can come and stay with us on Turpitude.'

'I don't want to leave Earth. I don't want to leave Trinket. This is my place. Look what I've found!'

She climbed over debris into a rear room. There was a shattered window frame through which she scrambled. Sighing, her father followed.

The long-dead planners of Trinket Gardens had made an error in design, or so it appeared to Colding. A wedge of ground was left between sheer walls on three sides. Just a wedge of ground, not much wider at its widest point than a fair-sized room.

'Real ground, Daddy, real soil!' She squatted in the grass. 'And just look what I've got!'

A green thing had seeded itself. Colding knew that it was a tree or a bush. Something moved under it and came towards them, so that for an instant he was alarmed. It waddled towards Rosey's outstretched hand, making small soothing noises at her.

'A chicken!' he said.

She looked up, laughing, her face all alight and unfamiliar in the open air. 'It's a goose, Dad, a real live goose. I call her Jinny. Jinny, come and meet my pop.'

The goose walked about them, craning her neck and opening and shutting her beak.

'Isn't it dangerous. Doesn't it bite or peck or something?'

'She's hoping I might have brought her some food. I generally do.'

He leaned against one of the walls, taking in the miserable wedge of derelict land, the bedraggled bird, the green growth, the sky overhead, fighting against another urge to weep.

'Your old grandfather keeps dreaming about horses.'

'Don't you think I'm lucky to have this little garden all to myself, Dad? It's mine alone, my secret. I found the goose. She wasn't here. She was in a lorry that crashed a way from Trinket, and I rescued her, or else she would have died, and carried her here. The lorry driver was dead, so it wasn't stealing or anything. I come to see her every day. Jinny's safe here, aren't you, Jinny?'

The destimeter readout had even included the goose, terming it 'a feathered animal' – at least an 87·5 per cent success.

'Look, Rosey, let's get back, you can't hang around this filthy scrap of ground – it's unhealthy, and dangerous.' The readout had implied there was someone else here, doing something.

'Nonsense, Dad, don't say that! This is my own special desert island, I love it here.'

He grasped her hand. 'You can't say here with this chicken, girl, now don't be so silly. Suppose someone discovers you? Aren't there any parks left you can go to?'

She stood up and looked sadly at him. 'Daddy, this is *my place*, do you understand? Do you ever understand?'

Colding moved his leg away from the bird and said, 'I don't know. Maybe I understand better than you. You'll go crazy here. You're still only a child. Now, please, let's get back. I'll take you to see your grandfather in hospital; you'd like that, wouldn't you?'

As they returned through the cavernous perspectives, she said, 'I do get sad sometimes. Not so much that you're away, just that you never understand. And I'm not a child any more, either, so it's no good your going on thinking so.'

'Dear, dear Rosey, come and live with us and I will attempt to understand, or I'll keep quiet when I don't. I'm trying to work out my life, and I'm on the verge of a big breakthrough. I'm getting old ... I get confused. I don't know, it's such a petty world.'

'No that's not true, either. To me it's not petty, and it hurts me to hear you say it.'

'Now you don't understand.' He achieved a smile.

Rosey stood right where she was, so that Colding was also forced to halt. He looked at her with love and impatience.

'That makes me sad, Daddy ... You see, I've now come to the end of my childhood. It's going from me, I can feel it – slipping away. Everything's changing, so I must cling to what I've got ... '

'You've got so little – I've given you so little.'

'No, I've got – most things. Only ... my dear secret garden isn't quite such a secret any more. Look, you'd better know, but I've got a boy friend. I'm grown up now. He comes here. He loves the garden, and Jinny, and ... ' She read his face, put a hand up to her mouth, inclined her head, and started to weep.

'Oh, my darling ... ' He put his arm about her shoulder.

An awful black thing rose inside him, choking him. He seized her hand, staring at the lines there, to see if what she said was true.

From a great distance, he heard himself say, 'It's time to go to the hospital. Let's go together.'

Two days later, Colding caught a shuttle belonging to the Chinese line which had virtual monopoly of the Earth–Turpitude route. His father had not died, he had found no alternative to Trinket for his daughter, he had managed to make himself see that the green suit assault had simply been a Lyra-2 paranoia onslaught; he contained his despairs and behaved like an average man, ergatoid among his fellow passengers.

Sitting in the soft-class lounge, he watched Turpitude float closer in the big screen. It was shaped like a rose petal which, falling, turns towards the sun that has been both its reason and its downfall. Colding was moved by the sight. The planetoid had been designed and built by a Japanese-Brazilian consortium; they had wrought well. He jotted down a note on his pad to call Kai Tak at Gondwana and discuss the design of the production model of the destimeter. There were, after all, little important things to be done; one could hide from oneself.

And was predestination – 'the exact science of the future' – really being built there, on the energy-loaded surface of that petal, to spread outwards and transform the minds and habits of men? Was there really something new under the sun? How would Rosey's generation accept it?

The petal was changing contour and shape now, as the *Verbeña Star* swung in towards its homing boom. It was becoming a confusion of sine curves, growing like a three-dimensional drawing in a computer, just as its precise ergonomic shape had once been conceived in a computer.

For a moment, Colding felt himself to be in the computer, *knew* he functioned only as a statistic, *knew* predestination was truth: all of science, and in consequence all of religion, all of thought. He might suffer, and feel himself alive through that suffering; but the biochemistries of his system secreted a specific, predetermined, and consequently computable meed of suffering. Of happiness, too. The ration was not random. Every emotion that ever moved mysteriously through whatever life could now be charted with as much rigour as a comet, visiting and fleeing from the sun on tight celestial schedule.

Something of that moment of perception lingered with him as he stepped out into the transportation station and caught a tube home, whistling through the plastic core of Turpitude towards Urbstak East.

He bought a pill on the train, warding off tachycardia and other maladies which afflicted him after space flight, and in consequence was feeling no more than slightly sick as he stepped off at Equinoctial E and grafted home.

Part of his ill-ease was the final wording of his destimeter readout: *Unfaith causes Resignation.* At Gondwana, they'd have to sort out the way the destimeter's language grew vaguer as its event horizon grew more distant and probability levels sank.

Unfaith causes resignation? His lack of faith in himself? Gloria's unfaithfulness to him? His betrayal of everyone close to him? Or did 'unfaith' simply imply doubt? And what sort of resignation? Was he going to resign from Gondwana, or Gloria from their compatibility contract? Or did it mean a sort of philosophical acceptance?

There was that clear face of hers, the features so beautifully formed. She stood and smiled at him. All innocence.

Colding always had to remember, as he took her into his arms, how small she was, how tall he was. Physically, they were not well matched.

She kissed him on the lips. He knew by her breathing and the moisture index of her mouth that she was in a special mood. Holding her, he placed his left palm across the cervical plexus at the back of her neck, so that the resonances in his palmar arch told him that her central nervous system was on the high.

He smelled and listened, catching vibes from under her parietal bones.

'Lovely to have you back,' she said quickly. 'I'll put on some musuc and make a fuss of you. How was Rosey – and your father?' Her movements over to the veeps system were too fast. 'Is he getting better?'

'Who was here just now?' he asked. 'He's still dying.'

He was aware of the buzz of the fluorescents and conditioning before she said, 'Someone from Gondwana – your boss, actually.'

'Tab Polymer? What did he want?'

'Nothing. Just a social call. Don't be so uneasy!'

'You've promiscued again, you rotten bitch! It's what the destimeter predicted.'

'You'd believe its word rather than mine, wouldn't you? You get more like a machine every day, Colding, you know that?'

'I am a machine. So are you. We just happen to be human machines, treading a computed path. That's how the destimeter can predict events. That's how I know you've betrayed me again.'

Gloria started the musuc automatically. It was a modal hushkit vibration, and instantly the chamber seemed to fill with cloud that saturated all but objects under direct gaze. She had always enjoyed the tunnel-vision effect better than he.

Facing him, she said, through the long white perspective, 'All right, all right. You want a computer that will do all your living for you. You'd like a machine for a wife. You want pre-destination because it gives you all sorts of excuses. I did go with Tab, I admit it. Your damned oracle is right. I want to be human, I want to *feel* – this vision of myself weeping in a black-and-gold room, I can't stand it, I can't stand to be shut out. I love you, Coldy, but I want to be human … '

He went to her. He stooped. 'We'll work it out, Gloria. I'll try to understand. You must have your secret garden. I don't forget that you're a Sensitive of the Unrealized Multi-Schizophrenic Type B. It's terrible being a failure of a husband

– one of the terrible things about it is that you know you're a failure – '

'Don't tell me that again! I know what you're going to say.' She turned away from him. 'Don't you ever understand?'

'I don't know. I honestly don't know. Maybe I understand better than you do. You say you want to be human. What you have to do is revise your understanding of what a human being *is* … '

'Don't give me that sort of argument – comfort me! You just stand there talking and talking! Comfort me!'

Making a great effort, he moved forward through the solid sound, stretching out his hands to her. Like all the others for whom he felt pity and responsibility, she was being left in an obsolescing version of the present, unable to face the future.

'I love you, Gloria,' he said. Even if it was not as much as 86 per cent true, he thought hopefully, it just might provide her with some sort of workable hypothesis for existence.

He kissed her, letting his hand stray down her body, sensing the tautness of her muscles, searching for warmth in her and in himself.

The Monster of
Ingratitude IV

The day was so beautiful that I left the teleceptual studios during the lunch hour and walked along Terrazza Terrace. One delight about being on Ingratitude, of all the Zodiacal Planets, was that the Shield was faulty, giving superb solar distortions. Tourists came from parsecs around just to see the effect of supersonic peacocks plunging in and out of the sun, like javelins growing foliage before they burst into fire.

There on the terrace I turned suddenly and saw a man who stared at me through kookaburra glasses before coming forward and extending his hand. I recognized him by his hand-print. 'Lurido Ponds!' I said. 'After all these years!' Where had I seen him last?

'Hazelgard Nef, incarnate and aglow ... How are you, Nef?'

'In a state of rapture, dear boy. Let's have a nostril of striped aframosta, shall we?'

I sensed immediately that Ponds was going to be important to me; the wiring in the ulna of my left arm was signalling. As we sat down in the nearest afrohale bar, I tried him out with some trivial conversation. 'I suppose you've heard about the new cult spreading through the Zodiacals? It claims that human beings are merely corpses, or revenants of foetuses, that what we think of as unborn children are in fact the dominant and adult stage of the human life cycle, and that what we have always called life is actually an Afterlife.'

'What's the name of this cult?'

'I forget. Their leader calls himself Mister Queen Elizabeth.'

'I don't doubt it. It has a sort of inevitability about it.'

'Wombud, it's called. Wombud. And what are you doing in this phase of your Afterlife?' I still could not recall when we had last met.

As we sat and sniffed and watched the lovely lacerating peacocks overhead, Ponds told me about the clinics he was running with the aid of a man called Karmon. Since Experimental Experience had caught on, people ran through psychotic phases very much faster than ever before, sometimes in a matter of hours or even minutes. The Ponds-Karmon clinic catered for these dramatic and often terrifying occasions. The name of the clinic was vaguely familiar to me.

'I may have to call on you myself.'

'You said you were in a state of rapture.'

'Look, here we sit, Lurido, our limbs disposed as we will. We talk, we communicate, our senses flow like silent water, and our nails grow. We experience sound and sight and touch. Isn't that rapture? Is anything more harmonious than being yourself? Also I have a lovely wife at home, sweet of breath and nature. But still I'm being driven mad.'

I told him how I'd come to Ingratitude IV to set up my studio and escape the colossal rentals charged in the cities of Earth. But my theories of painting were not popular and I had been forced into designing sets for telecepts. Currently – there seemed no point in withholding the news from Ponds – we were involved in making a musical version of Wittgenstein's *Tractatus Logico-Philosophicus*.

'What are you going to call it?'

'We're thinking of calling it *Wittgenstein's Tractatus Logico-Philosophicus*. It has novelty. Or maybe just *Steintrack*.'

'*Startrek?*'

'*Steintrack*. No doubt that sort of thing is much too frivolous for you. You were always an intellectual.'

'I enjoy telecepts when they are complex, as I'm sure yours

will be. They become something like waking dreams, which can transport you to a different level of reality. The entire spiritual history of this century has lain in the pioneering of new LORs. That's the line of mental health in which I specialize.'

I remembered then something he had said to me years back, before my marriage, about the colonization of cislunar space so expanding mental horizons that mankind had propelled itself into an age of neocortical evolution. Such talk always depressed me; besides which, Ponds had been better at getting girls than I had.

Something of my thought evidently got through to him, for he said, 'You okay? Co-ordination rating down?'

'No, dear boy. Just a touch of ecliptic allergy.'

We parted. He headed back to his clinic. As he went, I noticed for the first time a monstrous thing rolling and sprawling after him, moaning as it moved and dragging its genitals along the ziberline mothproof grass.

I went back to the studios, sneezing.

Something throbbed under my zygomatic arch.

My wife awaited me that evening when I staggered home, exhausted by the nonsense of *Steintrack*. Millimetre music was playing and she had on an entire frontal. We embraced passionately, matching respiratory rates and interlocking toes.

'Teresa, my darling!'

'Ally, my love!'

We fled together into the amniotic room, floated in the semi-dark, swallowed the fibre-lights, eagerly chased down into each other's digestive systems, rating the fizzy bacterial jazz of the upper intestine with the sombre melody of peristalsis. In rapture through the y-rays I saw the rare rose of an ovary on the great labyrinthine shores of her circulatory epithelia raise its homoblastic head in bud, felt the event celebrated in a minute eustatic movement of hormones through every uterine dell and declivity.

Oh, the divine delight of that decrustating decubitus!

Later, we dressed; as I made my way to the sun-room, I

came across my son Chin Ping, flat out with a flicker-book.

'Lazing here again! Why don't you get some exercise, play with other boys, do something instead of just hanging about?'

'You say I'm rotten at games.'

'That doesn't stop you playing them, does it? You might get a little better at them if you played more often.'

'Equally I might get better at them if you didn't keep telling me I was no good at them.'

'You *are* no good at them. The truth never hurt anybody.'

'Don't give me that old uni-level crap, Pop. Truth's just the salt at the banquet, not the whole feast.'

I began jumping slowly up and down. 'Aphorisms in an eight-year-old I will not stand!'

'I make your life a misery, don't I? And I'm glad, because you make mine a misery. Do you know why lizards and reptiles remain so still? It's because they don't have what are called saccidic eye movements; so, when they become stationary, they adapt visually and their environment becomes uniformly grey. You must be all saccidic eye movement, Pop, because you're never bloody stationary and your environment is a permanent puce!'

'You little permanent puke!'

'Witty!'

'Repartee you might dig in your dumb child mind!' I snatched up his flickerbook and found it was Theodor Reik's *The Unknown Murderer*, with the paragraph showing about crocodiles eating people in Madagascar, where nobody believes in natural death, and the formula of condolence to a dead man's family is 'Cursed be the magician who killed him!'

I switched the current off and flung the book at him, catching him just under his left eye.

'You stole this from my library, you little swine! Why are you reading such fantasy? Reality's too big for you, I suppose?'

'No, it's not big enough,' he screamed. 'It's just a rotten cage! There should be laws against reality.'

He ran screaming to his mother, clutching his face. I stopped to retrieve the book, noticing there was blood on one corner.

As I did so, something snapped in my back. I could not move, could not straighten up, could not sit down, could not kneel, could not cry out.

Teresa entered the room, saying in her gentle voice, 'Ally, stand up, please, because you and I and little Chin Ping are going to see a friend of mine.'

'Mmmmurrrr ... ' By pressing the small of my back with two fingers, I caused the pain to lessen and was able to straighten up. Immediately, I was myself again.

'I must tell you about the fun we had with *Steintrack* today, Teresa. They have a new girl in to rewrite a lot of the lyrics, and she is first class.'

She took my arm, leading me towards the sub-station, saying as she did so, 'I remember when I was composing a choral – '

'Remember, remember! Christ, is that all the human race ever does? Why not forget for a change, or doesn't neo-cortical evolution stretch that far? What about the future? Doesn't that excite your intellectual curiosity just one tiny bit?'

She burst out laughing and I remembered that she had been fond of greyhounds before I knew her. Chin Ping came running to her side, his cheek badly inflamed, and hid his face in her dress.

'What did you do to your cheek?' I asked him.

He would not answer. Then you wonder why fathers get angry with sons.

We climbed into the first car that came; Teresa punched buttons and we dived into the heart of the urbstak. Somewhere a voice was calling.

'I'm worried about *Steintrack*, love,' I confided, smacking Chin Ping across the head. 'Perhaps the trouble is that it's not complex enough. I enjoy telecepts when they're complex, as I'm sure you know. They become something like waking dreams, which can transport you to a different level of reality. After all, the entire spiritual history of this century has lain in the pioneering of new LORS, compatible with the expanding horizons of neocortical evolution.'

'That's what re-thinking courses are for,' she said vaguely.

'You worry too much, Ally. Maybe we should move to Self-Indulgence VI – I've heard it's fun.'

'It's the boy's future that bothers me.'

We stopped at an intersection station high on the outer face. As we climbed out, a sign lit nearby and a glass door swung open. The sign said, in letters of self-assertive discretion,

PONDS-KARMON CLINIC
Accelerative Psychoses

'Hey!' I said.

'We have an appointment,' Teresa said to a sweetly fragrant receptionist who met us in the foyer. She removed our masks and frontals.

In a short time, we found ourselves confronting a slight man in a stiff suit of silver, who introduced himself as Aldo Karmon. His main eccentricity was, as he explained, that he was a fringillidaephile; cardinals fluttered round the room as he spoke, followed by buntings and greenfinches. As we were admiring them, Lurido Ponds entered the room by another door and nodded familiarly to me.

'Hope you didn't mind my following you this morning,' he said.

After him crawled a strange creature which I could hardly believe to be human, so grotesquely did it drag itself over the carpet, groaning as it came. Its eyes were blurred pools of phlegm. Teresa backed away from it in horror, but Chin Ping ran forward in delight and went down on his hands and knees to it, as if the monster had been a puppy.

'That's right! We shall have Geoffrey cured in no time,' Ponds said. 'He likes a friendly reception. There's never a cure without love, even in phase-schizophrenia.'

I ran angrily across to my son, bending to grasp his collar and drag him away from the creature. My back snapped. I found myself stuck where I was, unable to stand erect again, unable to sit or kneel. A finch settled on my left ear.

My vision seemed to be going. As I toppled forward on to the monster, who made gestures of terror at my approach, I was able to see that the finch was in fact a woodpecker, and that its beak was digging cleverly into my ear, bringing out huge ripe maggots, which it gobbled. Its claws were sinking into my shoulder, pulling away loads of fluff and fur. Further down the tree, a weaver bird was knitting the fur and fluff into a protective blanket. I fell into the blanket, but it gave way and I plunged into the undergrowth below, landing painfully on a shingly strip of beach.

Only the mewling cries beside me forced me to retain my senses. Still sprawling, I saw a baby seal rolling about beside me, fat and white and weepy-eyed. I struck out at it, trying to blind it, but at that moment an angry bark made me pause. Heaving herself out of the waves, all anger and open mouth, was a mother seal. I saw the salty drops of water on her whiskers and recognized Teresa. I tried to call her but could not, for the waves were reaching me.

They were waves of an unknown sea. They were not of water nor of flesh. They were of a substance like jellied flesh, a flesh that had not properly formed. Each wave, as it crawled to overwhelm me, took the shape of ferns, deformed fingers, organs of an outré anatomy, all obeying biochemistries untold.

In fighting to get away from them, I fell over white dead things on the beach, and the waves were upon me. My skin experienced scalding sensations. My ulna was picking up signals from Cygnus 61. Even as I fought with the wave-things, my own flesh and blood were churning in metamorphosis – in them I was drowning, not in the waves, as my identity slipped down and down into blue depths of disorder, overwhelmed by acrocyanosis and the agar-agars of an extreme anguish.

Yet in the intensity of the feverish fathoms was a womb-like impetus that drew together again all that had become dissolved. The separate elements of me remarried and became a working entity, even as the tides that had taken me left me, retching but renewed –

'Two minutes, fifty seconds flat!' said Karmon, pocketing a stopwatch and jotting a note genially on a pad. 'Something of a record in the way of accelerative psychoses. Congratulations, Hazelgard, how do you feel?'

The unknown psychic sea had gone; Cygnus had rung off.

'My back feels great – Geoffrey looks better too,' I said. My breakdown had triggered the monster through his crisis; he looked human again. I picked myself up from the floor and embraced Teresa and Chin Ping, kissing his bruised face. He smiled at me, all open and beautiful.

'Can we have a crocodile for a pet, Dad?'

I cupped his chin in my hand.

'The Afterlife is hard for you, son. You're only eight years past your death. But we shall slowly educate you to remember the timeless months of your real existence, experiencing the universe of life in your mother's womb. Do not despair – every year, we understand more of our mysteries.'

Lurido Ponds said genially, 'You sound so convinced about Wombud that you almost convince me, Mister Queen Elizabeth. It'll be interesting to see which of the two sides of your life eventually stabilize.'

Teresa said, smiling, 'You're a hell of a strain to live with as you are, darling, but I wouldn't change a thing. The more alternatives we can generate, the better. If only I could help more in your non-Wombud incarnation ... '

'Everything's fine,' I said, 'and I'm hungry – aren't you, Chin Ping? Eat, then meet my disciples.'

He began jumping slowly up and down.

I went over and shook Karmon and Ponds' hands; then I adjusted my nose-mask.

'Goodbye, Hazelgard. See you tomorrow as usual,' Ponds said.

As I left with Chin Ping, Teresa was beginning to go into her psychotic breakdown. Another hour, and her renewed personality would be writing some more *Steintrack* songs for us.

Outside, overhead, high above the urbstak, diatoms and divers peacocks phantasmally nested in the sun itself. I sneezed. Something throbbed under my zygomatic arch.

D

Enigma 3:

The Aperture Moment

Waiting for the Universe to Begin
But Without Orifices
Aimez-Vous Holman Hunt?

Waiting for the Universe to Begin

Chin Ping Neverson went through the indignities of Customs and emerged into a bustling street. Colour fountains flared. There was no view of Outside. He was in the heart of the urbstak.

He caught a petulent and moved according to the map he had been given. At Indigo Intersection, a man in a frilled blouse bumped into him.

'You in a hurry, sunshine?' Chin Ping asked.

'It's the whole going human concern.' It was the correct password.

They turned off together into an afrohale parlour. The man ordered two double nostrils of polkadot aframosta and they sniffed. Floating, they moved into the gents' room. Nobody else was there, except a guy flat out in the drying chamber, being massaged by a molycomp.

'Hand it over, Earthie.'

'Let's see my inducement.'

The man in the frilled blouse wore a flesh mask, a tissue of sentient, symbiotic skin which clung to the outlines of his face, making him unidentifiable. Chin Ping scanned the eyes, but they gave nothing away. They did not even have a colour.

Unblinkingly, they watched Chin Ping as their owner extended a jewel to him.

Chin Ping whipped a pen from his pocket, snapped it open and peered through it at the jewel.

'Spectral signature says it's a doppler,' he agreed.

'Now the goods.'

Going over to a splash-basin, Chin Ping ran warm water round his skull and brow. He brought a damp tissue from a cachet and rubbed it on the same area. Then he peeled off his toupee.

Stuck to the underside of the toupee was a thin envelope. He flung the toupee into a trash basket and handed the envelope to the man in the frilled blouse. The man took it, passed over the doppler, and was gone.

And Chin Ping was free to visit his father.

Two men were working amid an organized clutter of machines. So intent were they on what they were doing that speech was rare between them. The main noises were electronic hums and sighs, the flicker of figures through various synthesizers, and the occasional clatter as data readouts moved up on a monitor screen. They were near the end of one stage of their work; a certain intensity in their attitudes revealed the fact.

The room was a mixture of workshop and luxurious rest room. The machines were grouped at one end, with coaxial cable and flow charts littering the floor. The other end of the room contained thick plummy floor sofas, a bar, still and movie projectors, and a screen. There was a tall window with striking views of the great outer sweep of the urbstak of Magnanimity IX, on which the sun always shone.

On the wall hung a large oil painting. It represented an historical scene. A Roman soldier clad in armour and gripping a spear stood on guard at the entrance to a narrow alley; or perhaps it was part of a gateway. Over his shoulder, in the street behind the gateway, a scene of terror and chaos was observable. Molten lava and cinder rained from darkened skies, overwhelming people who tried to escape from what was clearly a doomed city. A man and a woman struggled down the littered way in panic. Only the sentry stood fast. Orders to leave his post had not reached him and he remained on duty, eyes turned apprehensively to the sky.

Copies, charts, dissections, and abstractions of this picture lay about the room, often in stacks. Magnetic lettering on a whiteboard announced APERTURE MOMENT FOR FAITHFUL UNTO DEATH, with colour charts and diagrams appended.

'We're ready, Archie,' Hazelgard Neverson said. 'Switch on the processor.'

Archie depressed a key. A new humming note. The two men went and stood together, looking down at a delivery chute in the side of the faxprod machine. Neverson lit a mascahale. Ten seconds passed.

Neverson was a tall man with an air of battered calm about him. Although solidly built, he could look flimsy at will. Friends who knew him, women who loved him, claimed they loved but never knew him.

Colour slides clicked neatly down the chute, stacking themselves for presentation. When there were twelve of them there, Archie switched off the instrument and picked out the slides. He took them over to the other end of the room and inserted them in the projector. Neverson dimmed the lights.

On the screen, volcanic ash leaned steeply up against the walls of a town, while a volcano distantly jetted fire. An inconsequential view of a gate, lit by fire, part veiled by smoke. A view of two Roman soldiers, one about to leave. A street, an old man with his robes aflame. A building toppling, partly covering the corpse of a young girl. The sentry at his gate, looking up apprehensively, horror in the background. Dark shot of a tavern interior, with an aged woman huddled in a corner, trying to quiet a frightened dog. The sentry again, at the other end of the passageway, stones and ash falling about him. A knot of people, hurrying, led by a man with a grey beard. The greybeard trying to pull the sentry from his post. The street again, its houses burning, more fire raining from the clouds, with a flaming cart. The sentry, overcome by fumes, sprawled unconscious in the darkening passageway.

The pictures were crude, constructed by a pointilliste tech-

nique which proved, on close inspection, to consist of myriads
of tiny squares.

The two men stared at each other. Finally, Archie rose and
held out his hand.

'Congratulations, Hazelgard. It is going to work.'

'We've a long way to go yet,' Neverson said. 'Let's have a
drink.'

He stood staring out at the curve of Magnanimity IX.

'The frozen present,' he said.

'An illusion of the Zodiacal Planets, just because they have
no diurnal revolution.'

'More than that. They have no diurnal revolution because
we built them in our image. They are the expression of our
inward state.'

'You know I don't feel that at all.'

'Nevertheless, even for you the present is frozen, Archie!'

'And when your paintings move, will that free you from the
ice?'

'A start has to be made somewhere. We have made that
start.'

They spoke passionlessly, sipping their drink at the same
time. They had had this conversation many times before in
the course of the present project. In the same indifferent tone,
Neverson said, 'Let's have the rest of the day free. You can
go and join the junketing in the streets. I have to go to my
life-adviser.'

'Don't forget your son is supposedly arriving on Magnanimity today.'

'I'm so busy ... '

The two men looked each other in the eyes.

'Archie, you have reservations about the tremendous
developments we are cooking up here, haven't you? Won't
you see we are opening new dimensions of art? Why won't you
understand?'

The younger man cast his eyes down and said, 'Our sets
of values may be very different, sir.'

Neverson encountered his son in the hall, and did not bother
to display his annoyance.

'I'm off to the life-adviser, and I'm late already.'

'Your usual loving welcome, Father! I'll come along with you, if I may.'

'Please yourself.' As he and Chin Ping climbed into the feeder, he said, 'Why are you wearing that absurd uniform?'

'It happens to be all the fashion on Earth, Father. Why are you living on Magnanimity IX under an assumed name?'

'When one registers as One-Year Resident or Inhabitant, it is customary on a Zodiacal Planet to change one's terrestrial name. It is the courteous thing, let's say. As to why I'm here, I believe that Aldo Wattis Karmon is one of the best life-advisers anywhere, and so I settled near him.'

'Does he make you feel any happier, Father?'

Neverson stared into the distance. 'He is helping me to live with myself.'

His look was so weary that silence fell between them. The feeder had been programmed, and was travelling now in fast tube along the outer surface of the man-made planetoid. Below them, they could see festivity, which Chin Ping watched through binoculars. A long procession was wending its way through a public place, bearing effigies of a beaked creature, either animal or bird.

The vehicler branched into a slower tube and entered a pile-apt, slowing as it went.

'How did you get here from Earth?' Neverson said. 'The fare's expensive. You haven't been ... '

'No more theft offences, Father,' Chin Ping said bitterly. 'I'm on bigger things now.'

'I don't know what's to become of you. I've done my best.'

'You – ' Chin Ping checked whatever he was about to say. The feeder had arrived at the heart of the building, had signalled, and had been admitted into an apartment.

Father and son climbed out and Neverson announced them at an elevator door. As they were cleared, the door opened; they entered, and were carried down one floor.

'If you've never been in a life-adviser's before, you may find this one interesting.'

'I've never had need of one, thank God.'

'Just keep thanking him.'

The receptionist who greeted them was a standard polyclone female.

'Herr Karmon won't be long,' she said, showing them into a dim room with crimson drapes. Electronic music played faintly. They sank into lounges.

'Are you writing any more fiction?' Chin Ping asked.

'No.'

'I'm sorry.'

'You needn't be. I'm involved in something much more important. Do you understand how petrified we all are in Time? The popular understanding of Time is that it flows, that present moments always turn into past moments, that days and weeks slide by. That idea is erroneous. We age, our brains store and lose information, but that is Change, not Time, and is internal, not external. Time, I believe is frozen. We are inside an iceberg. We do not know it, but we are waiting for the universe to begin. The Big Bang has yet to occur and set cosmic time in process. Till then, we retain in our heads the broken dreams of a past universe.'

'How then do we live, converse, have children?'

'We do not. We merely dream that we do. Our belief that we eat, talk, procreate, is false, a belief shaped by distorted legends of greater and more meaningful acts which we as instruments will be able to accomplish when Time does finally begin. We cannot fully understand yet.'

Chin Ping was silent. Then he said, 'Father, I did not mean to speak sharply to you. Please forgive me. I never seem to give you the correct password. I was upset by the journey here.'

'It is absurd to believe that one generation follows another. They all coexist, like cards in a new pack. As yet, Time is congealed, unidimensional. Do you understand me?'

'You've been overworking.'

The polyclone reappeared. 'Herr Karmon will see you now, Mr Neverson.'

'Will you wait here for me, Chin Ping?' Neverson asked, rising.

'Of course, if you want me to.'

'I shall be a long while. You'll be gone when I come out.'

'No, I won't.'

'Well, we'll see.'

Aldo Wattis Karmon was a slight man who managed to combine a cold reserved manner with outgoing facial expressions. It was difficult to tell whether it was the cold reserved manner or the outgoing facial expressions which had been acquired, or both. He wore a long silvery alchemaical gown, trimmed with fur, under which were black trousers and a white shirt. A whimsical figure but still a considerable one.

One end of his long consulting-room was given over to his finches, fifty of them, which fluttered about in bursts of colour.

'How's the animation going?' he asked.

'We've had the first crude results in this morning. They do suggest that eventually I shall be able to achieve complete sequential high-probability animation for any painting I wish.'

'Or any photograph?'

'My interests at present lie entirely in Victorian paintings of what I call the Aperture Moment variety.'

'All the same, your company will have to develop. And you will need funds and investments at all stages.'

Neverson made no answer. After a silence, he said, 'Let us talk about my soul rather than my work.'

'By all means. Though they are not readily separable.'

Karmon crossed to a screen and it lit at a wave of his hand. He pointed to a line of figures on it.

'As you will observe, we have now analysed your schizophrenia group. You are a Schizo AM 26a, which is rather a rare group. We have examined the enzyme content of platelets in your blood samples, and determined the percentages of monoamine oxidase, or MAO —'

'Just a minute. What has monoamine oxidase to do with the state of my soul? I told you, since my wife died, I just need a mad woman, or a succession of mad women. Something a little violent.'

'Your obsession with copulation with the insane is directly

related to MAO. Deficiency of MAO is directly related to a number of schizoid states. The MAO deficiency index in your brain has affected your responses to temporal stimulae to such an extent that – '

Neverson held up his hand. 'I admit I'm sick. I admit I'm in need of help. That's why I came to you. I'm in pain and misery and depression. All the same, you'd better not forget that I'm a dedicated artist, and my work – my genius, if you like – means more to me ultimately than my happiness. I'm in a state of rapture. I'm not having you tamper with my enzymes, even if it "cures" me, so – '

'The treatment would be quite painless and entirely trouble-free. You must have been subject to a genetic weakness and, in the grief of your wife's death, your secretion of MAO fell below normal. A monthly booster shot – '

'Normal? My dear Herr Karmon, don't make me teach you the facts of life! Normality is a statistical fiction. I'm proud to belong to my schizoid group if it means I can see further than other people in some directions. My art relies upon what you call my responses to temporal stimulae. I'm glad of your diagnosis but you can keep your cure.'

The physician nodded in mandarin fashion. He went to sit on a dais close to the finches and rested his hands on his knees.

'Such was what I anticipated your answer would be. It is entirely characteristic of your schizoid group. We grow to love our chains. Freedom is for suckers. So I have prepared to help you in another way, which I hope you will find more accept-able.'

'I'll listen, of course.' He lit a mescahale.

'The finch-alternative method is for you. By rejecting a cure, you have, in effect, chosen a certain mode of living, of en-gaging with future events, the course that will conform to your group, bearing in mind a number of other factors. Had you accepted the offer of cure, then you would have chosen an alternative course. You understand?'

'Continue.'

'The course you will take through life will not be random. We could chart it absolutely, given all the other life factors

D*

you will encounter. Naturally, we are not given those factors, but we have enough data on you – your age, weight, disposition, predilections, financial circumstances, history, ancestry, etc. – to give us a very good idea of what the future may hold for you. You understand?'

'The process you outline sounds not dissimilar to certain techniques I am investigating myself. You are going to synthesize all these factors through a computer and give me, in effect, later time-phase versions of my present self?'

Smiling, Karmon said, 'I do not use a computer. My birds are my computer. These homoeopathic finches, as you know, have a life-cycle of two days. I have four of them already prepared, their systems loaded with toxics which will influence their actions in such a way that, when released, they will perform flight-paths to correspond with the possible parameters of your later career.'

'Ah. Now you've lost me!'

'We shall find you, Mr Neverson, a number of years from now.'

He walked over to the desk and fanned the bell-contact. In came the polyclone, bearing a plastic box containing four inert finches. Karmon, meanwhile, pulled back a curtain to reveal a large glass-fronted cage, three sides of which were covered with small square shutters lined in rank after rank. The shutters were painted in various colours, apparently at random.

Taking the plastic box over to the cage, Karmon pressed a plunger on its upper surface, releasing a crimson gas into the box, where it immediately disappeared. He placed the box on the bottom of the cage before the finches could revive.

As the birds came to life, they struggled to their feet. The lid of the box sprang open. Out flew the birds.

In strange erratic flight, they flew this way and that with a great flutter of wings. Whenever their plunging bodies touched a shutter, it fell open, revealing a number underneath.

'This is where the calculator comes in,' Karmon said. 'It is noting the numbers in the order that they are revealed, and keying them to a behavioural code. Watch – the birds are almost exhausted now.'

The finches were flying more slowly, making more frequent attempts to settle on the bottom of the cage. They fluttered up, releasing more shutters. Then they fell dead to the floor in four untidy little mouthfuls of feathers.

The polyclone tore a print-out from the compterminal on Karmon's desk and gave it to him. He read it, striking out a line here and there, nodding as he did so, frowning, pushing his bottom lip far out over his top lip.

'And what has this mumb-jumbo *proved*?' Neverson asked sarcastically, after a moment's silence.

'Oh, perhaps I let you think that the method was totally reliable. Of course it cannot be. We do have errors … I'm sure this time we have an error.'

'Why?'

Karmon cleared his throat and stroked his chin. He also looked at his watch and nodded dismissively towards the polyclone. 'The homoeopathic finches appear to forecast so many disasters for you. People's lives are not full of disaster – only in films and cinecasts – however much they may want them to be. I think we must have a few more sessions, and then we will try again. I reject these projections.'

In a stride, Neverson was at the other's side and had grasped him by the wrist. Immediately, a stinging shock ran up his arm and he staggered back.

Nursing his hand, he said, 'Since I have no intention of believing this mumbo-jumbo, you'd better tell me what it says.'

'Just keep your hands off me. You will be worse injured next time. My body electricity is marshalled to repel foreign bodies. The finch-alternative method, if you insist on knowing, predicts that you will very shortly meet the sort of woman you are hoping to meet, and that she will fulfil and more all your wishes. Your friend and helper will turn against you, eventually to reveal himself as one of your unassuageable enemies. You will manage to turn your present theories into reality through the strength of your obsessions. But those obsessions will cause the emotional ruin and perhaps worse of those who depend on you. Moreover, your success will prove a disaster for the very art you vociferously claim to love. I have also to tell you that I see here your death – blood and a flight of shallow steps are involved, somewhere in the open air – at the hands of the woman who you think loves you dearly.'

'Give me that rubbish!' Neverson jumped forward and snatched the strip of paper from Karmon's grasp, sustaining another shock as he did so. 'You damned quack, you're just trying to scare more money out of me!'

He screwed up the scroll and flung it at the finch cage.

'You'd better come back next week and hear the rest!' Karmon exclaimed, but his patient was already bursting out of the door.

The feeder took them back to Neverson's pile-apt. Traffic-flow control directed the vehicle down to lower levels, so that they slid evenly among gigantic structures.

'I gather the guy in the cloak upset you,' Chin Ping said, interpreting his father's silence. 'That was a real nuthouse in there – you shouldn't take stick from anyone in a shower like that.'

'Why don't you talk correct English? That slobby talk is only an affectation, and you know it. How did you manage to get here to Magnanimity, in any case?'

'If I told you I was smuggling go-go you'd believe me, wouldn't you?'

'I wouldn't put it past you. You know it's criminal.'

There was silence between them. They threaded their way through a square where dancing and festivity unwound to the sound of a band. Some of the onlookers carried effigies of a white beaked animal.

'What are they all feeling so good about?' Chin Ping asked.

'This is a great day on several Zodiacal Planets. They are sporting their domesticity emblem, Donald the Duck. This is his day.'

'Never heard of him.'

'A matter of mythology – not your strong point.'

'Uh – like you, Father, I'm waiting for the universe to begin … Do we have to be at each other's throats like this? Let's take that white bird for a symbol of peace. I came here because I genuinely wanted to see you. I understood you were ill.'

'You understood correctly. Did you also understand you could cure me?'

Chin Ping waved his arms a bit. 'Look, de-freeze, will you? See me real, will you? Like, I didn't kill Mother, I am not responsible for her death, and you can't make me be! I grieve for her more than you do. *You* killed her with your lack of concern – did your phoney life-adviser ever happen to tell you that?'

'Ah, here we are now at my home,' Neverson said pleasantly, as the feeder slowed. 'I'm sure you won't want to come in?'

They climbed out into the hall and stood looking at one another, both locked in the hopeless complexity of a relationship gone sour.

'You're caught in yesterday's cobwebs, Father. Step out of them, step right out of them and go on living again! Before it's too late for both of us.'

'What does that mean exactly?'

The boy hung his head. 'Life isn't easy for me either.'

'You always made things difficult for yourself.'

Archie appeared, putting on the flowery outer coat which he affected. He looked surprised.

'Are you back already? It's later than I thought. I've been running the Faithful slides through again. Are you going to stay with your father, Chin Ping?'

'No, he is returning to Earth immediately,' Neverson said. 'I'm sorry, Chin Ping, but I've just had a disturbing diagnosis, and your presence upsets me too much. You must go.'

'If you want it that way. Don't forget I've warned you.'

Archie put a hand on Neverson's arm, which was immediately withdrawn. 'Hazelgard, he is your son – '

But the outer door slammed. Chin Ping had left. Neverson turned away.

'You know the boy loves you … '

'Don't reproach me, Archie – I can't bear to be reproached. Perhaps I was too standoffish, but I have just been informed that I'm liable to be murdered by a woman. Why isn't there just work, why all this other side of life, this messy side! I love him, too, but there's time enough to sort all that out when our work here is done.'

'There may not be time enough for your son. Not all of us live in your frozen time, Hazelgard.'

Neverson stood stiffly, his face grim. 'For all your money, you're my assistant, not my life-adviser. Why don't you see if Karmon has a job open for you?'

He hastened towards his workshop and the safety of his art. Outside, the beaked creatures went by unnoticed, people thronged the streets, solar energy beamed down almost inexhaustibly.

But Without Orifices

Keith Road said to Miss Brangwyn and her daughters, 'I've travelled a long, long way ... '

The words hung for a while in Miss Brangwyn's living-room and were finally removed by a molycomp.

'A curious reaction to the only genuine Tiepolo-Nef inside or outside an art gallery!' said Miss Brangwyn. Her manners were always formal.

'Oh, I do like it ... I admire it immensely ... ' Keith said. 'It's all that Tiepolo is, and oh, how much besides!'

She switched it off; the screen went blank and hanging on the wall was merely a bulkily framed Tiepolo etching, 'Castle Scene with Penitents'. She stood silently by. Her daughters, Polly and Polkadot, stood silently by her, half-looking at Keith Road, as if aware that all four of them were merely a study for some ideal group of four, arranged with careful regard for the long unused light of evening coming horizontally through the glass wall behind them.

'Why I said what I said was that ... the Tiepolo-Nef seemed to sum up for me the distances of my life. That's why I said I'd come a long way. It was purely in admiration of your Nef, Miss Brangwyn.'

'I understand,' said Miss Brangwyn. 'Nef gave this work to

my grandmother, Faith Brangwyn. That is how it came into my possession.'

The room was full of precious porcelain.

'Mr Road has travelled a long way, Mother,' Polkadot said. She was the one Keith liked.

'Yes, and by *road*, too,' said Polly. She was the one Keith did not like.

Both girls wore blue.

'I'll walk with him back to his car,' Polkadot said. 'You'll probably be glad to get out of the Experimental Experience area, won't you, Mr Road?'

'Oh, I like it ... I mean, yes, it is my first time in an EE area, yes, Miss Brangwyn. I've been among the Zodiacal Planets.'

'What were you doing there?' inquired Miss Brangwyn.

'I was on a Re-thinking course, Miss Brangwyn.' He tried to copy their correctness.

He walked through the grounds with Polkadot. 'It was great of your mother to let me see her treasure, Polkadot, I mean, Miss Brangwyn. I do much appreciate the privilege.'

'Shit, we pretend to keep up conventional behaviour – it's all the rage – but you go too shit-holing far, Mr Road. Don't you want to seduce me or something, or not even so much as get a finger up?' Sunlight made her dress blink.

'Yuh, uh, well, you're a pretty girl, Miss Brangwyn, I mean Polkadot, but I mean, why, we've only just been reprod- uh, introduced ... '

'Fuck that, do you want to lay me or do you want to lay me not?'

The grounds were beautiful. There were stately pink flamingoes walking by the lakeside, not a dozen paces away.

' 'Course I bastarding well want to lay you!' he shouted. He clutched her. Their lips met. Her mother and sister's applause came faintly to their ears. Her arms went round his neck, her hair curled against his cheek. His hands ripped away the blue dress. He groaned with pleasure and got her down on the lawn. The grass was thick with flamingo shit.

There ends, unfortunately, the last story ever to fall from the computer of Hazelgard Neff. The fragment has a title: *But Without Orifices.* It leaves us with a mute surmise, as does Charles Dickens's *Mystery of Edwin Drood,* also uncompleted at death. Was Polkadot to prove without orifices? Would she prove to be a simulacrum (artifice-fiction – the so-called 'artifiction' – of the third decade of the twenty-first century is full of simulacra)? Or does Neff's title refer to some event as yet unrevealed, as seems more likely?

Neff's son, Chin Ping Neff, reminds us that Neff's earliest work was *The Golden Orifice,* and here the word was used in a metaphorical sense. Neff refers more than once to 'the fudged vents of the soul', a phrase later plagiarized by other writers.

Chin Ping says, 'Miss Brangwyn was probably an amalgam of women that Father knew, right? One of them was almost certainly Catherine Cleeve, known in certain circles as Capodistria Kate. They were lovers at one period, despite the somewhat cagey tone of their first meeting, see.'

NEFF: I like your dress.
CLEEVE: Do you? This is the first time I've worn it.
NEFF: It's beautiful.
CLEEVE: The boutique where I bought it called it 'très cad, presque snob!'
NEFF: There's a split in the seam by your left shoulder.
CLEEVE: It's designed for looks, not durability, darling.
NEFF: That goes for a lot of us.
CLEEVE: I have to be going myself now.

The conversation has come down to us because both Neff and Catherine Cleeve were wired for sound. Both had a mania for recording the transient; indeed, Neff's whole life was directed toward imposing order on the fleeting moment and banishing impermanence; it was the fulcrum of his art. This obsession it was which brought him and Catherine together. Her two daughters were already grown up and living in EE cities, Vienna, Austria, and Trieste, Italy.

NeffPanimation was the brainchild of Neff and Catherine

and their computers. The mating of their computers, charged as they were with life-data, was fully as traumatic as the mating of the two human beings.

And NeffPanimation exploited to the full that Neffian obsession with the transient.

'This all happened before I was locked away for anti-experimental behaviour,' Chin Ping says, inserting the thumb of his right hand in his left ear. 'Father had this thing about Victorian paintings, which were very fashionable again in the twenty twenties. He saw in them what he called the Aperture Moment, a frozen moment of time typically defined by artists from John Martin's day to Sickert's. Their whole range of pictures just don't make sense unless and until you ask yourself the sort of extra-artistic question, "What happens next?", right?

'I mean, like take one of the most famous paintings of the period, Holman Hunt's "The Awakening Conscience", well, it's not just a composition featuring some Victorian skirt rising from a piano – at least, it's only that from the narrower old academic art tradition. It's an Aperture Moment, my father said, where Hunt makes you expand a whole new section of your mind – new in Victorian times, I mean – and say to yourself, "What happened before now? How did this skirt get in this predicament at the piano with her boy friend? How long did they know each other? Why don't she like his tune, right?" And the Aperture Moment also makes you think about the future, right? So you say to yourself, "What happened after this? Did she give the guy the brush? Who got the house? What's that cat doing eating the pigeon? Was the artist there looking on all the time, like God?" What you'd call metaphysical questions, right?

'And Father said that it was by inventing – or at least perfecting, we'd better say, and accelerating, if you follow me – this Aperture Moment that the Victorian artists reflected the new dimensions of the age in which they lived, as exemplified by Darwin's theories, which widened the stage of human affairs, back far into the past and forward into the future. So painters like Hunt helped ordinary slobs to appreciate the new expansion of the mind of which we are capable.'

Chin Ping Neff was shot on Tuesday, May 1st, 2051, two centuries to the day after the opening of the Great Exhibition. The execution was carried out in 577 Buki Tinghi Street, Singapore, before a member of the World Judiciary.

'Sure I remember the dress,' Catherine Cleeve said. She was still beautiful in a Socratic fashion. She spoke without gesture, sitting absolutely composedly. A chill radiated from her. 'It was a nice dress. There was a split in the seam by the left shoulder the very first time I wore it. No, the right shoulder. It came from a boutique in Singapore. The girl who sold it to me said it was "très cad, presque manic", or something.'

'You worked with Neff on his first Animation, I believe.'

'Maybe it was the left shoulder. I know Hazelgard commented on it. Sure, I worked with him. Panimating Hunt's "Awakening Conscience" was my idea. Or my computer's, at least. He had done a Poynter before that, which he destroyed. I had a turquoise Tanzyme 5505 All-Digit. It never gave me any trouble. What we did, we fed into Hazelgard's big computer all the data we could get concerning Hunt's painting. Centrally, the data about the picture itself, of course, so that the comp could match colour values and everything – the proportions, relationships of figures to background, light readings, dynamism with frame – together with details about objects in picture, structure, type, make, material used, style, period and so on. Great fun to do. A lot of research needed. We were lovers at the time. My daughters still took up much of my life.'

Remaining immobile, she changed only the focus of her eyes, so as to gaze into some inaccessible distance.

'Hazelgard had always longed for an affair with a mad woman. And I was certified mad at the time. It is perfectly true that I had killed my brother to terminate our long and rather intense incestuous relationship. Oh, I can face the facts now. Hazelgard was marvellous. I owe my life to him. I can only say he treated me like a brother, in every way …

'We both had a mania for the transient. He was waiting for

the universe to begin. That was what brought us together. No, it was the seam on the right shoulder that went. Mind you, the side seam split the second time I wore it. I know I told Hazelgard that it was designed for appearance rather than permanence, and he said, "Aren't we all!" Very funny, I thought it was. His whole life was directed towards a study of the fleeting moment, with all its chaos and mystery. That was all he wanted from life.'

'That was why you animated Holman Hunt?'

'Basically, yes. We also fed the computer all the possible parameters of Hunt's life. First, his painterly technique, complete data on palette, brushes, mode of work, analysis of lengths of brush-stroke, all that kind of thing. Then his other pictures. Facts about his personal life, why he was blackmailed, how he ate the original scapegoat that died, his Christianity and his involvement with the slums through his mistress, Annie Miller – a very Victorian story! It all went in, together with a stack of information on the other Pre-Raphaelites and the society of the time.'

She sat stock still, not speaking, not thinking. Her hands were long and narrow.

'That business about the flamingo shit. A complete fabrication. I believe there was a goose turd somewhere, but nowhere near Bobbie and me.'

'And when you had fed all the data into the computer?'

'It was programmed on strict probability transference to produce a sequence of 4,320 reproductions of "The Awakening Conscience", using Hunt's original as central Aperture Moment, and using time as a factor of variance. These were to be projected in the form of film. At sixteen frames per second, we had a four and a half minute film which was in all respects a genuine Hunt original.'

'I believe there has been some argument on that score, Miss Cleeve.'

'Believe what you will. It was a genuine Hunt, its subject-matter enduring in time linearly as well as instantaneously. The brushwork was Hunt's and everything. Oh, I know what Sir Archibald McTensing said, but other critics were entirely on our side. Archie was a dirty little man, for all that he was the Great Panjandrum on Art. He buggered eskimo boys, it was well known.'

'At least the film was a great success.'

'Success? Success! My dear girl, it was a revolution! It was – it was a new art form, and we had invented it. It's the schizos who explore and extend the world. Yes, Archie actually buggered them in the snow, if you can believe it. In the end, he caught frostbite where he least wanted it.'

'What did your Hunt film show?'

'It showed "The Awakening Conscience" as it really would have been if Hunt had had access to our manipulative techniques. It was Hunt's film, not ours. The lady rises from the piano stool, where she has been playing *Home, Sweet Home* with the man she loves. No, *Come Into the Garden, Maud*. She goes to the door, opens it, walks into the hall, and –'

For a moment, her immobility is broken, she bends double in the chair to utter a coarse laugh.

' – and she nips into the lavatory for a pee! Ha ha ha ... '

The interviewer reaches out and slaps the ageing lady on the face, hard, three times, left cheek, right cheek, left cheek.

'Think what you are saying, Kate, you old bitch! You aren't in Capodistria now, or Koper either! This is Vienna, Austria, nor are we out of it, so you'd better answer my questions properly. Who am *I*, for a start?'

Catherine looked blearily up at her question. The woman was possibly in her late thirties, attractive, well-built, a splendid head of tawny hair. Something hard about her mouth.

'I know we've met before.'

'Of course, we've met before. I'm Polkadot, your daughter. Remember me now?'

The older woman in the wheelchair began to cry.

'You're trying to make me unhappy. I don't have any daughters. I had two but they died when they were small. I remember burying them in their party dresses, I remember how pretty they looked and how I cried –'

'You remember, you remember! Jesus Christ, is that all

the human race ever does? Why not forget for a change? What about the future, what about what's going to happen? Doesn't that excite your intellectual curiosity just one little titsy bit?'

'Not half as much as the past does, darling.' Catherine had pulled herself up in the wheelchair and was affecting a deep masculine drawl. 'Besides, you forget I'm mad, baby, and madness is all to do with the past, isn't it? You must have read your Freud and your Stekel and your Stockmeyer and your Rhukaiser if you're any sort of daughter of mine! The little webs in the grass, functional long after the spider's dead, the old fridge on the waste lot, still trapping kids ... Come on, will you? Why isn't there any air in here? You breathing it all?'

'In your presence I never breathed. You were always a suffocating presence, even when Polly and I were small. I remember running out into the fresh air and panting, clinging to the old Spanish chestnut and just trying to get the whole atmosphere of you out of my lungs.'

'Didn't do your asthma any good, did it?'

'You see, you do remember me! You aren't mad, you've been mad! You're just sick, aren't you?'

'Why do I have to remember you, just because you're my mother?'

Polkadot screamed and made a filthy face.

'I'm not your stinking mother, I'm your daughter! Oh Jesus, why do you make me live, why is there all this mess blowing round all the time, like I can never get free of it? I was mad to come here at this of all times, just when – '

She walked about the room, big and bleak, behind the wheelchair, gesturing as she went.

'– just when I'm in this dreadful emotional state, and my whole psyche seems to be breaking up. Do you know what I dreamed last night? I dreamed my little girl came all the way from Sacramento in a pink frock and she just went to the Rowlandsons' house next door to get her dolly, and she wouldn't come to me at all, and I thought she was coming, but when she got as near as the gate, she hitched a lift from a car and was gone, and I ran out to stop her, screaming "Dorothy,

Dorothy!", and there was her little dolly lying in the gutter, all bleeding and broken.' She broke into convulsive sobs.

Catherine started to laugh.

'Hazelgard had bad dreams too. He'd tell me about them at breakfast and we'd laugh at them over the grapefruit.'

Choking back her tears, Polkadot came round to confront her mother and said, 'You killed Hazelgard, didn't you? You shot him!'

'What gives you that idea? I liked him as well as any man I've ever known. He loved me, and he was faithful to me. Faithful unto me, "Faithful Unto Death" – that's the title of Poynter's dreadful Pompeii canvas, the first thing Hazelgard ever worked on ... '

'His Panimation Exhibition was so badly received that you shot him, didn't you? There are several nasty streaks in you, Mother, but the worst is that while you're a failure yourself, you can't bear failure in others, can you? You think I'm a failure, don't you?'

The older woman lit a mescahale. 'Go back to your husband, if he'll have you. I shouldn't think you're much of a lay. I *know* you're a failure. What's even more boring is that you keep on coming round every so often, begging me to tell you so. As for Hazelgard, he wasn't like you, he was a real man, he had a strong will to success, something every artist should have. When it seemed as if everyone turned against his invention, he couldn't bear that. He shot himself more in anger than sorrow. I was there, my dear child, I saw him run out on the terrace and do it. I went to him, but he'd blown half his head off. Before I had strength enough to call for help, I went back into the living-room and I remember his coffee still stood there, the cup half full. It wasn't cold yet.'

'If he shot himself, then why are you in this criminal institution?'

She was looking into the distance again. 'You know what Hazelgard always said? That reality was designed for looks, not durability! I really liked that remark. It was one of the things that won me to him. "Kate," he'd say, "reality is designed for looks, not durability." And the reality that killed

him wasn't at all enduring. If only he'd sweated it out a bit ...
The tide of opinion soon turned. People were soon on his side.
They wanted the product ... Poor Hazelgard! I loved him like
a brother ... '

Fidgeting, Polkadot said, 'Well, that's my cue to leave,
Mother dearest. We all know you killed your brother.'

'Do you remember that? I didn't think you were born
then? Funny how you get confused about such matters. Well,
give my love to little Dotty ... '

'I have a job now, Mother, believe it or not. I do Women's
Features for Eurovision. I'm going to write up this interview
for them.'

'Want a picture of me?'

'I have one. Shows you with your hair as you used to do it
when we were at Salzburg.'

'Oh, I remember. That big antique tortoiseshell comb I
had.'

'Was it genuine tortoiseshell?'

'The man said it was. And you and your sister used to wear
black-velvet bows in your hair. Fashions were so pretty then.'

'I guess that 2055 was about my favourite year.'

'That was the year we had those donkeys!'

'Oh, the donkeys! And that holiday in the Amundsen Sea!'

'Wasn't that fun, with the Polynesian music?'

'Lovely! Oh, Mother, let's do it all again some time! You're
not too old.'

'Of course I'm not! I'm still wired for sound. Just you wait
till they let me out of here – you'll see!'

'I'll wheel you back to your cell now.'

Aimez-Vous Holman Hunt?

The private viewing of the NeffPanimation Exhibition was
well under way, and some of the reporters and critics were
already glancing tipsily towards the exit, when Valery
Mallarmaine entered with Polly Neff and Sir Archibald

McTensing. Quimpax, Sir Archie's eskimo valet, followed close behind the trio. The two celebrated critics were having a loud and sophisticated conversation.

'He was a terribly talented young man, and I dearly loved him,' Sir Archie was saying. 'You know he was one of the founders of EE, one of the first to realize that whereas a majority of the population cling to Traditional Experience, there is nevertheless a considerable minority who prefer Experimental Experience, and that the two groups would be happier when separated. The New Renaissance dates from that perception.'

'A touch of Leonardo and Dirac about him, I agree.'

Sir Archie smirked. 'And Beardsley ... '

'He and his sister Kate did really have it off together?'

'Not a doubt! They were both so proud of it that they set many incidents on film. Careful what you say, though, Val — she'll be here, Kate'll be here, hanging on friend Neff's arm. He always said he yearned for an affair with a mad woman.' They tittered.

A gallery assistant brought them both catalogues. The men watched the beaten silver pages turn themselves over.

'No expense spared,' Sir Archie murmured.

'Neff always liked to impress,' Val said, catching sight of the artist in the far corner of the room wearing a silver alchemist's gown. Catherine Cleeve was with him.

'I see he's included Poynter's "Faithful Unto Death". Temperamental affinity, I always thought,' said Sir Archie. 'Neff's like Pompeii — all very quiet and Roman and enduring for a long time while, then suddenly, *puff*, the volcano erupts and everyone has to run from the boiling lava.'

'Of course, you used to work with him — you should know.'

'That was donkey's years ago. I bear no grudges. I doubt if he even remembers me.'

'We'd better go over and be nice to him.'

'He's okay if you give him the right password.' He gestured to the valet to follow.

There were ten Panimations on display in the exhibition, embodying single works by Turner, Egg, Wallis, Burne-Jones,

Millais, Waller, Poynter and Sickert, and two by Holman Hunt.

The private showing was a fashionable one, among those present being Naseem Bata, V. T. P. Naipaul, Anna Kavan, Francis Parkinson Hunt, and two especial friends of Catherine Cleeve's, Freddie Rhukaiser and Frank Krawstadt. Slightly apart from the others stood Heinlette van Ballison, the leading writer of artifiction, his android close behind him.

For once, many of the guests were paying closer attention to the exhibits than to each other. Although the attic in Gray's Inn with Chatterton dying caused some excitement, most of the interest centred on Hazelgard Neff's earliest completed creation, 'The Awakening Conscience'.

Albert is playing the piano.

The soft tinkling notes of Edgar Lear's *Tears, Idle Tears* come from the stuffy little room, over which the eye roves among dull indigos and reds. All is over-furnished; even the window open on to spring trees discloses only a claustrophobic little garden.

Suddenly, there is a break in the music. Annie Miller has pulled the sheet off the stand.

'You *are* in a pet this afternoon,' Albert says. 'That's what comes of lying in bed so late of a Sunday morning instead of going to church like a respectable girl.'

'You know why I was late getting up,' she says, half-sulking, half-coquettish.

He sniggers and starts to play *Oft in the Stilly Night*. The rosewood piano tinkles a little. She perches on the arm of his chair and sings with him. The tabby cat bursts savagely in through the window, a sparrow in its mouth. Her embroidery is unfinished. The wallpaper pattern of corn and vine is oppressive; thieving birds prey on the fruit. He had always longed to have an affair with a mad woman. Old webs capture prey long after the spider has gone. A slight breeze stirs the net curtain. A copy of Noel Humphrey's *The Origins and Progress of the Art of Writing* lies in elaborate binding on the table. Albert's novel, *The Golden Oriole*, has stuck on

Chapter Six, at the words, ' ... hoped that there would be more alternatives than his life had so far offered ... '

Annie's voice falters and stops. She rises, moisture trembling on her eyelashes like dew in grass.

'Come on, Annie! Let's hear you!

> "The eyes that shone,
>   Now dimmed and gone,
>   The cheerful hearts now broken ... " '

But Annie moves away, tall in her sad, silly, complex dress. Her face is a study in pained intensity. In Ruskin's words, the eyes are filled 'with the fearful light of futurity and with tears of ancient days'.

She strides from the room, closing the door behind her. The hall is dark. She passes a tall hall stand, crammed with coats and brushes; visiting-cards lie on a silver tray. A mirror catches a dim glimpse of her as she passes. She goes to a rear door and unlocks it, bending slightly to do so. There is a frosted panel of glass in the door, set round with lozenges of various colours.

Annie lets herself into the garden. There is an attempt at lawn, but the garden is east-facing and a high brick wall keeps out sunlight, so that the grass is thin or strangled by moss. Sun catches the boughs of their single plane tree. Two daffodils flower in a far corner. She closes her eyes, squeezing out a tear, and commences to walk back and forth. Once, a word comes from her lips, either a curse or perhaps the word 'Mother.' An inquisitive small boy peers at her over the wall from the next door garden. He wears a deerstalker hat. He clutches a hoop. The tinkle of the piano is thin in the Victorian air.

At the window, Albert appears, grinning. He rests his face on one hand and lets his jaw hang down in a mockery of Annie's dejection.

'Come on! Cheer up! I'll give you a drink, old girl!'

She hesitates, then looks towards him. Smiling, she begins her return to the house. All in genuine Holman Hunt brush strokes.

'It seemed to go quite well,' Neff said afterwards.

'I wonder how many of them realized that they were attending the birth of a new world of art?' Catherine said.

They were riding together on donkeys, moving steadily through the extensive grounds of the asylum. Huge black or white screens had been erected here and there to set off special trees or clumps of trees. Lights burned underground. A few people walked, many of them alone. It was very early.

The odour of cigars still hung about him from the night before, flat champagne cluttered his kidneys, making him pensive.

'See the schizos taking their exercise! They're our kind, yet not like us. The ability to turn sickness into art is a survival trait.'

'The schizos are exploring the real world, the world of artifice. You spoke to von Ballison last night, I hope?'

He was watching an inmate who had walked up to his donkey and was frowning as they rode by. 'Funny thing about reality. There's a split in the seam by the shoulder. It's designed for looks, not durability.'

She said dreamily, turning the donkey's head for home, 'Reality's for machines. We're coming to realize that now. Humans were never happy there. They just had to live there because we had no alternatives before. Now, with EE and all the rest of it, we have alternatives.'

His cloak was grey, her robes saffron. The long gold strikes of the early sun made them both the same colour. There was dew underfoot, and little clever webs made of minute pearls, which the hooves of the animals broke up. The grass bent and sprang upright again as they passed. Catherine sang wordlessly under her breath.

'Are you happy, Catherine?'

'I'm never happy, Hazelgard. We live so long, and we have to live so many lives, so many broken bits of miscellaneous lives. My daughters' lives ... Are you going to be able to face what the critics say?'

He gave no answer for a while. They rode back along an avenue of poplars, where sunlight painted the shadows behind their eyes red and green. The android at the stables took charge of their mounts. As they climbed the shallow steps into Neff's living-room, he said, 'Rapture. That's what I always feel. Used it not to mean "possession"? In that case, I'm possessed. Sometimes I think I really am a considerable artist, on that score alone. Whether happy or miserable, I am always in a state of rapture … '

'You don't care that these steps were the scene of a foul murder last week?'

He paused, looking into her eyes. Her face, her expression, still and always gave him a shock. There had never been anyone like her. The spider had created its web and left for ever.

'No, I recall no murder here.'

'Perhaps it's next week,' she said. In anyone else, the reply would have run like a feeble joke; from Catherine, the remark was merely confusing. For a moment, Neff saw dirty arterial blood everywhere. It stained the walls and curtains as he entered the living-room.

There he turned and confronted her. 'You can no more take my rapture from me than I can take your madness from you.'

'Isn't that why our relationship is impermanent? You always wanted an affair with a mad woman, but I as a person am meaningless to you. Only my madness awakes a response from you. Isn't that so?'

He cast his gaze down. 'Isn't it enough that … ' The sentence was never completed.

'Let's see what the critics have to say,' Catherine said.

She walked over to the fax machine, which had delivered six duplos. Looking through them, she selected one, pushed it into the go-slot, and switched on. The words of Sir Archibald McTensing spoke from the morning edition of *The European Times.*

What the NeffPanimation studio has done is little short of a miracle. Yesterday evening, I saw a new Holman Hunt. In many respects, it was a genuine Holman Hunt.

It was our old friend, 'The Awakening Conscience', that mawkish bit of kitsch of the Pre-Raphaelite School, which shows a woman having a touch of remorse about the things that were. I have never admired the quality of the thought or the handling of this picture. The paint surface is meretricious. But, yesterday evening, we were not invited to dwell on such exacting considerations, or to stretch our minds far towards an aesthetic response to an aesthetic act. What we were invited to do was to admire – and admire we did – the ingenuity of NeffPanimation in endowing the Holman Hunt with life. This was a world of peep-shows, not painting.

Accordingly, we saw the woman and her lover at the piano. We heard the piano playing, as the fancy man (wearing his gloves, mark you) gave us *I Stood on the Bridge at Midnight* and the woman sang. Then she broke off, went outside and walked about the garden until the fancy man called her in again.

All this in the peculiarly beastly palette of Holman Hunt, in suffocating pinks and indigos. It was a Holman Hunt we were watching, a Holman Hunt given the extra dimension of time.

You may think there was nothing particularly momentous in what we saw, that this was just one more tiresome technical trick. I disagree. I believe I have never seen anything so momentous.

We were witnessing the death of art, nothing less. As photography killed the portrait, so now the computer has killed the whole aesthetic of pictorial composition. I was assured by Mr Neff that his computer could have been programmed to produce the whole life-story of Hunt's wretched woman and her banal involvements. All he needs is backers; and can we doubt that in an age like ours backers will be forthcoming? When painting is transformed overnight into a tarted-up version of the comic strip, can we doubt that the Philistines will be there in their hordes?

For what we see here may be, in many respects, a

genuine Holman Hunt; but it entirely subverts the artist's original intention, which was precisely that his subjects and subject matter should not move, that the piano should make no sound, that the light at the window should be for ever frozen. Only thus could he achieve his intention of forcing the viewer to reflect on such profundities and delights as he, Hunt, had to offer. There was room, even in Hunt's limited art, for the connoisseur. Now the connoisseur is banished for ever. Thanks to Hazelgard Neff's computer, the connoisseur has been elbowed out of the way by the rubber-neck.

It would be vain to claim much majesty for Hunt's original conception, but at least he strove to present us, as honestly as he could, with the dilemma of a fallible woman. All that has been banished now. Instead, we have the privilege of following her into the toilet.

There are nine other pictures in this exhibition, all of which have been subjected to the same perverted ingenuity. One may watch – to name the most saddening victims of Neff's technique – the horses led off and the old house closed in Samuel Waller's 'Day of Reckoning', Chatterton, the golden boy, quaff down his poison as dawn comes up in those hues uniquely Henry Wallis's; Poynter's Roman sentry overcome by the disaster at Pompeii; and J. M. W. Turner's little steam train cross a viaduct in a storm and its passengers alight at Maidenhead.

As yet, we may remain, if not entirely calm, at least composed. For as yet the Neff studios have desecrated no major artist, with the exception of Turner. But I give warning now. Rembrandt, Giotto, El Greco, Botticelli, Titian, Tiepolo – none can rest easy in his grave. Within five years, I predict, we shall have the Mona Lisa smiling and waving at us, and shall be able to follow her as she trips away to sweep down her back porch.

The long struggle between art and science is at last over. Science has won. Given a few more years, it alone will possess the field.

Hazelgard Neff took off his cloak without speaking.

Catherine walked over to him and laid a hand on his shoulder.

'How's the rapture, honey?' she asked.

'There's a split in the seam,' he said. He hid his face in his hands. 'You try and give – you try and give … You devote your life to it. And they don't understand.'

She clutched at him, but he brushed her away.

'That is the artist's role – to strike out always for something new, to break away, to defy, to – to grapple with the unfamiliar … '

He staggered out to the terrace, confronted the long shallow steps, stared towards the ever-changing aspect of parkland.

Only the familiar ghosts confronted him, the deserted webs of other lives, other epochs.

She went to make some coffee.

Backwater

Frank Krawstadt was almost at the end of his monumental work and his tether. After a month's rest on an obscure Zodiacal Planet, he returned to Earth to secure a footnote to Chapter Five: 'Other Low Grade Arts of the First Great Depression'.

'The dimness of your life!' his friend Reemy Morris said as he saw Krawstadt off. 'What's the point of all this dumb research into dull subjects stuck in bygone periods of history? Look ahead, Frank, look ahead! Be positive!'

Krawstadt, who did not see Morris's job as administrative director in HER (Human Exudations Recycling) as the most scintillating or positive of occupations, muttered something vague and friendly about compulsion, and fastened his safety belt.

The *Celestial Barracuda* fell away from its station. Momentarily, the roar of its jet sounded. Its nose tilted and it began the long spiral which its computer conceived as a beeline fo Chinese Earth.

Yuma was a thriving port. Millions of whale and seal were bred every year in the northern waters of the Gulf of California; many of the cachalots, pilots, and bottle-noses were trained in

Yuma to patrol the oceans and keep surveillance over their own kind.

The Yanki quarter of Yuma also throve according to its lights. Those lights became very dim in the Imperial Street area. As you were working your way past the trash cans piled with refuse in Holy Jack Lane, the lights went out altogether. And at the far end of the lane, below the sign that used to say HOTEL: BLACKS AND WHITES ONLY was the door to Jimmy Petersen's place.

Inside the old hotel, Jimmy sat in what had once been the accounts office, looking at the sheet of paper in his electric typewriter. The sheet read: 'Branzi Maisel had never looked more beautiful than she did this evening. Her pale face was oval, with freckles sprinkled lightly across her nose; her eyes were a grey tone of blue, her lips were red. Her black hair reached her shoulders without a curl. Nobody looking at her would have guessed how deeply ... '

He put his head between his hands and sighed. Anna was coming downstairs. He listened with boredom to her tread, recognizing the note of individual stairs as, uncarpeted, they voiced their ages and inadequacies. She reached the last step and manoeuvred her way among the coffin-like piles of old pin-ball machines, uttering an odd word of impatience as she came. He waited for the complaints. This was all routine, a drama played out every night Anna Kavan was with him.

'Why don't we go out, Jimmy? Do you wonder I don't stick around for long? I get so bored. It's so dark in here. The goddam air's so old it's got whiskers on it.' At this point, she appeared in the office. She was wearing the blue cheong-sam with her habitual sandals and the yellow lipstick. 'Darling, there you are working, over that old novel. That old, old novel. Nobody *writes* novels any more.'

'Novelists do.'

She leaned on the table, picking at his hair, lifting a strand, letting it drop. 'Don't think I'm in any way sticking the knife in, but you are so indistinct ... A serious writer, is that what you are?'

It was his decision to smile at her. This he did, showing his

E

grainy teeth. 'I have to take myself seriously. You don't. No one does. As for indistinctness … What was that book I picked up? It quoted Freud as saying something about "We can't dictate to things their characteristics. Like the indistinctness of dreams is a characteristic of them like any other." Or something similar. My characteristic is to persevere – which you don't seem to care for, right?'

She ignored it all. She smelt of a scent called Antidote, hoping to cover the traces of the drinking she did up in her room. She walked round absently, hands floating at shoulder level.

'Yeah. Two books in twelve years. No reviews, no interviews. No fame. No income. With a record like that, you can't be anything but serious.'

He stroked her cheek. It was slowly withering. He knew she knew it.

'Yet you keep coming back here, don't you? Why do you like the odour of my failure? Does it serve as a foil for your success? Or are you just my wayward female persona? If not, why do I love you and your everlasting mother-loving torment?'

She inserted a finger irritatingly into the dry core of his ear.

'Everyone's going off into space, relationships are kind of dated. Outside of this dump – in Peking – I'm free. Here, I make a period piece with you – I guess it is a relationship of a sort … Or death. Maybe I enjoy death more than I know.'

He put a hand up the cheongsam and tweaked. 'Cut out that perverted stuff on my ear. You just like playing out your roles on me. Is all. You just like playing out your roles.'

The door chimes went. They whirred, they clanged off-key, just above Petersen's head.

Anna Kavan and Jimmy Petersen looked at each other.

'Someone at the door, honey.'

'I'll get it,' he said. 'Now who could that be?'

He shrugged his shoulders. Petersen was a tall, bony man; shrugging came easily to him. He pulled the rim of his old blue sweater down to meet his jeans, worked the lugubrious lines of his face into a simulacrum of a smile, unbolted and opened the door.

Outside stood a small, neat, colourless individual, with sandy hair and an alert expression on his flesh-free face. He wore clothes which Petersen recognized as of the type worn on the Zeepees.

'My name's Krawstadt, Frank Krawstadt. I'd like to interview you. You are Mr James Petersen?'

'You political? From the fuzzmen?'

The neat individual showed his teeth and started to move in. 'Nothing like that. Your fame has spread, Mr Petersen. I want to interview you as a celebrity. I'm a synthesist.'

Since Petersen looked blank and barred his way, Krawstadt added, 'I am a theories-critic, to tell it another way. I'm putting together a work that will – well, I guess you'd say *assemble* and *construe* all the constituent facets of twentieth-century art – paintings, films, TV, writing, whatever ... '

Petersen's face cleared. 'Writing? A critic! And you've heard of me? Sure, come right in, Mr Kronshaw. Forgive the state of the house, but I've been moving the furniture around ... '

He bolted the door while Krawstadt looked about with interest. Everything was shadowy. And behind the shadows of the junk was the shadowy outline of an old hotel. And behind that the shadows of a vanished way of life.

'Maybe I should explain a little. My thesis takes in history, science, politics, economics, as well as all the arts. All in all, I'm piecing together a theory I call Total Environment. TE for short. Arts, science, history – these are what I call reactives. See, no coherent understanding of which reactives predominate in cultural terms has ever been established. Some say technology shapes history, some say politics shapes economics, some economics politics, some literature history, and so on. My theory is that, in a sense, all these views are correct. All reactives react. Like chemicals, they combine with other elements.'

'Uh, you mean like politics becomes history?'

'I like to leave the past tense out of my consideration,' said

Krawstadt grandly, staring into the shadows where Anna Kavan stood. 'I mean that the reactives themselves change character with time. For instance, journalism at the beginning of the twentieth century concerned the straightforward conveying of information from one part of the world to another; under such masters as Josef Goebbels it developed into a system for manipulating beliefs, and so diversified into sub-reactives, like propaganda. Or, take a minor art, science fiction began as a palatable way to serve up science-fact to the young, and later spawned futurology and what is now called philo-fiction. I find, paradoxically, that the most neglected arts are often seen to be the most potent reactives when viewed in the light of my theory – '

'Oh, this is most interesting, and most valuable,' said Petersen, rubbing his hands together with a dry noise. 'Please come and sit down in what I call my den, and I'll get you a drink.'

Ushering his guest towards the door behind the old reception desk, he pushed his way between the pin-tables and moved to where Anna stood in the half-dark by the foot of the spiral stair. She was patting her lower lip with two fingers.

'Anna, you hear that? This guy is interested in my novels. He says they're reactive. He recognizes their contribution to the thought of our times. Now, be a good girl, don't play up, and go and get me a bottle of booze out of your room.'

She looked narrow-eyed at him, still tapping the lip.

'Why should I play up?'

'Of course you wouldn't, Anna. I didn't mean that. I just wanted you to fetch me a bottle of whisky, or gin, or anything, and tomorrow you and me'll go and have lunch at one of those fish cafés down by the quayside, okay?'

'Wow! What are we celebrating?'

He gestured helplessly. 'Look, this gentleman is obviously of some standing. He has read my books. *I could be rediscovered!* That matters a lot to me, Anna.'

'Go and talk to him then. Don't waste time talking to me.' She went slowly upstairs, swivelling her narrow hips inside the cheongsam.

Petersen found that Krawstadt was leaning on the reception desk, looking into the gloom of the foyer. 'How many pin-tables do you have here, Mr Petersen?'

Petersen brushed the question aside. 'Drink's on the way. Damned place is full of them. I used to collect them when they went out of fashion. I'll get some ice. Just a hobby while I got on with my life's work.'

'Which is?'

'My writing, of course. If I may, I'd like to outline briefly for you the ideas basic to my third novel, the one I'm working on now. It was in fact my first novel, but it got turned down by every publisher on the continent, barring none. My second novel was published first. That was *Years with the Wilsons*. But the first one I am now reworking; it has considerable potential. It was called *The Day of the Jekyll*, though that will be changed. Possibly to *Transformations*. Briefly, it is about an ordinary family living in the more peaceful days before the Union. The Harman couple – the name's symbolic, of course – the Harman couple have three children. They are fine children, sweet-natured, healthy, intelligent. But as they grow up they become increasingly unpleasant, violent, destructive, evil. There's nothing the parents can do. It's the Jekyll and Hyde syndrome. Gradually the bad comes out – pours out of them. I try to show that we go the same way as we grow older, until all that is left of goodness is a little lost child imprisoned somewhere inside of us, like – '

He was interrupted by harsh laughter. Anna Kavan came towards them, pushing her way among the old machines, a bottle grasped in one hand.

'It's his autobiography he's writing! What a fool theory! Did you ever hear the like? You men are such goddam fools, chasing fool theories like dogs after leaves! Jesus, Jimmy, can't you see that's just an old Christian hangover, all that stuff about kids being little saints – '

'Stay out of this, Anna, will you, shit you!' Petersen ex-claimed, jumping up. He attempted to grab the bottle from her, while at the same time planting his other hand on her flat chest and pushing her away.

Looking on with some interest, Krawstadt said, 'Christian myths have a fair percentage of effectiveness. As reactives, I give them a Three grading of potency.'

Anna handed over the bottle, evaded Petersen's arm, and moved towards Krawstadt.

'Potency, mister? What the maddening old monkey puzzle do *you* know about potency? You don't look like you could fecundate a female ferret! I heard your silly theory too, and I wouldn't give you that for it.' She snapped her fingers derisively. 'All theories are alike – they kill you in the end.'

Petersen said, keeping his voice calm, 'She's a little drunk, Mr Crumshaw, don't – you know, don't worry. She's acting out a role, playing barmaid or something. The old hotel atmosphere does such things to her. Uh, sorry about it.'

Anna laughed again. 'Oh, no, sonny boy, I'm not acting. I'm not acting, I'm *real*. You're the ones who aren't real, the pair of you – theory-mongers. Life, let me tell you, life is meant to be lived, not theorized upon.'

'Platitudes as reactives,' said Krawstadt, looking towards the veined ceiling. "Life is meant to be lived … " Fantastic!'

'Fantastic, am I? Believe me, I'm good red meat. Good red meat doesn't need theory. You're just imitations of real men – and that goes for the Harman family too!'

'Normally she's very quiet,' Petersen said. 'Plays patience quite a bit.'

In order to avoid Anna's breath, Krawstadt had backed round the counter, setting his spine against a stack of piled-up wicker chairs. He smiled as if he enjoyed the contact.

'Perhaps we could go somewhere quieter,' he suggested.

'Quieter?' Anna screamed. 'Quieter? Ye gods, what place is quieter than this wall-eyed flea-ridden joint, tell me that, will you? Short of the grave, mister, no place, but no place – '

She broke down and started to weep, curling up in an old wicker chair of oriental origin.

'It's the word grave,' Petersen said sympathetically. 'The word grave always throws little Anna. She figgers it'll close in on her soon, and I guess she's right.'

With the same studious air of sympathy, he poured two

whiskies and passed one over to Krawstadt with a solemn, even elevated air, as if the liquor was embalming fluid.

'Great, your health,' Krawstadt said, downing the drink fast and holding out his glass for more. Petersen filled him up, sipping his own glass noisily at the same time.

It was so dark in the place, under the green and purple shades, that Krawstadt leaned forward to see his host's face clearly.

'Now, would you mind if I had a look at your pin-tables, Mr Petersen? I can't wait to inspect them, it's such an amazingly large collection.'

'Sure, you can look at them if you want, I guess ... I'll explain more about my novel as we go. It sure is dusty here ... '

As the two men moved into the gloom, and Krawstadt began pulling wraps off the tables, Anna called shrilly, 'There they stand in the pale glare of history and what do they do? They look at old pin-ball machines. The whole solar system outside their doorstep and what do they do? Grown men, they look at pin-ball machines. Small wonder women weep, small wonder I say ... Gimme that bottle, Jimmy, you Jesuit!'

Krawstadt was tearing off wraps with increasing excitement, jumping about. 'Fantastic, fantastic, can't we have more light? Jesus, what a trove ... A Williams *Four Aces* ... Genco *Wizard* itself! ... Fantastic graphic work ... Jesus, fantastic, a Bally *Olympic Champ* ... Wow, fantastic early Ballys – look at the backflash on this *Riviera Rider* ... a masterpiece in its own genre ... Yeah, wow ... '

All this Petersen tolerated for some while, finally saying, 'By the way, Mr Crumbstraw, if you were wanting to interview me about my novels, I have to go out in a few minutes. My time's precious. A writer's time is precious, no denying that.'

Pausing in his excitement, Krawstadt said, 'I didn't know you also wrote books, Jimmy. Will you look at the way these thumper bumpers and roll-over buttons are integrated into this design! I came across an interview with you in an old issue of *Wacky Collector*, dating, oh, maybe eleven years back and gone. That's where I learned about your fantastic collection of pin-tables. Why, you've got one of the original Alwyn-de-luxes here!'

'You mean to say ... Look, mister, hold on, let's get this straight – you mean to say you came here just to look at these old obsolete *pin-tables*?' Petersen went pale as he spoke. 'They were just a *hobby* – what about my *writing*, my life's work?'

Looking him in the eyes, blinking rapidly, Krawstadt said, 'I came to Port Yuma all the way from the Zeepees to inspect your precious collection of pin-tables. I know nothing about any fiction. I greatly regret if I have upset you some way. I mean your novel sounds great, but where I'm at right now is securing a footnote to Chapter Five: "Other Low Grade Arts of the First Great Depression". You see, my reactives react most vigorously in times of crisis, and during the first great depression, late 'twenties, early 'thirties, many new arts were born: big-band, talkies, family radio, science fiction, and of course pin-tables. The art of these pin-tables is akin to Red Indian art, to Benin bronzes, African masks, even cave paintings. It springs from the people, and its reactive influence is enormous. Now you take this playfield here – this was a very famous machine in its time – a Bally *Wizard*, sold millions. This fine vivid design is by Dave Christensen, one of the finest pin-ball artists of all time, as well you know.

'Notice how a spiritual meaning, a message of protest, is conveyed. Even the name, *Wizard*. It dates from the 'seventies. Fantastic combination of realism and mysticism. What's the customer think subliminally when he plays Bally's Christensen's *Wizard*? Why, he thinks, The world has something to offer me personally, win or lose. Reactives like this capture and thus reinforce, redirect, all other reactives. The whole equation moves. The influence of this one table alone on the recovery from the Second Great Depression is inestimable – but I'm going to estimate it, and that's why I'm here ... What else have we here? Jesus, what a trove ... here's an early Italian machine, a Zaccaria – note the swastikas, very unusual ... '

While he was talking, Petersen was subsiding into a small

decaying chair, burying his face in his hands, shrinking gradually inside his sweater.

Anna had taken several swigs from the whisky bottle and was sobering up rapidly. She came over to Petersen in a series of lurches.

'Y'know, it's only a week since I was in a vision studio talking to one of the most famous guys in this planet, guy called Ted Lim Hsua. Maybe you heard of him. Or in your case, maybe not. He's in energistics, he's been every place in the system, including the asteroid belt. He spent five years in the asteroid belt. And his touch ... The way he looks at you ... Jesus, when I compare him with you and this creep here, sniffing round flipper machines ... Ted doesn't work out his aggressions on a table – he has all space ... '

She sank her claws pityingly into Petersen's hunched shoulders, and lapsed in interior monologue.

'No good talking. Ted Lim Hsua didn't talk all that much. A doer; everywhere, but everywhere. Seen those tungsten fish on Mercury, imagine that. The touch of his hand ... Culture-free guy. None of this past stuff – all future. Jesus, little lost child inside us, so there is, it's true to a point, but strangle the little horror, strangle it ... It's the fault of the West. Freud. Kill that inner kid. America should have burnt up its whole past, every damn bit. Instead the Chinese did it for us. They don't give a piss about pin-ball machines. Not a piss. Nor these stinking theories. Just do. Get out there and do. What we had once. Nation of go-getters. Gone, gone, everyone with their stinking noses in *Wacky Collector* ... '

Petersen said, 'That guy Kumshaw's gone upstairs now ... I've got to talk to him. He thinks he knows everything. If he'd only mention my books – just a footnote, just a damned footnote, I don't care.'

'Let him go. The world will blast on, believe you me, Jimmy boy, the world will blast on without you or him. You got to look forward, outwards.'

He rubbed his face as if it were a plastic mask which would come off by abrasion.

'Maybe there's nothing to life but life ... In which case,

E*

why not suicide? Life and death are just the same, aren't they, if there's nothing to life but life? I don't get it.'

'What the hell you expect, angels with trumpets, you nut? It's your Christian hangups. Life isn't even life with you – you never even see daylight, stuck in here, hunched over that lousy typewriter. You don't need Jesus, you need a fucking shrink.'

She took another swig at the bottle and passed it over to Petersen. He raised it to his lips and drank. He stared up at the stained ceiling.

'Yeah, the sun's out there, pouring out its fluid. The human race pulls nearer to it, sucking up the juice like there was no tomorrow, or no yesterday. Everything's changing. Butterflies bursting out of chrysalises, birds out of eggs – all due to the sun. The sun giveth and the sun taketh away ... Anything positive now takes place out in orbit. I know it, don't tell me. So I live in a backwater – you know what came out of back-waters? Life, life on land, the lungfish trundled up from stagnant pools to conquer the world. So Earth's a backwater – that means nothing, it's still *the* place and space is still just space. It's the difference between life and death ... '

Anna looked down at him sceptically and relieved him of the bottle.

'You still got me, Jimmy. On and off, now and then.' She kissed him.

Upstairs, Krawstadt ran through room after room, pulling wraps off old machines. Here were whole galaxies of art, of yesterday, of theory and delight, crammed into deserted bedrooms and corridors.

Mad caricatured faces smiled up at him from amid the bulbs, the thumper bumpers, the roll-over buttons – faces of glamorous women, lean men, Spanish dancers, hula girls, musicians, baseball players, gamblers, apes as big as the Ritz, supermen, rocketships, riders, clowns, queens, musicians, switchboard operators, magicians, jockeys, divers, singers, soldiers, jostling with the zany lettering. On the now dead back-flashes, enormous scores still stood, memorials to the valiant dead. The great old names unrolled before his eyes. Chicago Coin, Jennings, Williams, Bally, Williams, Williams, Bally,

Gottleib, Chicago Dynamic, Marx, Yatashi, Bally, Alwyn, Pierrot, Love Bay, Bally, Daval Chicago Coin ...

'You'll see,' Petersen said. 'I'll finish the novel. Everyone will read it, everyone. I'll dedicate it to you, Anna ... '

'Why don't you call it *Now that the Future is Safely Past*?' she suggested. She raised the bottle to him and drank again.

Together, they listened to the running feet overhead.

Enigma 4:

The Eternal Theme of Exile

The Eternal Theme of Exile
All Those Enduring Old Charms
Nobody Spoke or Waved Goodbye

The Eternal Theme of Exile

Anna Kavan believed that I was persecuting her. Rather, she believed that she was being persecuted and that I was in some way responsible for the persecution. Sometimes, I was the chief agent of it; sometimes, I was no more than an innocuous bystander who acted as a focal point through which some insidious form of vengeance was channelled.

In order to prove to her that I was entirely innocent, I decided one morning to travel to the Outer Zodiacal Planets. My secretary informed me that an ion-jet was leaving for OHG 3RL in an hour's time. I registered with the Ministry of Slavery and checked aboard the I. J. *Silence* as a Propulsor.

We arrived at OHG 3RL, a distance of sixteen point four light minutes, fourteen minutes later. Resuscitation took a little over half-an-hour, and then I was allowed on to the face of the planet.

One never becomes used to the changes in metabolism which take place as one treads ground which is not Earth's, not even when one has travelled to as many exotic scenes as I have. On OHG 3RL, I was burdened with the miseries of an entirely imaginary past, details of which, crowding in on my senses, almost drowned out what I thought of as my normal person-ality.

The impressions were so evanescent that, once I left the planet, they could never be recaptured. I retain a memory of them only because, as it happens, I stopped at a booth offering narcissistance and made a cassette of my troubles.

'Father, I still grieve that the state closed down your business just at a time when, in middle age, you were at last making a success of your life. We were so proud of you, your ailing family. We too felt the bitterness of an edict pronounced just because our skins were of a different colour from our neigh-bours. Our hearts bled for you – mine particularly, because Erik and Franz had their own jobs, whereas I, your youngest, worked only for you.

'Now that you are dead, I realize how bitter you were that you could no longer provide as head of family. Perhaps it was a mistake that we left the country and went to start life anew in K—— in Africa. We always held the move against you, hating K—— as we did. Only now do I see how truly you hoped for a freer life for your sons, unable to understand how your bitterness was imprisoning us all in your old European world we seemed to have fled.

'The constant journeying broke Mother's health. First the slow boat down the East Coast, calling in at all those squalid ports. Then the attempt to settle in Johannesburg. Well, we were happy there for a while. That was where I first saw Anna. Then the two-year trek north, the succession of horrible vehicles ... '

So the catalogue went on, always with the eternal theme of exile – one perhaps nearer to the human heart even than love and hate. All the while, I earned a slender living working in the great earth kilns of Kubanjitully, the capital of OHG 3RL. I knew I had to live there for a year. Then I could return to my native planet. So great were the relativity gradients on OHG 3RL, owing to the Black Class sun, that when I set foot again on Earth, Anna would be an old lady, and no longer in fear of me – if indeed she remembered at all.

The year passed, I laboured through it with many lifetimes on my back – not only mine but those of a bedridden mother, rambling on about her idyllic childhood in the Ukraine, and of my brother Franz and his wife and two children, all of them completely imaginary. Franz lost his job because of his inability to master the complex atonal language of OHG 3RL; he drank and soon became unemployable. His wife, Hettie, a wan and consumptive girl, more and more sought my company.

At last, I returned to the space port and registered for passage to Earth. As I was boarding, Hettie ran up and begged me to take her with me. Compassion forced me to consent. In a moment, she was crowding into the cryobunk by my side. Our joint decision was to settle in New Zealand, there to forge a happier life together.

Earth again. My old personality hardly fitted me. I came down the ramp alone, conscious of irredeemable loss. What had I dreamed? I looked up, but heavy cloud covered the night sky. Every star was a life, so they said.

Well, at least there was Anna. She would be old. She would be at my mercy. To all my old armoury of tortures, I could now add the insult of my youth.

I bought a pale flower for my buttonhole.

All Those Enduring Old Charms

To escape the attentions of Anna K——, my master journeyed to the Remade Planets, where he served his time as a demographer in the state of Aphos, on Caphoster. He took on to his staff two beautiful young females, whose names were Vittoria and Venice; their job it was to classify data and tend to my master's Madagascan Indris.

The Remade Planets had been in existence in their present form for many thousands of years. They had been set in orbit about Profabdos; there were sixteen of them, most of them burnt-out cores of old suns. On Caphoster, most of the states specialized in one predominant emotion. My master had chosen the state of Aphos because its predominant emotion was severity, which was congenial to him.

'Tomorrow, we visit Hostas, the city beyond the Tiger Glacier,' he told me. 'You will accompany me. Vittoria and Venice will remain here with the animals.'

The Tiger Glacier was so called because of the stripes that ran along much of its length, painted by moraines brought down from the mountains. We crossed it in a day and found ourselves in Hostas, a strange city where one sailed over magma to get from house to house. No windows were built into any of the buildings, in order to keep out the permanent drifting smoke. It proved a congenial city to my master: he settled quickly into its vices and duties, investing in its fashions and obsessions.

During our second year there, he came across his own name carved on a memorial. After extensive inquiries, he discovered that Hostas was the city of his family's origin, or had been, several thousand years earlier.

'Send a message to Vittoria and Venice to come at once,' he told me. 'We will reside here for a term. There are connections I must explore.'

No sooner was the message sent than he made another discovery. The cryotomb of his ancestors stood in another part of the city. Indeed, it had been added to within recent date. After application to the city fathers, my master entered the cryotomb; there he found his grandmother in D S A, clutching to her side an immense lily as she endured phases of minimum biological activity.

Busy although he was, he decided to fall in love with her and have her reanimated. No doubt he was attracted by the perversity of the idea, while the fatal disruptions in his family, dating from early in his father's lifetime, probably encouraged his intentions.

By the time the necessary papers came through, and the tomb was set to Regeneration, Vittoria and Venice had arrived in Hostas. Celebration was in order. All my master's new friends came to see how beautiful the girls and their animals were, so that other projects were forgotten for a while. The

Festival of Enshrouding Smoke was held, commemorating the original programming of the city.

My master was in a tavern on Culpice Street when he saw his grandmother on the other side of the room.

'My faith, but she resembles Anna,' he said. She was haggard but still possessed charm, despite her advanced years. She had been endowed with a fine bone structure; it was simply that this same bone structure was now more prominent than formerly. Unfortunately, she took offence at the sudden amorous advances of a hitherto unknown grandson, and would have nothing to do with him.

Daily, my master sent her one lemuroid after another, hoping to win her heart. One by one, the animals were returned, decapitated. My master sent her flowers, mathematical disputations, five-dimensional objects, sweetmeats, metaphors, plumes, plums, live jewels. All were returned. Grandmother was not to be moved.

'How vexatious,' said my master to the girls, 'that I should leave one planet to escape the attentions of a woman, only to find myself on another planet where another woman plainly wishes to escape my attentions!' He besought Vittoria to go to his grandmother and present his case personally. Vittoria was not returned.

Venice now begged my master to forget his madness, relinquish his exile and head back to Earth. Such were the charms of his grandmother – in his eyes at least – that my master would agree to this only if Venice would go first and make one final attempt to convey his feelings to the romantic old lady. Resignedly, Venice went. She was never returned.

Overwhelmed by amusement as well as remorse, my master wrote an elaborate suicide note to the elusive charmer; he then relinquished his post as demographer, and we left the Remade Planets.

But he remained attached to his beautiful suicide note, which seemed to embody for him many of the eternal truths of love. On the voyage home, he recast it as a love letter, posting it to Anna K—— as soon as we docked in Tellus City.

Nobody Spoke or Waved Goodbye

No, I was never in love with the man I still call 'my master', not even during those few months when we were married to each other. Differences in ages, temperament, position – especially the fact that we had been born on different planets – all such things make us completely incompatible.

Why, then, am I never free of him?

Only today he was here, as ever more keen to be clever than kind, bringing with him that blank-faced clone-serf of his.

'Anna, I'm leaving tomorrow. I came to say goodbye.'

'Where are you going? Back to Caphoster?'

'Ten years in DSA. I'm hiring out my personality while I'm gone. If you have patience, life can teach you a lot about the human condition you'd never understand in any other way.'

Always those baffling remarks of his. I would not kiss him. He left me his silver coffee service, many volumes of Anna Diary, some anatomical studies, gutta-percha figurines, foils, veils, and an eidetic dream-memorizer. Despite which, I felt myself alone.

Consolation was something I always found in the melancholy Masked Gardens of Santarello. I chose a lemur mask and walked along the wall.

The eternal conspiracy had penetrated even there. Among the crowds, someone spoke my name. Soon it was taken up on all sides. I ran among the trees, dropping one of the volumes of Anna Diary as I went. Someone would find it with all its vile explicitness; their life and mine would be ruined.

I sank under a chestnut tree. A short-haired man stood there, smiling.

'I can tell you are a hunted being,' he said. 'But at least you live at the centre of your world; people find you worth persecuting. I live only on the outer perimeters of my existence, a nomad unfit for persecution. My spirit is grey, yours cerulean.'

Faintly, I said, 'Please go away; I can tell that your personality is hired.'

Although I absorbed myself in my work, and in particular in a town I was redesigning in Wildgreif, my emotional life was empty. Some months later, I met the smiling man again.

'Are you still on the perimeters of your existence?' I asked boldly.

'Working towards the outer suburbs. I find you in my subtopia, in uncertain light.'

'Cerulean no more?'

'The human face is the most spectacular of all objects. Yours includes much of the sky.'

We became lovers before I discovered that, in his double life, he was famous. Wherever he went, crowds of short-haired men and women followed him, all more handsome and youthful than I could tolerate. I asked him what he could possibly find in my small pale being on which to nourish himself.

'Only surprise me!' Sometimes he quoted obscure poetry.

When I began evading him, he followed me to Wildgreif. I computed his face obsessively into the façades of public buildings. Every gesture he made could be expressed in the rhythms of thoroughfares and traffic-flow lanes. His hired characteristics I expressed in the tensions of bridges and spaceways. To his persecution of love I supplied an answering persecution of function. Soon he was pervaded by interpretations of himself; the whole city became his anagram. The original population moved out, while all his followers moved in, delighted with the fantasy of existing within the spirit of their hero made concrete.

His will broke before mine. 'It is well to remember that evil is a pretty bad thing,' he said. 'I shall leave tomorrow for the Outer Zodiacal Planets. In any case, my present avatar expires next week,' He moved 1·03 light minutes away, but I could still see him.

All his admirers came to the spaceport to see him off. Nobody spoke or waved goodbye. There were ashes in the air, and traces of older destinations.

Now someone else wears the hired personality. My city expires under its borrowed mannerisms, like machines whose wheels are velvet. My master sleeps for another seven years. I age. Shortly, I will revisit the environs of the Paranoid Sun, and then again dreams will be worth the memorizing and vitalities will fall from the atmosphere.

Meanwhile, I preserve my taste for the curious. A fame of my own has come my way; the lost volume was published, to immense acclaim. Now, on buildings expressing his animus, I find my anatomy sketched. Time has many revenges, but seven years will not pass too soon.

All that I was, he is. All that he was, I wish I were. As long as he remains asleep, I remain in exile; the foils and veils cannot comfort me.

The Expensive Delicate Ship

But for him it was not an important failure; the sun shone
As it had on the white legs disappearing into the green
Water; and the expensive delicate ship that must have seen
Something amazing, a boy falling out of the sky,
Had somewhere to get to and sailed calmly on.

W. H. AUDEN

In the old days, there used to be a suspension bridge across from Denmark to Sweden, between Helsingør and Halsingborg. It's scrapped now. It became too dangerous. But it had a moving walkway, and my friend Göran Svenson and I often used to use it. At one time, taking the walkway grew into a pleasant afternoon habit.

We got on the bridge one day, complaining as everyone does occasionally, about our jobs. 'We work so damned hard,' I said. 'When do we have time to live?'

'I've got a theory,' he said, 'that it's the other way about.' When Göran announces that he has a theory, you can be pretty sure that something crazy is going to come out. 'I think we work so hard, and do all the other things we do, because living – just intense pure living – is far too painful to endure. Work is a panacea which dilutes life.'

'Good old Göran, you mean life is worse than death, I suppose?'

'No, not worse certainly, but the next most severe thing to death. Life is like light. All living creatures seek the light, but a really hard intense white light can kill them. Pure life's like that.'

'You're a fine one to talk about a pure life, you old lecher!'

He gave me a pained look and said, 'For that, I shall tell you a story.'

We climbed on to the accelerating rollers, and so up to the walkway proper. We were carried out over Helsingør docks, and at once the Øresund was beneath us, its grey waters looking placid from where we stood.

Ths is Göran's story, as near as I can recall to the way he told it, though I may have forgotten one or two of his weird jokes.

He was aware that he was on a boat in a fearful storm. He thought the boat was sailing up the Skagerrak toward Oslo Fjord but, if so, there must have been some sort of a power failure, because the interior of the ship was miserably lit by dim lanterns swinging here and there.

Maybe is was a cattle boat, to judge by the smell. He was making his way up the companionway when a small animal – possibly a wallaby – darted by. He nearly fell backwards, but the ship pitched him forward at just the right moment, and he regained his balance.

When he got on deck – my God! What a sea! It couldn't be the Skagerrak; the Skagerrak was never that rough! Göran had spent several years at sea before the last vessels were completely automated, but he had never encountered an ocean like this. The air was almost as thick with water as the sea, so furiously was rain dashing down, blown savagely by high winds. There was no sign of coast, no glimpse of other vessels.

An old man made his way up to Göran, going hand-over-fist along the rails. His robes were dripping water. Something about his wild ancient look gave Göran a painful start. What sort of vessel was he aboard? He realized that the rails were made of wood, and the companionway, and the entire ship as far as he could see – roughly made, at that!

The old man clutched his arm and bellowed, 'Get up to the wheel as fast as you can! Shem needs a hand!'

Göran could smell strong liquor on the old man's breath. 'Where are we?' he asked.

The old man laughed drunkenly. 'In the world's pisspot, I should reckon! What a night! The windows of Heaven are open and the waters of Earth prevail exceedingly!'

As if to emphasize his words, a great mountain of water as big as an alp went bursting by, soaking them both completely.

'How – how long's this storm likely to last?' Göran asked.

'Why, long as the good Lord pleases! What a night! I've got the chimps working the pumps. Even the crocodiles are seasick! Keep your weather-eye open for a rainbow, that's all I can say. Now get to the wheel, fast as you can! I'm going below to secure the rhinos.'

Göran had to fight his way first uphill and then downhill as the clumsy tub of a boat wallowed its way through the biggest storm since the world was created. He knew now that the Skagerrak would be a mere puddle compared to this all-encompassing ocean. They sailed on a planet without harbour or land to obstruct wind and wave. Small wonder the seas were so monstrous!

Forward, Shem was almost exhausted. Between them, the two men managed to lash the wheel to hold it. Every moment was a fight against elemental forces. The cries of animals and the groan of timbers were almost lost in the roaring wind, picked up and scattered contemptuously into the tempest.

Finally, between them, they had the ship heading into the storm, and clung to the wheel gasping for breath.

Göran thought himself beyond further fear when the ship was lifted high up a great sliding mountainside of water, up, up, to perch over a fearful gulf between waves. Just before they sliced down into the gulf, he saw a light ahead.

'Ship ahoy!' That was Shem, poor lad, pointing a finger in the direction Göran had been looking.

Ship? What ship? What possible ship could be sailing these seas at this time? What para-legendary voyage might it be on?

The two men stared at each other with pallid faces, and in one voice bellowed aloud for Noah. Then they turned to peer through the murk again.

At this point in his narrative, my friend Svenson broke off, to all appearances overcome by emotion. By now, the bridge had carried us half way across to Sweden; beneath us sailed the maritime traffic of the tranquil Øresund. But Göran's inner eye was fixed on another rougher sea.

'Did you catch a second glimpse of the phantom ship?' I asked.

You've no idea what it was like to sail that sea! The water was not like sea water. It was black, a black shot through with streaks of white and yellow, as if it were a living organism with veins and sinews. There were areas where fetid bubbles kept bursting to the surface, covering the waves with a vile foam ...

Yes, we saw that phantom vessel again. Indeed we did! As the ark struggled up the mile-long side of yet another mountain of water, the other vessel came rushing down the slope upon us.

It was as fleet, as beautiful, as our tub was heavy and crude, was that expensive delicate ship! And it was lit from stem to stern; whereas the ark – that old fool Noah had not thought to provide navigational lights, reckoning his would be the only boat braving those high waters.

We stared aghast, Shem and I, as that superb craft bore down on us, much as two children in an alpine valley might gaze at the avalanche plunging down to destroy them.

Japheth had fought his way through the gale to cling beside us. His arrival made no impression on my consciousness until I heard him scream and turned to see his face – so pale and wet it seemed luminescent – and it was only on seeing him that I could realize the extent of my own terror!

'Where's your father? Where is he?' I shouted, seizing him by the shoulders.

'He stubbed his foot down below!'

Stubbed his foot! In sudden wild anger, I flung Japheth from me and, turning, pulled out my sheath knife. With a few slashes, I had cut the wheel free and flung it over with all my might, fighting the great roar of tide under our keel with every fibre of my being.

Sluggishly, our old tub turned a few degrees – and that great beautiful ship went racing by us to port, slicing up foam high over our poop, missing us, as it seemed, by inches!

It went by, and, as it went by – towering over us, that incredible ship – I saw a human face peer out at me. For the briefest moment, our gaze met. I tell you, it was the gaze of doom. Well, such was my deep and ineradicable impression – the gaze of doom!

Then it was gone, and I saw other faces, faces of animals, all staring helplessly across the churning waters. Those animals – it was an instant's glimpse, no more, yet I know what I saw! Unicorns, gryphons, a centaur with lashing mane, and those superb beasts we have learned to call by Latin names – megatherium, stegosaurus, a tyrannosaur, triceratops with beaked mouth agape, diplodocus ...

Of course, they all sliced by in a flash as the miraculous ship – that doppelganger ark! – sped down the waters. And then they were lost in the murk and spume. A flicker of light, and once more our ark was all alone in the hostile sea, with the windows of Heaven open upon us.

And I was wrestling with the wheel, on and on – maybe for ever ...

I burst out laughing.

'Great story, great performance! You are trying to persuade me that you sailed on the ark with Noah? Who were *you*? Ham, no doubt!'

He looked pained.

'You see, you are so coarse, old chap! Your scepticism does you no credit. Concentrate your attention on that fine ship which almost rammed us. What was it? Where was it sailing? Who built it? And what happened to it, what happened to all the creatures aboard?'

'An even bigger mystery – did poor old Noah's toe get better?'

He made a gesture of disgust. 'You refuse to take me seriously. Just consider the tragedy, the poetry, the mystery, of that apocalyptic encounter. I sometimes ask myself if the wrong vessel survived that gigantic storm. Remember that God was very angry with that drunken old sot, Noah. Did the wrong set of men and animals survive to repopulate the Earth?'

'I can't imagine a pterodactyl bringing a sprig of olive back into the ark.'

'Laugh if you will! Sometimes I wonder what alternate possibilities and possible worlds flashed past my eyes in that moment of crisis. You haven't my fine imaginative mind – such speculations would mean nothing to you.'

'You began this sermon by talking about just pure intense living – I suppose in contrast with all the muddled stuff we get through. Are you saying that this moment when you saw this – "doppelganger ark", as you call it, was a moment of intense living?'

He glanced down at the docks of Halsingborg, now rolling under our feet. The new art museum loomed ahead. We had almost arrived on the Swedish shore.

'No, not at all. Being so imaginative, my moment of intense living was to invent this little mysterious anecdote for you. I live in imagination! Too bad you are too much of a slob to appreciate it!'

Then he dropped his solemn expression and began to laugh. Roaring with laughter, we moved down the escalator to terra firma.

Next day, we saw in the newscasts that two small children, a boy and a girl, had been drowned in the Øresund just outside Halsingborg harbour, and at about the time we were passing regardlessly overhead.

Enigma 5:

Three Coins in Clockwork Fountains

Carefully Observed Women
The Daffodil Returns the Smile
The Year of the Quiet Computer

Carefully Observed Women

From my position, her bed looks like a ruined countryside, covered with a miserable dapple of fields. Occasionally, fields heave, rise to a great height above sea level, or sink from view, as Harrion stirs in her agony.

Much of the time, all I see of her is the old yellow of the roof of her mouth as she lies panting for breath. Sometimes, a great slack arm hangs down towards the floor, twisted and gritty like a stalactite in veined sandstone. Bits of her broken past come upon her; for days at a time, she labours among the fragments of a bygone year. She smells bad of nights, so that I lie as far from the bed as my chains will allow. I could have done better.

Outside I hear the plash of clockwork fountains. Toy fish swim there, learning to devour each other.

Time streams by as always. Although now there is no one to check it at its source.

The women come to see Harrion. Some of her regular friends, like Bettron, Citrate, and old Ma Kandle, unable to give up a lifetime's habit of visiting. There are relations, like Mylene, Temple, Floret, Marriet, and the two aged sisters,

Emilor and Chatelait, who are so fat they bump together as they walk, like buoys in a light swell. Neighbours appear, the blind Ma Audopar, little Pi, Cathwal, Eadie, Gaffrey with the port-wine mark from next door. There are women with whom Harrion once quarrelled, now come to make their peace, sleek Perchince, Porly, and deaf Dame Caper. Many of these women are accompanied by their daughters.

When they come from a distance, some even bring their men. I know when men are chained up outside, can hear them pulling restlessly at their rings or scuffling among each other. They do not enter the building. Only women and girls flock into the sick-room, bringing little gifts with them, a flower or a carved stone. The shelves are full of needlework and knick-knacks, dolls and daffodils.

In comes Perchince, smart as ever, with a loose-woven shawl over her long costume, ushering in before her Scally, the dark-eyed daughter, whose elegant legs show a flaking of dark hair over the calves. Perchince brings a tiny prayer embroidered on green cloth and set about with artificial sea shells. She gives it to Harrion, whose arm comes up yellow and stringy to grasp it.

'You're looking better than when I last saw you, my dear. I'm sorry I've not been to see you for so long, but we've had so much trouble.'

'Recovery's only one stall in the market place,' says Harrion, speaking in her usual elusive and epigrammatic way.

Somewhere, Harrion finds the strength to pull herself up, wild-eyed and sweating, her lank fair hair raining down into the pits of her cheeks. Perchince helps adjust her pillows.

While Harrion fights for breath, Perchince tells her things she would like to know – how the price of fish has gone up, the scarcity of benjamins, the dangers of going out at night, the afflictions of her family, and the alarmingly high tides in Gobblestone.

To all this, Harrion listens after a fashion, her vacant and feverish eye rolling here and there. I watch her, but I also look at the visitors, Scally especially. Scally smells good and fresh. She has a small nose, wide dark-brown eyes, pleasant lips which sometimes purse together mischievously, and curly hair which clusters round her head in a lively way. I'd like to get her in my pad, I'd like to throw myself on her, I could eat her. She's getting fat.

She does not join in the conversation. She sits and is aware of my interest. She moves round slightly in her chair by the bedside, so that I can admire her knees. She opens her legs slightly, so that I can devour her thighs. She observes the effect of this on me.

Harrion interrupts the spate of Perchince's recital, saying, 'Scally is getting fat.'

'The trouble we have with her! We had just the same thing with her sister, seventy-five years ago. She's not fat, she's pregnant. Get up, Scally, show yourself.'

Scally rises and stands there indifferently.

'You naughty girl,' Harrion says. 'The taking of care never lost a friend yet. You've been in the ruins again, haven't you?'

Scally says nothing. I shake my chains but they take no notice.

'It'll be a cloud all the centuries of your life,' Harrion says, vaguely. 'And there's no repeal before the bar of your own conscience.'

'I don't feel guilty about it, Aunt Harrion, if that's what you mean,' says Scally defiantly, with a little flounce of her body that sets the saliva squirting in my gums.

'She's still very proud,' sleek Perchince says. 'That's the worst of it. And she would not confide in me until she was all of twenty-three months gone.'

'Independence is of no merit where tears are,' says Harrion.

'Still, we shall make the best of things and see her through her trouble.'

'Those who love their own creations too much fall into bondage,' Harrion replies, shifting her position and glancing pointedly at me. She wants me to see where the remark really applies.

Perchince arises, smiling frowningly at her daughter.

'We must go,' says she. 'I've got to take her to the calibrator's and have her oriented. Always more expense, Harrion.'

'Folly's three-quarters of circumstance,' Harrion agrees. 'Take care of yourself, and remember that compassion makes captives.' Again a mean glance at me.

Off goes Perchince, taking Scally with her. Scally looks cheerful. I miss it when her fresh smell no longer cuts the fats of the room.

Harrion dies a little more in the night and, next day, while she drowses through the late afternoon, her cousin Temple appears. Temple's man, who is left outside, whines and scratches at the door. With her eyes still shut and one hand pressed to her fevered forehead, Harrion gives an account of what passed between her and Perchince on the previous day. She clutches her cousin's hand and elaborates their conversation endlessly, exhausted though she is.

'I'm sorry for Scally,' Temple says. I know she waits for her cousin to fall asleep; then she will occasionally slip over to me.

'It's all a mere dance of the ferret,' says Harrion. 'Scally is not really pregnant. She has a cushion under her clothes. They're just doing it for me, to distract me from the notion of dying. Anything, to keep my mind off that.'

'Oh, that would be wicked,' Temple says. 'Besides, you are not dying. You're getting better.'

'They no more deceive me than a bee a flower. Didn't my mother make me play the same trick on old Ma Bonnitrude seven or more centuries ago? She used to say to me, "Now that even God's fallen so low, we've each of us got to get out of life as best as we can." ' As she speaks, she struggles into a sitting position and opens her weary eyes.

She sees then that Temple has one arm in a sling, and that bloodstained bandages cover her hand.

'What have you done with yourself?' she asks. And her cousin tells her a hair-raising story involving several coincidences, a rail journey, and a man who escaped from a travelling circus. Harrion tut-tuts all the way through the recital.

When Temple has gone, she says to the room in general, 'They don't fool me with their tales. I never forget about death. I *am* dying, aren't I?'

'You're dying,' I say. I can't help panting and looking eager.

She fixes me with a glowing stare. 'And you know what happens to *you* when I go … '

'You've often told me.'

'You'll be as solitary as a stone, just like you were when you started.'

She revives. I watch her heave herself upward, reaching for the prod, which is just long enough to touch me. I scramble to the end of my chain, but she will get me again if she does not fall dead first.

The last rays of sunset are red on the walls above the bed, like an old stain.

Time still streams by. The fountain plays. But there is nothing to do; nothing can be done.

I try to recall those happy seven days when I created the universe.

The Daffodil Returns the Smile

Neece and Reneece will drink no ichor from Moolab tonight, since he has to hunt and kill a *kimarsun*. He will need all his energy against the intense cold of the Rind and the might of those beings.

Neece and Reneece dress their warrior, singing to him as they do so, being careful to hold always to the old forms. Moolab stands between them in a trance, all his mailed hands extended and slowly vibrating. They saved the last of his sloughs against this occasion; the chitinous armours have been beaten with prescribed bronze mallets, and carefully lined with the ordained coatings of claysyrup and boccarrd-fleece. Now the females clamp on the armour.

Beyond their broodhaven, chirplings set up the agonizing Sun-Slayer chorus.

By the time he is prepared, at the prescribed hour, Moolab is in the warrior's trance. They are ready to leave. Both females pause at the door. They encompass his neck with their mailed jaws, tenderly kissing the scars there. Then they move into the tunnels of the Great Warren.

Through the haze of smoke and gas, they see the buildings all about them. They disregard them. They disregard the crowds.

'The Rind!' cry the crowds. 'Moolab goes to the colds of the Rind to slay one of the eternal *kimarsunss*! He will bring us the night as a present!'

Moolab glances neither to right nor to left. He heads straight for the Fate Gate of the city, where the Hive Lord awaits him.

The Hive Lord stands with the Arch-Priest, a tremendous broad-spanned being, every one of whose eighty legs bears a plutonium ring on every claw. At sight of him, Neece and Reneece fall behind, adopting the shrivel stance.

But Moolab approaches the Hive Lord with no decrease in pace, only stopping when nil-distance separates them. The two beings lock jaws, black clashing on black. That's over in a trice. Without hesitation, Moolab side-steps, offering his occular vibrissi into the gaping mandibles of the Arch-Priest. The pose is held to the count of ten, accompanied by a shrill chant from the sanctified chirplings. Then Moolab slides back one pace, to stay confronting the Priest as the other snaps shut his mandibles, otherwise remaining immobile.

'Do you, Moolab, accept your sacred duty to slay a *kimarsun* and render night to us?' demands the Hive Lord in a singing tone.

'I accept my sacred duty and I will slay a *kimarsun* and render night to our kind until the purse is filled.'

Now the Arch-Priest begins to speak in a singing tone. Each of his phrases, Moolab echoes after him. 'By the nine beggared cripples. By the fragrance of the Old Pursuer. By the cyclic stains that burn against a closing wall. By the fifteen hundred generations underground. By the scales of the mother and the leavings of the dreaded brood. By the colds and unmentionable voices that infest the Rind. By spawn claw. By the things themselves. Above all, by the stars that blaze above the world, and the Wheel of Evil. Till ichor festers.'

Despite his clumsy caparisons, Moolab throws himself flat before the Priest.

'I will take notice of the hated constellations, of the Bat, the Devil Bull, the Boulder, the Night Worm, and the Queen's Scar. This night shall see a report here of my death or my success. I will return with eye of *kimarsun* or my own eyes shall roll for ever down the crippled glaciers of the outside.'

'Take success with you, Moolab of the Core, bring back fire for our fire.'

The simple ritual is over. Lord and Priest both raise their prows high. Moolab rises and scuttles off at high speed through Fate Gate without a backward look. Whistling, the two brood-sisters, Neece and Reneece, rush after him, kicking dirt. The great gate slams behind them.

With unpausing ferocity, Moolab hurls himself forward, through the dreary and smouldering tunnels of the mantle. The brood-sisters gallop behind. Crevasses, molten rock, roof-falls – nothing can halt them. Moolab is going to slay a *kimarsun*.

Sometimes the tunnels divide. One way leads to the Rind, one to another hive. Kicking cinders, they gallop ever upwards.

At one junction, a Mother is crossing their path. She is in the huge serrated softness of Metamorphosis 1. At the sound of their terrible progress, the Mother turns, flicking her sepia head, opening her mandibles. She is unhesitatingly ready to fight.

Moolab tears into and through her soft body. He does not pause.

Following, Neece and Reneece plunge through the pulped remains, covering themselves with a viscid cream as they go. The still-chattering head of the Mother is flung aside by Reneece's shoulder as she passes.

They scent cooler parts of the world. The walls are more opaque. Movements about them have a duller grind. They know the world lives, just as they live.

Because of the increasing cold, the three beings move more slowly.

Moolab sniffs the terrible world ahead, where solids cease

and emptiness comes down to the Rind. That is the region of the *kimarsunss*. He recites the Oath of Death or Success.

'By the nine beggared cripples.

By the fragrance of the Old Pursuer.

By the cyclic stains that burn against a closing wall.

By the fifteen hundred generations underground.

By the scales of the mother and the leavings of the dreaded brood.

By the colds and unmentionable voices that infest the Rind ... '

They come up to a trapdoor. Without pausing in his stride, Moolab goes at it full tilt, stopping dead with his occular vibrissi almost touching the solid stone.

He moves forward slowly. He presses himself against the stone. He heaves. Hind pairs of legs drum in the tunnel for additional purchase. The stone rolls aside.

Moolab climbs out on to the Rind, beneath the awful emptiness. The brood-sisters follow, bellies flat to the ground. Their antennae swivel in dread.

They feel the colds, hear the unmentionable voices.

Overhead, the Wheel of Evil grinds.

The warrior Moolab feels the living Rind beneath him. He clings to the great carcass with all claws, knowing that his body now forms part of the division between Good and Evil. Below is all Good – the farther below, the more good, until the deep hives are reached, nestled for ever among the greatest good. Above is all Evil – the farther above, the greater evil, until the high stars are reached.

He fixes his multiplex vision now upon the high stars. He must reach the place of the *kimarsunss*. To get there, he must use the directions pointed by the high stars; in this way, Evil is used for Good; that is part of the pattern.

Above him in the emptiness, he makes out the constellations, the Bat, the Devil Bull, the Boulder, the Night Worm, the Queen's Scar, and others.

The Night Worm is in the ascendant. Its hated length spirals up from horizon to zenith, marked by stars whose names Moolab recites to himself: Boylat, Crabarty, Prosshing,

F

Hrozne, Ramarkkan. Ramarkkan burns in the fangs of the mouth of the Night Worm. It is a baleful orange star.

And Moolab knows it threatens his life. He sees that it is tonight's enemy.

He uses Ramarkkan to betray itself. Taking it as a bearing, he sets off in the direction of the plateau where the *kimarsunss* are.

Neece and Reneece are left behind. They stay by the trap. They will die if he does not return. They will never move again if he does not return. Their bodies will be possessed by the *kimarsunss* and the high stars, and they will stride the empty plains of the Rind on rear legs whenever Ramarkkan rises in the clotted west.

Moolab travels in an intense wave motion best suited to the undulating terrain. He is without fear. In him live the fifteen hundred generations underground.

The ground slopes upward in an antique and unbroken goemetry, its euclidean symmetries taking it towards the plateau of the mighty *kimarsunss*. Nothing changes. Even the light that falls becomes permanent with time.

When everything withers, the stones retain their life.

He flows over the step separating the incline from the plateau. He stops.

Here are the monstrous creatures. The radiance of the high stars falls on the sine curves of their flanks. Their shoulders are dwarfed by distance. Their skulls are lighthouses, blinking from a far headland. Their colossal size makes them abstract. The night upon their carcasses makes them legendary.

Low rumblings of hatred start somewhere amid the joints of Moolab's abdomen and work forward towards his thorax. He channels the rumbling through his glands, so that its help ferments the poisons he will soon need. He rejoices to feel his own chemistries at work, knowing their cyclic stains will aid him against evil. Until they are ready, he waits.

As he waits, he observes the monstrous *kimarsunss*. They have stayed on this starlit plateau for ever. Although Moolab has never been here before, he has a folk-memory of the beings. He knows their very positions on the plateau. None of them has ever moved.

When the season comes about in the core, when the axis grinds round on the impulse, when the desire falls on the hive, then comes the Swarming. Then the hives go forth, breaking through the Rind, soaring aloft in the emptiness between Good and Evil. The Swarming flies over the plateau of the *kimarsunss* and those that survive will recall the dispositions of the enemy. But most will fall, dying, their wings bursting into flame as they plunge down to dust. One *kimarsun* can bring about twenty thousand deaths.

Moolab will revenge the deaths. As he waits, he turns some eyes again at the high stars. The Mottled Egg, the Queen's Scar, they are to his left shoulder. The Night Worm still burns overhead, the orange tooth of Ramarkkan still flaring in the fanged mouth.

The stars, revolving on the great Wheel of Evil, have more motion than their guards down below. No Swarming has ever reported the movement of a single *kimarsun*. Moolab sees that they are still with an immeasurable stillness.

That terrible immobility is because the *kimarsunss* work on a different time scale to the rest of the living things in the universe. For there is no doubt that the *kimarsunss* are alive. They can be killed.

Occasionally, dull internal glowing overtakes one of the colossi. Moolab is fortunate. As he waits for his chemistries to become effective, he sees that one of the more distant *kimarsunss* is undergoing this colour-change.

To the oblique concave surfaces of the colossus comes a dull crimson flush. It travels like a wave across the bulk of the being, over the abstractions which serve for limbs, abdomen, shoulders. The wave is like a signal of anger. Anger is communicated to Moolab; he raises his belly from the ground and flexes his rear segments over his head, preparing to charge.

The eyes of the *kimarsunss* watch him. They will turn him to stone if he entertains a moment's doubt. Doubt is defeat in a moral war.

The flushing colossus is now a dull red all over. But the colour seems to fade slightly. Then, a sudden shock. The creature emits a helium flash. The blaze of white light extends all over its bulk, bursts outwards, illuminating the plateau for an instant.

The flash serves as a signal to Moolab. He waits no more, but launches himself savagely across the powdered plain. He hits top speed, his multitudinous feet pulverizing ground as he runs between the living mountains. The noise of his progress is such that it wakens echoes among the surrounding canyons of rib and flank. Avalanches of stardust roll down the ancient sides of the nearest *kimarsunss*.

But Moolab does not see. He directs all his vision at the target ahead, which appears to swell monstrously as he approaches, eclipsing the Twin Cinders, the Queen's Scar. It is still undergoing colour-change. Now a dusky red expands over its surface again, lit from inside with shots of brighter colour. The sight would be terrifying, petrifying, if Moolab did not close his mind with incantation.

Now it's near. He goes in for the kill. His antennae vibrate, his maxillae sweep back, his poisoned mandibles open wide. He directs his travelling bulk at one grotesque corner of the *kimarsun*. The sound of his charge is left to rattle far behind him. Noiseless, he bears in towards the motionless foot, the heel. Jaws wider still. He bites.

Without pause, he plunges on, bearing away with him part of the substance of the colossus. Then he halts, turning right around in one moment. The great clatter of his charge sweeps about him and is gone.

Silence falls.

The high stars shine.

The *kimarsun* begins to shed matter as Moolab's poisons take effect. It seems to grow, become unstable. Bits fall off it and die into the plateau. An eye tumbles down, to lie there, glowing and white. The whole process is pitiful, insignificant. In a few moments, there is nothing left but a little white eye. Evil is defeated. Good has triumphed.

Moolab goes back and picks up the eye. He will take it to the Arch-Priest.

He is almost too tired to feel the stir of victory. But he looks up through the unmentionable piles of emptiness to the great revolving Wheel of Evil.

There he sees the high stars comprising the Night Worm. The Night Worm's hated length still spirals up from horizon to zenith. Boylat, Crabarty, Prosshing, Hrozne, still burn. But Ramarkkan no longer blazes in the Worm's fanged mouth. Ramarkkan has gone out.

In time, the forces of Good will eradicate all the high stars. The hive will possess everything.

The Year of the Quiet Computer

Whispers of a faint boutique and the band playing its own tune, endlessly, on and on. Every now and then, someone takes a musician out to the beds of daffodils, brings him to orgasm, garrottes him, and buries him among the spring flowers. The ground is wonderfully warm for the time of year.

Toy fish swim in clockwork fountains. They are learning to devour each other.

Alphonse Didcot reclines on a self-invented chair, reading some tales from the quiet computer. He has his own music. The magic word Cathay hangs in shades of T'ang gold over the food-divider. And his great-great-grandfather, five foot two and the best potter of his day, smiles down mummified from above the fireplace; the teeth are rather yellow now, but the gums still shine with a redeeming blue.

Outside the tall flanks of the tower, the ceremony of Fluctuating Lanterns is still in progress. Children flounce in long lean grass.

'We will bear them away, we will bear them away. Transience will be banished, banished to the eternal hills,' chant the little holy orphans. Surely enough, mists roll in about the gaunt building.

'Let us move to Gorica 57901,' Alphonse says. Already, he can feel the start of the multiple births. The great-great-grandfather nods, its backbone creaking comfortably, like a familiar board in a family house.

One man walking sniffs the familiar flavours of the sky. Despite the lanterns, the trains are still coming in, burrowing through interstellar gas in a fury of speed; their great broad firemen bend their backs, shovelling in the helium-coal. Some engines are black, some red. In their rattling trucks, they bear the last of the stars to the depot, Betelgeuse, Procyon, Aldebaran, poor Vega, lying on its side. Already, the wreckers wait in the yard.

When the whistle blows, Alphonse is ready. He pulls back the heavy curtains. From the outside of the windows, things fall away, crying, crying. The mist is all about. Some trees appear, stifled by the mist, entangling it in their unkempt gestures. The musicians have all been finished now.

The mist clears. Gone is the old clutter of habitation, with its lockers and appearances. Instead, the castle stands on a flat unclothed plain. It stretches away into all distances. Only to one side stand the mountains. The mountains stand aloof. Strange lights of sunrises and sunsets, interplaying, confuse their contours. Something skips from peak to peak, looking for destiny.

Alphonse takes up a daffodil and smiles. The daffodil returns the smile.

An Appearance of Life

Something very large, something very small; a galactic museum, a dead love affair. They came together under my gaze.

The museum is very large. Less than a thousand light years from Earth, countless worlds bear constructions which are formidably ancient and inscrutable in purpose. The museum on Norma is such a construction.

We suppose that the museum was created by a species which once lorded it over the galaxy, the Korlevalulaw. The spectre of the Korlevalulaw has become part of the consciousness of the human race as it spreads from star-system to star-system. Sometimes the Korlevalulaw are pictured as demons, hiding somewhere in a dark nebula, awaiting the moment when they swoop down on mankind and wipe out every last one of us in reprisal for having dared to invade their territory. Sometimes the Korlevalulaw are pictured as gods, rising with the awfulness and loneliness of gods through the deserts of space, potent and wise beyond our imagining.

These two opposed images of the Korlevalulaw are of course images emerging from the deepest pools of the human mind. The demon and the god remain with us still.

But there were Korlevalulaw, and there are facts we know about them. We know that they had abandoned the written word by the time they reached their galactic-building phase. Their very name comes down to us from the single example of their alphabet we have, a sign emblazoned across the façade of a construction on Lacarja. We know that they were inhuman. Not only does the scale of their constructions imply as much; they built always on planets inimical to man.

What we do not know is what became of the Korlevalulaw. They must have reigned so long, they must have been so invincible to all but Time.

Where knowledge cannot go, imagination ventures. Men have supposed that the Korlevalulaw committed some kind of racial suicide. Or that they became a race divided, and totally annihilated themselves in a region of space beyond our galaxy, beyond the reach of mankind's starships.

And there are more metaphysical speculations concerning the fate of the Korlevalulaw. Moved by evolutionary necessity, they may have grown beyond the organic; in which case, it may be that they still inhabit their ancient constructions, undetected by man. There is a stranger theory which places emphasis on Mind identifiable with Cosmos, and supposes that once a species begins to place credence in the idea of occupying the galaxy, then so it is bound to do; this is what mankind has done, virtually imagining its illustrious predecessors out of existence.

Well, there are many theories, but I was intending to talk about the museum on Norma.

Like everything else, Norma possesses its riddles.

The museum demarcates Norma's equator. The construction takes the form of a colossal belt girdling the planet, some sixteen thousand kilometres in length. The belt varies curiously in thickness, from twelve kilometres to over twenty-two.

The chief riddle about Norma is this: is its topographical conformation what it always was, or are its peculiarities due to the meddling of the Korlevalulaw? For the construction neatly divides the planet into a northern land hemisphere and a southern oceanic hemisphere. On one side lies an endless territory of cratered plain, scoured by winds and bluish snow. On the other side writhes a formidable ocean of ammonia, unbroken by islands, inhabited by firefish and other mysterious denizens.

On one of the widest sections of the Korlevalulaw construction stands an incongruous huddle of buildings. Coming in from space, you are glad to see that huddle. Your ship takes you down, you catch your elevator, you emerge on the roof of the construction itself, and you rejoice that – in the midst of the inscrutable symmetrical universe (of which the Korlevalulaw formed a not inconsiderable part) – mankind has established an untidy foothold.

For a moment I paused by the ship, taking in the immensity about me. A purple sun was rising amid cloud, making shadows race across the infinite-seeming plane on which I stood. The distant sea pounded and moaned, lost to my vision. It was a solitary spot, but I was accustomed to solitude – on the planet I called home, I hardly met with another human from one year's end to the next, except on my visits to the Breeding Centre.

Wind tugged me and I moved on.

The human-formed buildings on Norma stand over one of the enormous entrances to the museum. They consist of a hotel for visitors, various office blocks, cargo-handling equipment, and gigantic transmitters – the walls of the museum are impervious to the electromagnetic spectrum, so that any information from inside the construction comes by cable through the entrance, and is then transmited by second-space to other parts of the galaxy.

'Seeker, you are expected. Welcome to the Norma Museum.'

So said the android who showed me into the airlock and guided me through into the hotel. Here as elsewhere, androids occupied all menial posts. I glanced at the calendar clock in the foyer, punching my wrisputer like all arriving travellers to discover where in time Earth might be now.

Gently sedated by alpha-music, I slept away my light-lag, and descended next day to the museum itself.

The museum was run by twenty human staff, all female. The Director gave me all the information that a Seeker might need, helped me to select a viewing vehicle, and left me to move off into the museum on my own.

Although we have many ways of growing unimolecular metals, the Korlevalulaw construction on Norma was of an incomprehensible material. It had no joint or seam in its entire length. More, it somehow imprisoned or emanated light, so that no artificial light was needed within.

Beyond that, it was empty. The entire place was equatorially empty. Only mankind, taking it over a thousand years before, had turned it into a museum and started to fill it with galactic lumber.

As I moved forward in my vehicle, I was not overcome by the idea of infinity, as I had expected. A tendency towards infinity has presumably dwelt in the minds of mankind ever since our early ancestors counted up to ten on their fingers. The habitation of the void had increased that tendency. The happiness which we experience as a species is of recent origin, achieved since our maturity; it also contributes to a disposition to neglect any worries in the present to concentrate on distant goals. But I believe – this is a personal opinion – that this same tendency towards infinity in all its forms has militated against close relationships between individuals. We do not even love as our planet-bound ancestors did; we live apart as they did not.

In the museum, a quality of the light mitigated any intimations of infinity. I knew I was in an immense enclosed space; but, since the light absolved me from any sensations of clausagrophobia, I will not attempt to describe that vastness.

Over the previous ten centuries, several thousand hectares had become filled with human accretions. Androids worked perpetually, arranging exhibits. The exhibits were scanned by electronic means, so that anyone on any civilized planet, dialling the museum, might obtain by second-space a three-dimensional image of the required object in his room.

I travelled almost at random through the displays.

To qualify as a Seeker, it is necessary to show a high serendipity factor. In my experimental behaviour pool as a child, I had exhibited such a factor, and had been selected for special training forthwith. I had taken additional courses in Philosophicals, Alpha-humerals, Incidental Tetrachotomy, Apunctual Synchronicity, Homoontogenesis, and other subjects, ultimately qualifying as a Prime Esemplastic Seeker. In other words, I put two and two together in situations where other people were not thinking about addition. I connected. I made wholes greater than parts.

Mine was an invaluable profession in a cosmos increasingly full of parts.

I arrived at the museum with a sheaf of assignments from numerous institutions, universities, and individuals all over the galaxy. Every assignment required my special talent – a capacity beyond holography. Let me give one example. The Audile Academy of the University of Paddin on the planet Rufadote was working on an hypothesis that, over the millennia, human voices were gradually generating fewer phons or, in other words, becoming quieter. Any evidence I could collect in the museum concerning this hypothesis would be welcome. The Academy could scan the whole museum by remote holography; yet only to a rare physical visitor like me was a gestalt view of the contents possible; and only by a Seeker would a significant juxtapositioning be noted.

My car took me slowly through the exhibits. There were nourishment machines at intervals throughout the museum, so that I did not need to leave the establishment. I slept in my vehicle; it was comfortably provided with bunks.

On the second day, I spoke idly to a nearby android before beginning my morning drive.

'Do you enjoy ordering the exhibits here?'

'I could never tire of it.' She smiled pleasantly at me.

'You find it interesting?'

'It's endlessly interesting. The quest for pattern is a basic instinct.'

'Do you always work in this section?'

'No. But this is one of my favourite sections. As you have probably observed, here we classify extinct diseases – or diseases which would be extinct if they were not preserved in the museum. I find the micro-organism beautiful.'

'You are kept busy?'

'Certainly. New exhibits arrive every month. From the largest to the smallest, everything can be stored here. May I show you anything?'

'Not at present. How long before the entire museum is filled?'

'In fifteen and a half millennia, at current rate of intake.'

'Have you entered the empty part of the museum?'

'I have stood on the fringes of emptiness. It is an alarming sensation. I prefer to occupy myself with the works of man.'

'That is only proper.'

I drove away, meditating on the limitations of android thinking. Those limitations had been carefully imposed by mankind; the androids were not aware of them. To an android, the android umwelt or conceptual universe is apparently limitless. It makes for their happiness, just as our umwelt makes for our happiness.

As the days passed, I came across many juxtapositions and objects which would assist clients. I noted them all in my wrisputer.

On the fifth day, I was examining the section devoted to ships and objects preserved from the earliest days of galactic travel.

Many of the items touched me with emotion – an emotion chiefly composed of nosthedony, the pleasure of returning to the past. For in many of the items I saw reflected a time when human life was different, perhaps less secure, certainly less austere.

That First Galactic Era, when men – often accompanied by 'wives' and 'mistresses', to use the old terms for love-partners – had ventured distantly in primitive machines, marked the beginnings of the time when the human pair-bond weakened and humanity rose towards maturity.

I stepped into an early spaceship, built before second-space had been discovered. Its scale was diminutive. With shoulders bent, I moved along its brief corridors into what had been a relaxation room for the five-person crew. The metal was old-fashioned refined; it might almost have been wood. The furniture, such as it was, seemed scarcely designed for human frames. The mode aimed at an illusionary functionalism. And yet, still preserved in the air, were attributes I recognized as human: perseverance, courage, hope. The five people who had once lived here were kin with me.

The ship had died in vacuum of a defective recycling plant – their micro-encapsulation techniques had not included the implantation of oxygen in the corpuscles of the blood, never mind the genetosurgery needed to make that implantation hereditary. All the equipment and furnishings lay as they had done aeons before, when the defect occurred.

Rummaging through some personal lockers, I discovered a thin band made of the antique metal, gold. On the inside of it was a small but clumsily executed inscription in ancient script. I balanced it on the tip of my thumb and considered its function. Was it an early contraceptive device?

At my shoulder was a museum eye. Activating it, I requested the official catalogue to describe the object I held.

The reply was immediate. 'You are holding a ring which slipped on to the finger of a human being when our species was of smaller stature than today,' said the catalogue. 'Like the spaceship, the ring dates from the First Galactic Era, but is thought to be somewhat older than the ship. The dating tallies with what we know of the function – largely symbolic – of the ring. It was worn to indicate married status in a woman or man. This particular ring may have been an hereditary possession. In those days, marriages were expected to last until progeny were born, or even until death. The human biomass was then divided fifty-fifty between males and females, in dramatic contrast to the ten-to-one preponderance of females in our stellar socities. Hence the idea of coupling for life was not so illogical as it sounds. However, the ring itself must be regarded as a harmless illogic, designed merely to express a bondage or linkage – '

I broke the connection.

A wedding ring ... It represented symbolic communication. As such, it would be of value to a professor studying the metamorphoses of nonverbality who was employing my services.

A wedding ring … A closed circuit of love and thought.

I wondered how this particular marriage had ended for both the partners on this ship. The items preserved did not answer my question. But I found a flat photograph, encased in plastic windows, of a man and a woman together in outdoor surroundings. They smiled at the apparatus recording them. Their eyes were flat, betokening their undeveloped cranial reserves, yet they were not unattractive. I observed that they stood closer together than we would normally care to do.

Could that be something to do with the limitations of the apparatus photographing them? Or had there been a change in the social convention of closeness? Was there a connection here with the decibel-output of the human voice which might interest my client of the Audile Academy? Possibly our auditory equipment was more subtle than that of our ancestors when they were confined to one planet under heavy atmospheric pressure. I filed the details away for future reference.

A fellow Seeker had told me jokingly that the secret of the universe was locked away in the museum if only I could find it.

'We'll stand a better chance of that when the museum is completed,' I told her.

'No,' she said. 'The secret will then be too deeply buried. We shall merely have transferred the outside universe to inside the Korlevalulaw construction. You'd better find it now or never.'

'The idea that there may be a secret or key to the universe is in any case a construct of the human mind.'

'Or of the mind that built the human mind,' she said.

That night, I slept in the section of early galactic travel and continued my researches there on the sixth day.

I felt a curious excitement, over and above nosthedony and simple antiquarian interest. My senses were alert.

I drove among twenty great ships belonging to the Second Galactic Era. The longest was over five kilometres in length and had housed many scores of women and men in its day. This had been the epoch when our kind had attempted to establish empires in space and extend primitive national or territorial obsessions across many light-years. The facts of relativity had doomed such efforts from the start; under the immensities of space-time, they were put away as childish things. It was no paradox to say that, among interstellar distances, mankind had become more at home with itself.

Although I did not enter these behemoths, I remained among them, sampling the brutal way in which militaristic technologies expressed themselves in metal. Such excesses would never recur.

Beyond the behemoths, androids were arranging fresh exhibits. The exhibits slid along in transporters far overhead, conveyed silently from the museum entrance, to be lowered where needed. Drawing closer to where the new arrivals were being unloaded, I passed among an array of shelves.

On the shelves lay items retrieved from colonial homes or ships of the quasi-imperial days. I marvelled at the collection. As people had proliferated, so had objects. A concern with possession had been a priority concern during the immaturity of the species. These long-dead people had seemingly thought of little else but possession in one form or another; yet, like androids in similar circumstances, they could not have recognized the limitations of their own umwelt.

Among the muddle, a featureless cube caught my eye. Its sides were smooth and silvered. I picked it up and turned it over. On one side was a small depression. I touched the depression with my finger.

Slowly, the sides of the cube clarified and a young woman's head appeared three-dimensionally inside them. The head was upside down. The eyes regarded me.

'You are not Chris Mailer,' she said. 'I talk only to my husband. Switch off and set me right way up.'

'Your "husband" died sixty-five thousand years ago,' I said. But I set her cube down on the shelf, not unmoved by being addressed by an image from the remote past. That it possessed environmental reflexion made it all the more impressive.

I asked the museum catalogue about the item.

'In the jargon of the time, it is a "holocap",' said the catalogue. 'It is a hologrammed image of a real woman, with a facsimile of her brain implanted on a collapsed germanium-alloy core. It generates an appearance of life. Do you require the technical specifics?'

'No. I want its provenance.'

'It was taken from a small armed spaceship, a scout, built in the two hundred and first year of the Second Era. The scout was partially destroyed by a bomb from the planet Scundra. All aboard were killed but the ship went into orbit about Scundra. Do you require details of the engagement?'

'No. Do we know who the woman is?'

'These shelves are recent acquisitions and have only just been catalogued. Other Scundra acquisitions are still arriving. We may find more data at a later date. The cube itself has not been properly examined. It was sensitized to respond only to the cerebral emissions of the woman's husband. Such holocaps were popular with Second Era women and men on stellar flights. They provided life-mimicking mementoes of partners elsewhere in the cosmos. For further details, you may –'

'That's sufficient.'

I worked my way forward, but with increasing lack of attention to the objects about me. When I came to where the unloading was taking place, I halted my vehicle.

As the carrier-platforms sailed down from the roof, unwearying androids unloaded them, putting the goods in their translucent wraps into nearby lockers. Larger items were handled by crane.

'This material is from Scundra?' I asked the catalogue.

'Correct. You wish to know the history of the planet?'

'It is an agricultural planet, isn't it?'

'Correct. Entirely agricultural, entirely automated. No humans go down to the surface. It was claimed originally by Soviet India and its colonists were mainly, although not entirely, of Indian stock. A war broke out with the nearby planets of the Pan-Slav Union. Are these nationalist terms familiar to you?'

'How did this foolish "war" end?'

'The Union sent a battleship to Scundra. Once in orbit, it demanded certain concessions which the Indians were unable or unwilling to make. The battleship sent a scoutship down to the planet to negotiate a settlement. The settlement was reached but, as the scout re-entered space and was about to enter its mother-ship, it blew up. A party of Scundran extremists had planted a bomb in it. You examined an item preserved from the scoutship yesterday, and today you drove past the battleship concerned.

'In retaliation for the bomb, the Pan-Slavs dusted the planet with Panthrax κ, a disease which wiped out all human life on the planet in a matter of weeks. The bacillus of Panthrax κ was notoriously difficult to contain, and the battleship itself became infected. The entire crew died. Scout, ship, and planet remained incommunicado for many centuries. Needless to say, there is no danger of infection now. All precautions have been taken.'

The catalogue's brief history plunged me into meditation.

I thought about the Scundra incident, now so unimportant. The wiping out of a whole world full of people – evidence again of that lust for possession which had by now relinquished its grip on the human soul. Or was the museum itself an indication that traces of the lust remained, now intellectualized into a wish to possess, not merely objects, but the entire past of mankind and, indeed, what my friend had jokingly referred to as 'the secret of the universe'? I told myself then that cause and effect operated only arbitrarily on the level on the psyche; that lust to possess could itself create a secret to be found, as a hunt provides its own quarry. And if once found? Then the whole complex of human affairs might be unravelled beneath the spell of one gigantic simplification, until motivation was so lowered that life would lose its purport; whereupon our species would wither and die, all tasks fulfilled. Such indeed could have happened to the unassailable Korlevalulaw.

To what extent the inorganic and the organic universe were unity could not be determined until heat-death brought parity. But it was feasible to suppose that each existed for the other, albeit hierarchically. Organic systems with intelligence might achieve unity – union – with the encompassing universe through knowledge, through the possession of that 'secret' of which my friend joked. That union would represent a peak, a flowering. Beyond it lay only decline, a metaphysical correspondence to the second law of thermodynamics!

Breaking from this chain of reasoning, I realized two things immediately: firstly, that I was well into my serendipitous Seeker phase, and, secondly, that I was about to take from an android's hands an item he was unloading from the carrier-platform.

As I unwrapped it from its translucent covering, the catalogue said, 'The object you hold was retrieved from the capital city of Scundra. It was found in the apartment of a married couple named Jean and Lan Gopal. Other objects are arriving from the same source. Do not misplace it or our assistants will be confused.'

It was a holocap like the one I had examined the day before. Perhaps it was a more sophisticated example. The casing was better turned, the button so well-concealed that I found it almost by accident. Moreover, the cube lit immediately, and the illusion that I was holding a man's head in my hands was strong.

The man looked about, caught my eye, and said, 'This holocap is intended only for my ex-wife, Jean Gopal. I have no business with you. Switch off and be good enough to return me to Jean. This is Chris Mailer.'

The image died. I held only a cube in my hands.

In my mind questions flowered.

Sixty-five thousand years ago …

I pressed the switch again. Eyeing me straight, he said in unchanged tones, 'This holocap is intended only for my ex-wife, Jean Gopal. I have no business with you. Switch off and be good enough to return me to Jean. This is Chris Mailer.'

Certainly it was all that was left of Chris Mailer. His face made a powerful impression. His features were generous, with high forehead, long nose, powerful chin. His grey eyes were wide-set, his mouth ample but firm. He had a neat beard, brown and streaked with grey. About the temples his hair also carried streaks of grey. His face was unlined and generally alert, although not without melancholy. I resurrected him from the electronic distances and made him go through his piece again.

'Now I shall reunite you with your ex-wife,' I said.

As I loaded the holocap into my vehicle and headed back towards the cache of the day before, I knew that my trained talent was with me, leading me.

There was a coincidence and a contradiction here – or seemed to be, for both coincidences and contradictions are more apparent than real. It was no very strange thing that I should come upon the woman's holocap one day and the man's the next. Both were being unloaded from the same planetary area, brought to the museum in the same operation. The contradiction was more interesting. The woman had said that she spoke only to her husband, the man that he spoke only to his ex-wife; was there a second woman involved?

I recalled that the woman, Jean, had seemed young, whereas the man, Mailer, was past the first flush of youth. The woman had been on the planet, Scundra, whereas Mailer had been in the scoutship. They had been on opposing sides in that 'war' which ended in death for all.

How the situation had arisen appeared inexplicable after six hundred and fifty centuries. Yet as long as there remained power in the submolecular structure of the holocap cells, the chance existed that this insignificant fragment of the past could be reconstructed.

Not that I knew whether two holocaps could converse together.

I stood the two cubes on the same shelf, a metre apart. I switched them on.

The images of two heads were reborn. They looked about them as if alive.

Mailer spoke first, staring intensely across the shelf at the female head.

'Jean, my darling, it's Chris, speaking to you after all this long time. I hardly know whether I ought to, but I must. Do you recognize me?'

Although Jean's image was of a woman considerably younger than his, it was less brilliant, more grainy, captured by an inferior piece of holocapry.

'Chris, I'm your wife, your little Jean. This is for you wherever you are. I know we have our troubles but ... I was never able to say this when we were together, Chris, but I do love our marriage – it means a lot to me, and I want it to go on. I send you love wherever you are. I think about you a lot. You said – well, you know what you said, but I hope you still care. I want you to care, because I do care for you.'

'It's over a dozen years since we parted, my darling Jean,' Mailer said. 'I know I broke up the marriage in the end, but I was younger then, and foolish. Even at the time, a part of me warned that I was making a mistake. I pretended that I knew you didn't care for me. You cared all the time, didn't you?'

'Not only do I care, but I will try to show more of my inner feelings in future. Perhaps I understand you better now. I know I've not been as responsive as I might be, in several ways.'

I stood fascinated and baffled by this dialogue, which carried all sorts of overtones beyond my comprehension. I was listening to the conversation of primitive beings. The image of her face had vivacity; indeed, apart from the flat eyes and an excess of hair she passed for pretty, with a voluptuous mouth and wide eyes – but to think she took it for granted that she might have a man for her own possession, while he acted under similar assumptions! Whereas Mailer's mode of speech was slow and thoughtful, but without hesitation, Jean talked fast, moving her head about, hesitating and interrupting herself as she spoke.

He said, 'You don't know what it is like to live with regret. At least, I hope you don't, my dear. You never understood regret and all its ramifications as I do. I remember I called you superficial once, just before we broke up. That was because you were content to live in the present; the past or the future meant nothing to you. It was something I could not comprehend at the time, simply because for me both past and future are always with me. You never made reference to things past, whether happy or sad, and I couldn't stand that. Fancy, I let such a little matter come between our love! There was your affair with Gopal, too. That hurt me and, forgive me, the fact that he was black added salt to my wound. But even there I should have taken more of the blame. I was more arrogant then than I am now, Jean.'

'I'm not much good at going over what has been, as you know,' she said. 'I live each day as it comes. But the entanglement with Lan Gopal – well, I admit I was attracted to him – you know he went for me and I couldn't resist – not that I'm exactly blaming Lan … He was very sweet, but I want you to know that that's all over now, really over. I'm happy again. We belong to each other.'

'I still feel what I always did, Jean. You must have been married to Gopal for ten years now. Perhaps you've forgotten me, perhaps this holocap won't be welcome.'

As I stood there, compelled to listen, the two images stared raptly at each other, conversing without communicating.

'We think differently – in different ways, I mean,' Jean said, glancing downwards. 'You can explain better – you were always the intellectual. I know you despise me because I'm not clever, don't you? You used to say we had nonverbal communication … I don't quite know what to say. Except that I was sad to see you leave on another trip, going off hurt and angry, and I wished – oh well, as you see, your poor wife is trying to make up for her deficiencies by sending you this holocap. It comes with love, dear Chris, hoping – oh, everything – that you'll come back here to me on Earth, and that things will be as they used to be between us. We do belong to each other and I haven't forgotten.'

During this speech, she became increasingly agitated.

'I know you won't want me back, Jean,' Mailer said. 'Nobody can turn back time. But I had to get in touch with you when the chance came. You gave me a holocap fifteen years ago and I've had it with me on my travels ever since. When our divorce came through, I joined a fleet of space-mercenaries. Now we're fighting for the Pan-Slavs. I've just learnt that we're coming to Scundra, although not with the best of motives. So I'm having this holocap made, trusting there'll be a chance to deliver it to you. The message is simple really – I forgive anything you may think there is to forgive. After all these years, you still mean a lot to me, Jean, though I'm less than nothing to you.'

'Chris, I'm your wife, your little Jean. This is for you wherever you are. I know we have our troubles but … I was never able to say this when we were together, Chris, but I do love our marriage – it means a lot to me, and I want it to go on.'

'It's a strange thing that I come as an enemy to what is now, I suppose, your home planet since you married Gopal. I always knew that bastard was no good, worming his way in between us. Tell him I bear him no malice, as long as he's taking care of you, whatever else he does.'

She said, 'I send you love wherever you are. I think about you a lot … '

'I hope he's made you forget all about me. He owes me that. You and I were once all in all to each other, and life's never been as happy for me again, whatever I pretend to others.'

'You said – well, you know what you said, but I hope you still care. I want you to care, because I do care for you … Not only do I care, but I will try to show more of my inner feelings in future. Perhaps I understand you better now.'

'Jean, my darling, it's Chris, speaking to you after all this long time. I hardly know whether I ought to, but I must.'

I turned away. At last I understood. Only the incomprehensible things of which the images spoke had concealed the truth from me for so long.

The images could converse, triggered by pauses in each other's monologues. But what they had to say had been programmed before they met. Each had a role to play and was unable to transcend it by a hairsbreadth. No matter what the other image might say, they could not reach beyond what was predetermined. The female, with less to say than the male, had run out of talk first and had simply begun her chatter over again.

Jean's holocap had been made some fifteen years before Mailer's. She was talking from a time when they were still married, he from a time some years after their divorce. Their images spoke completely at odds – there had never been a dialogue between them ...

These trivial resolutions passed through my mind and were gone.

Greater things occupied me.

Second Era man had passed, with all his bustling possessive affairs.

The godlike Korlevalulaw too had passed away. Or so we thought. We were surrounded by their creations, but of the Korlevalulaw themselves there was not a sign.

We could no more see a sign of them than Jean and Mailer could see a sign of me, although they had responded in their own way ...

My function as a Prime Esemplastic Seeker was more than fulfilled. I had made an ultimate whole greater than the parts. I had found what my joking friend called 'the secret of the universe'.

Like the images I had observed, the galactic human race was merely a projection. The Korlevalulaw had created us – not as a genuine creation with free will, but as some sort of a reproduction.

There would never be proof of that, only intuition. I had learned to trust my intuition. As with those imprisoned images, the human species was gradually growing fainter, less able to hear the programmed responses. As with those imprisoned images, we were all drifting further apart, losing definition. As with those imprisoned images, we were doomed to root through the debris of the past, because copies can have no creative future.

Here was my one gigantic simplification, here my union with the encompassing universe! This was the flowering before the decline.

No, my idea was nonsense! A fit had seized me! My deductions were utterly unfounded. I knew there was no ultimate 'secret of the universe' – and in my case, supposing humanity to be merely a construct of the Korlevalulaw: who then 'constructed' the Korlevalulaw? The prime question was merely set back one step.

But for every level of existence there is a key to its central enigma. Those keys enable life-forms to ascend the scale of life or to reach an impasse – to flourish or to become extinct.

I had found a key which would cause the human species to wither and die. Ours was merely an umwelt, not a universe.

I left the museum. I flew my ship away from Norma. I did not head back to my home world. I went instead to a desolate world on which I now intend to end my days, communicating with no one. Let me assume that I caught a personal blight instead of detecting a universal one. If I communicate, the chance is that the dissolution I feel within me will spread.

And spread for ever.

Such was my mental agony that only when I reached this barren habitation did I recall what I neglected to do in the museum. I forgot to switch off the holocaps.

There they may remain, conducting their endless conversation, until power dies. Only then will the two talking heads sink into blessed nothingness and be gone.

Sounds will fade, images die, silence remain.

Wired for Sound

Fog hung in layers over Southmoor. Christopher Woodham paid off the pedicab.

'It's six minutes past four,' he said aloud. 'I've arrived home.'

He could see a light moving in the house, where Ruth was preparing for the evening's ordeal. Before daylight drained away, he made an inspection of the grounds, checking that the remaining goat had hay, that the hens and goose were secure. The half-acre of garden had been turned into a smallholding ten years ago; Ruth no longer grew prize chrysanthemums, but her marrows were renowned.

A shaggy figure loomed in the mist. Woodham was immediately on the alert. Despite enforced personal bugging, lawlessness was current, particularly in areas of high unemployment.

'It's me, Chris. I was checking the pump.'

Fred Laws had been in the aircraft industry until the Fall. Now he was a general trader, operating just within the law, and helping with odd jobs for wealthy friends like Woodham. He was a big man; he wore an old helmet painted in stripes.

'Hello, Fred. I'm getting the batteries.'

They went to the windmill which Laws had built. Laws

made deaf-and-dumb signs as they walked through the chicken enclosure. At the windmill, which worked a generator charging the batteries that supplied much of the Woodham's power, Laws said, 'What's wrong here?' and leaned against the metal superstructure.

Covered by the vibrations which played through his body, cancelling his personal bugging system, he said softly, 'It's your big night tonight, isn't it? Are you going to have any trouble with him?'

Woodham shook his head, conscious of the wires about his neck and chest and the recorder in the small of his back.

Laws motioned him to press against the superstrucure too, saying, 'I was in Oxford today. I've got a haunch of venison, guaranteed from Magdalen deer park, if that would help you with him.'

'They like sausages. Ruth has got sausages.' Woodham hated these stealthy conversations which everyone indulged in, knowing they were wired for sound. He bent down and read the voltmeter. The batteries were ready. The windmill could generate 75 kilowatts in a forty k.p.h. wind.

As Woodham took two of the batteries off charge, preparing to drag them to the house on a sled, Laws said in a hearty, artificial voice, 'Everything's fine, then, Chris. I'm glad we live in heroic times! I'm fitter than I was ten years ago, sitting in an office from nine till five, lining up for a coronary. Outdoor life suits me. And thank heavens cigarettes have disappeared. Remember those disgusting fags we used to smoke? If this is a relapse into barbarism, I'm for it!'

'Yes, heroic times ... I never think of that wasteful old consumer society we escaped from,' said Woodham, despising himself for pandering to whatever member of the Conservationist Party might examine his tape tomorrow. He genuinely hated what everyone called the Fall of Europe, whereas Laws, nefarious by nature, genuinely enjoyed it. Laws would be in trouble one day; on that day, it might help not to have accepted his hijacked venison.

The men parted, Laws vanishing into mist as Woodham lugged his batteries towards the house.

With the batteries linked to the emergency lighting, the room filled with yellow light.

Woodham grunted. 'We'll have a log fire, so that it's warm here when he arrives.'

Ruth blew out her candle. 'What a relief when we have power through the grid again. A lot of use the Severn barrage is!'

Assuming an official voice, he said, 'The tidal power harnessed in the Bristol Channel goes to operate essential industry – Britain must export or die. We'll be getting a domestic supply next year, when the Solent barrage comes on the national grid.' He pulled a face, to show her that what he was saying was strictly for the bugmen.

She held a strip of paper before his eyes, on which she had written FOOD STORE CLOSED AGAIN TODAY SOLDIERS GUARDING.

She smiled wearily. Ruth had stood the challenge of the last years remarkably well. The girl he had married, so dependent on mother's helps, shopping sprees, TV, and hairdressers, had disappeared; in her place was this quiet dependable woman, thin of cheek but adept at gutting an occasional illegal rabbit. He patted her bottom as she went into the kitchen.

The room looked well enough, Woodham thought. They had brought out all their Arab knick-knacks. Vessels of bronze and copper, one inscribed A SOUVENIR OF ISFAHAN, stood on the mantelpiece, a fine hanging was draped down the wall, and an aroma which passed for Arab incense hung in the air. They had put themselves out for an honoured guest. It was now dark; nobody would see how shabby and paintless the place had become.

'Heroic times indeed!' he said aloud. There was always a hope that you might *bore* a bugman to death …

The magical sound of a *car* on the drive.

'Seven-fifteen precisely and guest arrived,' Woodham said.

He hurried to the door. A uniformed Pakistani was opening the car door – Rolls? Cadillac? Some other old-fashioned name? – and in no time, smelling sweet and herbal, impeccably tailored Munich-style, Shaikh Mahmoud Gheleb was striding into the Woodham house.

He seemed to throw off light and elegance, from the strands of burnished gold in his neat dark beard to the rings on his fingers. Although Ruth kept out of the way for etiquette's sake, the distinguished visitor had not forgotten *alva* for her, with Sumatran cigars for Woodham. Moreover, he was delighted with the room – surprised to discover how civilized it was, charmed by its warmth and the feel of genial Olde England.

Ruth's meal went equally well. Before they ate, a fragrance drifted in from the kitchen, and the Shaikh confided how much he enjoyed British sausages. Lo and behold, in came Ruth, bearing a great plate of goat sausages and poached goose eggs, bedded on rice! The two men belched delicately afterwards, as they finished their vintage apple wine, and Shaikh Gheleb confided that Britain was easily his favourite tourist country. No, no, he even liked the cold damp winters; they made a pleasant change after the heat of Jiddah.

'I fear you are playing the polite guest, Shaikh. This is a miserable little country, which people leave when they can get work permits for yours.' The rules were strict but clear: it was only seditious to run down one's country to a fellow-countryman; to a prosperous foreigner, advantage might be gained.

Yet his was a tactless remark. For the Shaikh could have rejoined that at least there was still a thin stream of Israeli refugees coming into Britain. The man was too courteous for such crudity; he said, 'We never forget how hospitable Britain was, in the days of her prosperity, to workers from all over the world, no matter what colour their skin.'

It was time for business. Ruth was working the manual-power record-player, but music could not drown out voices for little microphones clamped round the neck. Woodham seized the Turkish coffee-grinder and worked it with difficulty against the top of his spine.

'Forgive this absurdity of posture, Shaikh, but you know how law-abiding this country is. I have a confidence to share with you which I do not wish to get into the central computers. You forgive me, I hope, since the confidence could be mutually profitable?'

'The pleasure of your home is sufficient, but your confidence would be an added benefit. So let's talk turkey. You have some reclamation systems you can sell my firm? Oil by-products?'

'No. Not quite.' Grating away till his head hummed, speaking low so that Ruth's bugging would not catch his words he said, 'As you know, I own a re-cycling plant in Abingdon – part-own, since the government has compulsory shares. We re-cycle things: paper and glass. We mainly turn the glass into cullet, which then goes to a glass factory to make more glass. The paper we turn into cardboard and protein.'

The Shaikh nodded. 'I understand you are making steaks from the re-cycled paper.'

'Yes, and they are palatable when flavoured with dog or cat meat essence – you probably know that the British are no longer allowed pets since 1982, but laboratory animals exist, which we acquire cheaply. Now, my technicians have discovered a way of making crude but cheap containers out of a modified cullet. They're like tin cans, such as we used to drink beer from, before the Fall. I plan to can our steaks and sell them as a cheap storeable food-source.'

'Where do I come in?'

Woodham glanced at the clock. It was later than he thought. In an hour, curfew, and the day's tape poured in one loud high-speed scream into the computer terminal on the phone … its contents to be picked over at leisure by the buggers of Whitehall. He ground the mill more furiously at the thought.

'We need one vital thing which you can supply, Shaikh. A refrigeration unit. They can't be obtained in Europe, even on the black market. Get me one of those, and I will guarantee you twenty-five per cent of my profits. Here are some figures.' He handed over a prepared sheet.

Shaikh Gheleb appraised the figures with a keen eye, then said, 'It's difficult. You understand the Arab Bloc is at war with Japan. For me to get a permit for exports to Europe will be extremely complex in the circumstances.'

'For thirty per cent, perhaps?'

'Can you not obtain the permit through legal channels, since your objective is to increase productivity?'

The very words caused Woodham to tremble. He blurted out a Party slogan, 'Expansionist Thinking set Britain sinking!'

The Shaikh nodded. 'But they would accept a fait accompli, the authorities, right? Particularly if it were guaranteed by an Arab industrialist? That would entail a capital risk for me … '

'Thirty-five per cent?'

Leaning forward confidentially, the Shaikh said, 'One further doubt … This – this food product … '

'Yes? We shall market it initially as "The Cullet Cutlet" – if we obtain your support, that is.'

'This Cullet Cutlet … it cannot be very tasty. Where will you find a market sufficiently undiscriminating to buy your product?'

'Ah! We have just such a market! As you probably know, Shaikh, our massive unemployment has forced many Englishmen to form mercenary armies or join the British Legion. There are, I'm proud to say, three British mercenary battalions fighting for the Arab Super-State in the Pacific right now.'

'And four fighting for the Japanese … '

'That's seven battalions in the Pacific theatre alone. Cullet Cutlet will find a ready market, rest assured.'

'Okay. Sixty per cent.'

As they were saying farewell, Woodham glanced at the clock. Just gone ten. Half an hour to curfew and off-load. He would have twenty minutes of suspicious blanket-noises on his tape, but that could be explained away. Meanwhile, the deal had been completed. Mentally, he saw himself booking passages on a Korean sailboat and heading with Ruth for sunny retirement by the Red Sea. The Shaikh and he embraced with warmth, although Woodham was conscious of his own strong body odour.

The night was thick outside. Shaikh Gheleb produced a torch and shone it towards his vehicle.

Both men exclaimed. The chauffer lay gagged and bound in

the car. His eyes rolled helplessly. His body was lashed round with a green fencing wire which Woodham recognized.

Crime against property, foreign property! The car was propped up on bricks. Its tyres, synthesized from precious Arabian oil, had been removed. And on the doors of the vehicle were scrawled the words HEROIC TIMES!

There was still a place for unspoken crime, even in the best-organized society.

Journey to the Heartland

At certain times of day, the campus was full of people. Students and college professors alike paraded in the sunshine, talking, calling, flirting, reading – a bright flock almost as migratory as birds. Five minutes later, they would all be gone to classroom or playing field or canteen, leaving the area deserted.

The windows of the Dream Research Unit looked down on the parade. Andrew Angsteed looked down through the windows. He was head of the unit. He was tall, casually dressed; his hair was greying. People found him remote. The hubbub from below rose to his ears. On the whole, he preferred the campus empty.

Behind him, in the laboratory, his three assistants worked, transcribing and codifying the previous night's work. Angsteed walked past the row of caged cats with their shaven heads. A thin beam of sun, slanting in the end window, lit the last cage; its occupant rolled over on her back, purring as Angsteed passed. He went to the window and drew down the blind.

Then he retreated into his office and put his head between his hands.

Rose-Jean Dempson was woken by the yellow buzzer.

She opened her eyes. The scene that drifted in on her senses was without meaning, an affair of walls, angles, and corners in which she was not remotely interested, so vivid remained the perspectives in which she had just been namelessly moving.

Turning carefully so as not to detach electrodes, she pulled herself on to one elbow and reached for a microphone by the bedside.

'Four-seventeen. I dreamed I was on a train in the Jurassic Age. It was a funny train, all full of beautiful furry surfaces. They were like big moths. I don't think they were alive. I wasn't scared of them. It didn't seem to be Jurassic time out-side, at least, not at first.

'My husband was in the dream. We had been to a party with a lot of people. Maybe it was somewhere underground. I had left without him to catch the train. Yet he was also on the train. That sounds confusing, but it wasn't in the dream. He was at the party and he was also in the train. I kept wondering how I could save him. I loved him best in the world and I wanted to be perfectly possessed by him; but he would not come all the way towards me. That was why I was having to go into the Jurassic, I think.

'Someone was arguing with me. It was a ticket collector. He was old and grey but very solid, very fatherly. He could not seem to see my husband. He was telling me to get off the train.

'I said, "There are things which have never been done before. I have to tell my husband to let go of his strict self-control. He has to reject all the things he thinks he loves, or else he will die. He must be more random, as these moths appear to be."

'But I knew that was wrong, somehow. The ticket collector would not let me explain properly. He shook his head and said something like, "The essence of human life can only be a matter of cyclic repetition."

'I was trying to explain to people that my madness, my wish to roam, was a special, life-giving quality. My husband had to admire, accept, and emulate it. I knew this meant suffering for him, but only in that way could he make his inner life flower. Everything else in the compartment was flowering, the upholstery and everything, but he sat there almost like a pile

G

of luggage. I must have identified with him in some way, because I also felt like a thing of a sudden.

'There were strange lumpy people moving along the corridor of the train.

'When I lay down on the seat, I realized it was night outside. We were gliding through the outer suburbs of a huge city. The train was a blaze of flame and foliage and bright things. Just above the rim of the window, I saw cold lights that fled by in the dark – white, white, white, white, white, repetitive, chilled nine hundred times. Very threatening. They were lighting wide deserted roads. Then there were dark houses. Then spots of sodium lighting, threaded out thin. Then country. Blackness.

'A different blackness from my blackness. Mine was rich and warm, personal, unregulated. The outer darkness had been chilled by the little urban lights. I tried to explain to my husband that the mad and the sane met here, that the lights were the lights of the sane – in those two camps of the world, the sane were winning by sheer force of numbers, pushing their cold little non-radiant lights out into the countryside.

'There was a terrific noise as we went over a bridge. I was excited because I thought we were getting near the Jurassic. The moths were very thick and bright.

'Then the bell rang.'

Rose-Jean looked about the laboratory, thick with muted noises of machines. Then she settled her dark head down on the pillow and fell asleep. Ninety-two minutes later, the yellow buzzer roused her again.

Andrew Angsteed and Rose-Jean Dempson walked back from town. The sun was low, casting long poplar shadows across the fields towards the university, where a few windows were already lit against dusk.

'I'm going to be away next week,' Angsteed said. 'Or did I already tell you that? Do you want a break from work, Rose-Jean?'

'No, I'm not tired at all. Besides, I'm off duty tonight.'

'But you've been on nights for six weeks now, going on seven.'

'I can't exactly explain, Andrew, but I'm refreshed by my dreams. Since you've been recording them, they have become much more vivid. I feel as if – as if a whole new side of my personality were coming into being.'

A silence between them. Before it could grow too long and awkward, Angsteed said, 'You've become my star guinea-pig, Rose-Jean. As you know, our interest in the project is simply to categorize, not analyse, dreams. We've identified three main types, or think we have – sigma, tau, and epsilon, and over a five-year period we are specializing in the tau-type, which is a phenomenon of median second-quarter sleep. In other words, we are concerned with classification, not in the dream-content *per se*. What is begining to emerge is that the tau-type is a more multi-layered dream than the other kinds. But your dreams – your tau-dreams, Rose-Jean ... well, I happen to find them extraordinarily beautiful, interesting, and significant. I mean nothing personal – '

She looked up at his face and said, 'Dreams aren't exactly personal, are they?'

'No, let me finish! Just because I'm in charge of the project, I may seem remote at times. You know that our findings are being challenged by Dr Rudesci in St Louis.' He paused. 'Have I said this to you before?'

'No. Well – yes, in a way. Sometimes. People have been known to repeat themselves, Andrew, especially if it is something that's worrying them.'

They had come to the gate into New Buildings. He paused and took her hand.

'Don't let's go in yet! I have to talk to you. Rose-Jean, I have fallen completely for you. You must have noticed. You're so beautiful and your dreams are so beautiful. I've never been so close to anyone's inner world ... '

She looked searchingly at him, so that he could devour once again the sight of that perfect conjunction between nose, nostrils, upper lip, and mouth, and the unique placement of her eyes, eyes that he had so often surreptitiously gazed on when, closed and inward gazing, they were merely the most entrancing part of his research project.

'You'd better come up and have coffee in my room, Andrew,' she said.

Hers was the ordinary untidy room of a young faculty teacher. He noted books on her shelves that one might find in any of twenty adjacent rooms: Tilbane's *Lord of the Rocks*; *The Grand Claim of Being*; *Sex in Theory and Practice*; Orlick's *After the Post-Renaissance*; his own *Sense and the Dreaming Self*; *What I Know About Mars*; J. T. Fraser on Time; Krawstadt's *Frankenstein Among the Arts*; and others. There were also drawings and gouache paintings scattered about.

By the window was a framed photograph of her with a man, laughing.

He picked up one of the gouaches. It showed a girl sitting decorously nude against a panther. 'Did you do this?' he asked. The colours were crude.

'Please. It's not finished. Besides, it isn't very good.'

He watched her push her paintings away in a locker. She was right, that must be admitted; the painting wasn't very good; her dreams were much more striking.

Straightening, she said, 'I keep painting the same picture over and over again, as if that one image is all I have to offer, I don't know why. It's as if my essence was just repetitive.'

'The essence of human life can only be a matter of cyclic repetition, since all generations are similar, have similar experiences.'

'I mean repetitive within myself. Maybe all my dreams would boil down to repetition, if they were analysed.'

He suspected she was trying for pathos. He replied with a great effort at warmth, 'I would not think that at all. There are always certain recurrent archetypes in dreams, but much of the other content of your dreams I find highly original and thought-provoking.'

'Is that really so? What sort of things – I mean, may I ask – ?'

'Take your last dream, the one about travelling by train into the Jurassic. I've played your report over several times. I found it interesting the way you contrasted the mad and the cold sane. Your sympathies were with the mad. You evidently see our urban culture, nominally built by the sane, as a sinister thing – a threat to *true* sanity, which is allied to madness.'

She put her hand over her mouth. 'Do I really? Did I say that? Oh, it sounds very profound ... My subject's really domestic science ... Maybe I should get us some coffee, would you like that?'

'The dream world – right at its Heartland lies an extraordinary amalgam of sanity and madness ...' His attempt at explanation hung in the silence of her banal room.

He watched her preparing coffee, dearly wishing that she would offer him whisky. He recalled that she did not touch alcohol. Perhaps he could change that, given time.

She looked so cool, so lovely, in her simple outfit of slacks, blouse, and suede waistcoat. He went over to her and put an arm round her.

'Rose-Jean, the work has taken on new meaning for me since you joined our unit as a volunteer.' As he said the words, he thought how pedestrian they sounded. The language of dreams was so much more eloquent than the poor defaced coinage of waking.

She took the opportunity to ask, 'What do you hope to find out from these researches? You must believe in them – you've dedicated so much time to them.'

'There are things that have never been done. Haven't I said this to you before? It's some while since it was discovered that there were different kinds of sleep. Now we are sure that there are different kinds of dream – although the situation looks more complex than when I launched the project, nine years ago. I think at last I have the answer ... '

'And what's that? What sort of answer?'

'Oh, forget it. Let's not talk shop. Rose-Jean!' He grasped her and tried to kiss her. She struggled in his arms but he would not let her go. She submitted, bringing her lips up to his.

Although she stood unyieldingly, after a second she parted

her lips slightly, so that he could taste the warmth rising from within her, the furnace of her. He cupped her left breast with one hand before letting her go.

She retreated, hand up to mouth again.

'Andrew, I'm not psychologically prepared for this kind of assault!'

'Assault!'

'As you may know, I'm living separate from my husband, but he is still around and – I may as well tell you this, he still occupies much of my thoughts. Now, please let me pour you some coffee.'

He clutched his head. 'As I say – the essence of human life is cyclic – archetypal emotions, sensations, experiences. They don't change ... Sometimes I feel that the whole of modern existence is a fraud, a distraction from some deep and living thing. Maybe we help release that in our work.' He laughed, half angrily.

She gave him a mug full of black coffee, looking at him curiously.

'You were saying you have an answer to your work-problems. Can you tell me? I have a fascination for science, so I am genuinely interested, you know.'

'Are you? Do you care about me at all? Could you ever love me?'

'Could you ever love me, Andrew? Or is it just my dreams that you care about? I sometimes think my husband never cared about the real me. My dream side is surely impersonal – it contains all kinds of fascinating – snippets, I guess, from God knows where. The collective unconscious, I guess. But the real Rose-Jean Dempson only surfaces in waking hours.'

He looked at his watch. 'Listen, I'll tell you what I've told nobody. I think the unit is on to something really big. There are things which have never been done before, and we could be on to one of them.

'Scientific thought is finally acknowledging the complexity of a human being. As usual, the biological side has had to come first, with its gradual revelation of the intricately different times and cycles kept by the physical body. Since then, there's been progress in other directions, all reinforcing the same pattern.

'The further we probe into sleep and dreams, the more actual becomes the vast, rich complexity of the mind. It sometimes feels like – I sometimes feel like an explorer, trembling on the brink of an unknown world.'

'That must be a wonderful experience, Andrew. I'm truly glad for you.'

'We've had a whole year of frustrations. The work's got nowhere. Our findings have been challenged, as you know. Now we recognize that our earlier interpretation of the evidence was incorrect. We were working with a too-simple model of the mind. At last I can understand that we are on the threshold of something of much more startling import than I ever expected. Your dreams have helped me towards an understanding of that something.'

'Oh, how totally thrilling! And what is that?'

He set his mug down and said, slowly, 'Rose-Jean, I can't expect anyone but myself to grasp the entire picture yet, but I have discovered that there are several different time-flows running concurrently in the brain.'

'I don't understand. Time-flows?'

'We all occasionally acknowledge different time-flows, despite the horrible supremacy of clock-time in the modern world – the clock-time I believe you were escaping from in your last dream. That's why I think you are like me. There's the light, slow time-flow of childhood, the heavy, sluggish time-flow of the mentally deranged, the time that lovers appear to abolish, the speeded-up time of drunks, the suspended time-flow of catastrophe, and others. They're not imaginary, they're genuinely different internal circuitry. I believe I shall soon have proof of that, proof that many different time-flows exist within any one mind, in the same way that various time-mechanisms coexist in the body.'

Angsteed went to the window, absorbed in his vision. The campus, glimpsed here from an angle, was brightly lit. Several people were about. Some strolled leisurely, some walked briskly, one or two were running. Some went in groups and pairs. Many were solitary. Some chose the light areas, some the shadows.

She was looking at him wide-eyed. There was something curious in her manner.

'Do you mind if I draw the drapes?'

She crossed to the window. It was sunrise outside and a terrific noise was going on. The field was full of people. He understood that they were watching a comet which blazed in the sky. Attempts were being made to capture the comet in some way, in order to harness its energies for fuel.

He said, 'They are going to harvest its energies.'

She said, 'It is not time for the harvest yet.' He noticed that her husband was beside her, a small man standing behind some kind of flower arrangement.

Someone was asking what time the harvest was.

She came out from behind a rocking-chair, smiling, and saying that she had a record she wanted to play them over and over again.

It was already playing. It brought them all happiness. He danced with someone in the room, but it was not she. The room vanished.

They were outside, under the stars and a comet like a great Biblical sheaf of wheat. Trees were the colour of resin.

The yellow buzzer sounded.

Angsteed roused, staring round the familiar laboratory without raising his head from the pillow. He regularly used himself as his own guinea-pig, and had determined to do so again directly after his evening with Rose-Jean.

He reached out almost automatically for the microphone and began to record the details of his dream, after noting the time. Early. 1.56.

He completed the report, added the words, 'Typical sigma dream, preoccupied with digesting the experiences of the day,' and settled his head back on the pillow. Then he sat upright.

The interpretation of the dream flashed upon him. It had signalled itself as a special dream by the hint to begin with:

the drawing of the curtains symbolized the closing of his eyes. And the rest ... well, he needed to talk to someone about it. Rose-Jean! Why not? He had a pretext for visiting her at night.

Going to the dressing-room, he pulled on some clothes and slippers and shuffled out of the labs. He crossed to her block. Nobody was about, although a light shone here and there where a student hunched over a book or talked to or seduced another student. The moon shone. It was a perfect night. He could hear the continuous rumble of traffic from the freeway.

Before Rose-Jean's door, he hesitated, then tried the handle. The door opened – somewhat to his surprise, for warnings about theft were posted on every residential floor. He entered. This was the room in which he had kissed her only a few hours earlier. The experience came so freshly back to him that time seemed to be annihilated.

Angsteed stood there, taking in the scents and impressions of the room before moving towards the bedroom door. Opening it, he called softly, 'Rose-Jean, are you awake? It's only me, Andrew.'

He knew immediately from her tone that she had been awake. In her voice was a note almost of panic.

'Andrew? You can't come in here. It's the middle of the night. What the hell do you want?'

'I've had a dream. A revelation. I want to discuss it with you. I promise I'll only talk. Can I put the light on?'

'No! No, I forbid you to put the light on. Please go, Andrew – we can talk in the morning. I was asleep.'

'But listen, darling – suddenly I've seen my way ahead, and you gave me the clue in a dream. There was a comet in the sky, and you said – '

'Andrew, will you please get out of my room before I call the porter?'

He went nearer to the bed and sat down on it, reaching for her hand. 'Please attempt to listen to me. I didn't come here to seduce you! This is something really important. You know how on medical reports it is now considered vital to record at what precise time drugs are administered? The time is

G*

recognized as being as important as the quantity. Because the same dosage can have widely different effects at different times of day. You told me in my dream that you had a record which was played over and over. That refers to the record of all dreams kept by the unit. We have always entered the time of waking in the sleep records, but we have not applied the time in the classificatory data. Don't you see that we can check back over the last fifteen years' records and we should be able to turn up the new factor?'

She was still angry. 'You're babbling, Andrew! What new factor?'

'Didn't I say that? Look, we've only studied times of dreams as part of how long after the commencement of sleep they occur. But we need to study them as against body-time. The dreams come at certain regular intervals after the onset of sleep, but what we may have missed is that the *content* of the dreams may well be influenced by the subject's body-time! We can check on that. And my dream suggests that the answer will be epoch-making – hence the comet. We may well discover that the different sorts of dream come from different time-flows. In other words, it may be possible in future to key in to whatever level of personality we require – and of course with that new understanding, we shall be able to chart an entirely new picture of consciousness!'

He leant forward in his excitement to embrace her. The curtains were drawn together in the room. He could only vaguely discern the pale outline of her face. As he reached towards it, another face materialized next to it, and a rough male hand thrust itself into his face.

'You leave my wife alone!' a voice told him.

Next morning, Rose-Jean went to see Angsteed. She apologized for last night.

'We'd better forget it,' he said. 'And obviously you will want your name removing from the dream roster.'

'Don't be so stuffy, Andrew. I know you sleep around a fair bit, or used to. My friends told me. Don't start being unkind to me just because I have my husband in my bed once in a while. If you must know, I didn't even invite him in last night. I thought he was hundreds of miles away, but he dropped in on me.'

'I don't want to know about your personal affairs.'

'Of course you do. Why sulk? Listen, Andrew, I like you a lot. I have this thing about my husband, but sooner or later I reckon I have to shake him out of my system. You can help me, if you really wish. I'm just in no mood for – oh, forget it!'

He stood against her and took her hand. 'I'm sorry, Rose-Jean. Of course I'm peeved about last night, peeved with you and with *him* – and jealous, of course – and most peeved with myself. I'll get over it. Let's be friends. I need you. Think what my life has been, stuck in dreary research institutes – before I was here, I was studying dying flies and making moth pupae abort in order to learn about circadian mechanisms. A life for science! Well, it's been a living death. Your dreams have revived me, given me new imaginative insight. I really think I'm on the brink of a major breakthrough, and I'd like you to get some of the excitement too.'

She kissed him then.

'How's that for excitement?'

'Great. There are things which have never been done before, but they have no power to alter the essence of things.'

'I don't quite see what you mean.'

He looked at her in puzzlement. 'Have I said that before? Your dreams have altered something in my essence, brought me to life in some inner way.'

'I find that hard to believe; I'm so unimportant. Yet, why not? I feel refreshed by my dreams myself, as maybe I told you. Maybe the essence of one human life is cyclic in nature, and a new season is about to dawn in both our psyches, if that isn't too fanciful!'

'And a new comet in both our skies!'

At last he had broken the spell. He took her powerfully into his arms. Their mouths met. After a moment, they settled down on Angsteed's plum-coloured sofa.

The yellow buzzer woke Rose-Jean Dempson at 2.11 a.m., activated by her REMS.

Pulling the microphone towards her, she said, 'Two-eleven. There was an earthquake, and the university was in ruins. Everyone else seemed to have gone. It was night, and I wasn't at all frightened.

'I ran out across the field. The layout of everything was different. I saw a broken clock lying on the ground. It had stopped at ... I believe it was ten minutes past six. Evidently it had fallen off a ruined tower.

'I went towards the line of poplars. The sky was curiously bright and there seemed to be creatures running about near me. One of the poplars had fallen over. I appeared to climb along its horizontal trunk. Then I was looking down at its roots, which were earthy and dangling in the air. I could see something gleaming in the hole. It was a gold casket but when I lifted it out it had blood on it, so I gave it to someone who was beside me.

'Then it seemed that I was riding a horse. I was very excited. Maybe there was another earth tremor. It sounds silly, but the whole landscape was coming along with us. The horse started galloping round in circles.

'Reindeer were running nearby, beautiful creatures, brown and white, with terrific antlers. They ran with their heads down, breath pouring like steam from their nostrils.

'I was full of delight because in the morning the world was going to begin anew. I guess it all sounds like a typical epsilon dream, I'm afraid.'

Rose-Jean looked about the laboratory, thick with the dusk of shaded lights and the caterpillar sounds of machines. Her eyelids closed, shutting it all away. Her head went back on the pillow and she slept. Ninety-five minutes later, the yellow buzzer roused her again.

In the morning, Rose-Jean went to see her closest friend on the faculty, Alice Butley. Alice was head of the Philosophy Department, a stringy woman in her mid-fifties with a lot of life and humour in her. Rose-Jean had liked her from their first meeting, although Alice was almost twice Rose-Jean's age.

'Care for a drink, Rose-Jean?'

'Just a Coke, maybe.'

'It wants three-quarters of an hour before the time for my first Martini, but I guess I could run forty-five minutes ahead of schedule for once. Though "for once" is certainly not the phrase I should use there. Drinking early is getting to be a repetitive event ... I can stand just so much of this place ... You aren't coming to tell me you're quitting?'

Rose-Jean laughed. 'Far from it. I'm just getting interested. But I guess I was wanting to talk to you about a repetitive event.'

'Go ahead! This dump is stocked with nothing else but ... '

'Alice, you'll laugh when I tell you.'

'Try me.'

'I think I'm falling heavily for Andrew Angsteed, the head of the Dream Research Unit. Now – I know your opinion of him is mixed, and he surely does seem a bit dull at first but, when you get to know him better, why, he's just great. He's so understanding, and the work he's doing is just fascinating.'

Alice brought over the drink. 'It's not the work in your man's life, it's the man in your life's work that counts. Andrew's nearer my age than yours. Still, when could one ever say that and expect a hearing?'

'He really is tremendous, Alice. He's had a dull life, but now he feels that everything is going to change. I feel just the same way. Really new things are about to happen!'

Raising her glass, sipping, Alice said, 'Well, there are things which have never been done before, events that have never taken place, but they have no power to alter the essence of things. You may or may not resent that, according to temperament.'

'I don't follow you. You're saying the essence of things is repetitive?'

'No, but the essence of human life experience is largely a matter of repetition – or cyclic in nature, let's say, since generations do not differ in that respect, suffering the same miseries and pleasures, the same emotions, the same realities of birth, death, love, and so on … Not forgetting boredom – it's a worser killer than death, as my old pop used to say.'

Her phone warbled. She walked over to the desk and cut it off.

Perching on the edge of a chair, Rose-Jean said, 'But these cycles – they aren't concentric, are they? I mean, otherwise the same events would happen over and over again, without the participants being aware of it.'

'Well, don't they, dammit?!'

Rose-Jean's gaze dropped to the floor. Then she laughed. 'Maybe, I guess. At least – oh, I don't know. You're the philosopher, Alice. You see, I did want to talk to you about a repetitive event. You know the last place I was in, the University of Catrota, well, I also fell in love with a man there. He was very intelligent but sort of a hippie. No, not a hippie but at least a potential drop-out from society. He didn't accept the way society was run, any more than Andy does, in a different way. His name was Allan Dempson. We got married. I told you about it.'

'Sure. You told me it didn't work out.'

'Oh, we tried, but it was just impossible. He was gorgeous, but so tyrannical. Andrew's quite different. I had to leave Allan and Catrota. He's thrown up his job there too. He works as a transcontinental truck-driver, when he works at all.'

'Now you're afraid you're going to make a mess of things all over again with Andrew Angsteed?'

'I don't know. You said it yourself, the major events of life occur over and over. Still, Allan and Andrew are just so different. I guess Allan just had one major obsession, the state of society.'

Alice looked at the younger woman meditatively. 'I'd say that hit off Andy pretty accurately, too. He's obsessive, if ever I saw it.'

'Oh – I don't know … I just find him so fascinating … '

Alice took her arm. 'Honey, you spend too long on that dream machine. You're still married to Allan, right? So you *can't* marry Andrew. That takes care of that.'

'But I can divorce Allan. He said I could.'

'In order to marry Andrew? Maybe your trouble is that you are pursuing archetypes, not real people. That's when the going really gets difficult and events really start to repeat themselves. Let me lend you Anna Kavan's *Ice* to read, then you'll understand what I mean by pursuit of archetypes. You are seeing Andrew generically when you should view him as an individual. Let's talk again about this – I must go and see old Birkett. We have a deal of trouble regarding the appropriations fund.'

'You've nothing against Andrew?'

Alice looked away. 'No. I'm very fond of Andrew.'

Angsteed shut himself in his office and played back to himself the cassette on which he had recorded Rose-Jean's dream from the master-tape. The master-tape was university property; the cassette was his property. He now had records of one hundred and seventy-four dreams dreamed by Rose-Jean Dempson. In the work-files of his department, all dreams contributed to the bank by all volunteers were anonymous, and elaborately cross-filed in the computer according to dream-type, content, key-symbol, and so on. Now they were all being additionally classified according to time of dream.

All that was impersonal, and routine. Angsteed's private collection of Rose-Jean's dreams was both private and personal.

He let his mind wander as her sleepy voice reached him through the earphone in his ear. Her dream territory had become more and more familiar to him. He, possibly more than any man alive, was able to chart that territory. In every dream, he could tell whereabouts he was in her psyche, in which quadrant, how deep he was. He knew the colorations, he had come to recognize various meta-continents, in each of which certain archetypal emotion-events prevailed. All was cloudy, ever-changing, but he no longer went in fear of losing his orientation. As his knowledge and sensibility increased, he grew to comprehend something about the different time-flows of the different meta-continents.

Gradually, and without being aware of it, he was coming nearer to the Heartland, that interior into which no conscious thought – not even Rose-Jean's – had ever penetrated. The interior was beset with mystery and guarded with barricades, the foremost of which was the attentuation of consciousness into sleep. The effect came like an enchantment as one approached, and the brain-waves which it radiated served as tseste fly in maintaining the territory intact and virginal. But Angsteed was learning to move in ever deeper.

During the lunch-hour, he retired to his room, taking the cassette to add to his growing collection. He moved slowly and somnambulistically, often ignoring the greetings of his fellows.

He had plans for writing a ballet, for making a film, for painting a picture, which would embody the inner world of which he was the sole explorer. As yet only a few notes and diagrams existed. Sometimes Angsteed sat before his typewriter, sometimes he sat with his gouaches on the desk before him. Rarely did he do more than gaze into perspectives of which only he was aware.

When his phone warbled, he picked it up and spoke inattentively.

It was Rose-Jean.

At once he became more alert.

'We both have the night free of the lab. Let me drive you into Goadstown, and we'll have a meal together. You might even remind me how to dance. How's about it?'

'Why, that would be fine, Andrew, but – '

'No buts, honey! Let me for once pose as a man of action. Be round at my apartment at six, and we'll have a drink before we go. I had a letter this morning that I'd like you to cast an eye over. Things are going to change from now on, and you're a part of it.'

'Oh, okay, Andrew, whatever you say. Ciao.'

Although he set the phone down briskly, the smile on his face faded into abstraction, and he sat where he was, gazing into his own personal distance.

He was lying on his bed with the same expression on his face when Rose-Jean arrived that evening, brightly dressed for the trip to town.

'I'm meant to be showering, but I got lost in a fit of abstrac-

tion. I'm not always quite so absent-minded.' He kissed her
rather formally.

'You'd better go and shower now, then. I came at six as you
asked.' She was piqued that he offered no compliments about
her appearance after the long ritual she had subjected herself
to before her mirror.

'Sure, sure. Won't be long! Grab yourself a Coke out of
the icebox. Have a look at my books.'

She did as she was bid, mooching back and forth before his
well-worn collection of hardcover and paperback with a glass
in her hand. She saw no titles that particularly took her fancy,
except for some egghead movie paperbacks. The directors
discussed were Buñuel, Jancso, Tarkovsky and Bergman.
Since the latter was the only one she had heard of, and his
films bored her, she shovelled the volumes back into their
shelf. She put a Bonzo Dog Band record on the record-player
instead.

Just as Angsteed reapeared, looking unfamiliar in a grey suit,
the door bell rang. Alice Butley entered.

'Hi, Rose-Jean, you're looking great. I've picked a bad time
to call, Andy – I can see you're going out. I only dropped in
for an idle chat. I'll call around some other time.'

'Don't go. Great to see you again, Alice. I'm just getting
myself a Martini – let me make you one.'

'I can resist anything but temptation. Set 'em up.'

When they were drinking, Angsteed said, 'Alice, things are
most definitely going to be different, radically different, around
here. We're on the move at last. The psyche is going to expand
in a big way. Believe me, I'm on to something really new, aren't
I, Rose-Jean?'

'Oh, I do hope so.'

'Well, there *are* things that have never been done before,
though most of them are powerless to alter the essence of
existence,' Alice said.

'What about a new thing that goes direct to the essence of
existence?' He grinned and looked at Rose-Jean for her
approval.

'The essence of the human life experience is largely a matter of repetition. It's cyclic in nature, at the least, with every generation suffering the same miseries and pleasures.'

'Oh, sure, we all enjoy the same emotions, the same realities of birth and death, love, desire, hate. Haven't I said that to you before?'

Rose-Jean perched on the edge of Angsteed's sofa and said, 'These cycles, Alice – at least they can't be concentric, or else the same events would happen over and over again without the participants being aware of it.' She passed her hand across her brow, as if brushing a hair away.

Alice laughed. 'So they do happen over and over again! I guess reason suggests otherwise, but reason is fallible in these matters.'

'A fine thing for a philosopher to say! You've no proof of this repetition.'

She spread her hands and offered him a face of innocence. 'The major events of life occur over and over, perpetually. Rose-Jean agrees with me, don't you, Rose-Jean?'

But Rose-Jean had walked over to the window and was pressing her forehead against the glass. Angsteed went quickly across to her and put an arm round her shoulders.

'What's the trouble, honey? You okay?'

'I'm okay. I just hate what we're talking about. Sometimes, I get an awful sense of déjà vu. Let's go out if we're going out, can we, do you mind?'

'Just say the word, sweetheart.'

'I can take a hint,' Alice said. She shot Angsteed a significant and warning look, but he chose not to heed it.

Towards midnight, they finished up at Luigi's, where the juke-box was loud, the lamps were encased in lead, and the waitresses wore green leather pants and little else. Beyond the pool tables was a space for dancing. Angsteed was drunk enough to try a few steps. He enjoyed the music and the noise and the people.

'Too long since I did this!' he shouted at her.

'It does rather look that way, Andy. Wouldn't you rather sit down?'

'Come on, girl, I'm only just getting going! You know your trouble?'

'What is my trouble?'

He started to laugh as he swayed. 'You're just a babe-in-arms. You should learn to drink, that's what you should do! Coke's a kid's drink.'

'I happen to like it.'

'Okay, you like it. I tell you what – let me get you a Coke with a rum in it. How about that?'

'No, thanks, alcohol is a drug and I'm not having any.'

He stopped dancing. 'What's wrong with you, Rose-Jean? What was that you said the other day about not being a person? Alcohol never did anyone any harm in moderation. Now come on, come and have a Coke-and-rum. What do they call it? A Cuba Libre! I'll have a Cuba Libre with you!'

He dragged her away to a table, shouting for a waitress. Finally, two Cuba Libres were brought and set before them.

'I'm not going to drink it, Andy, so you'd better make up your mind.'

'What you afraid of? Come on, pour it down, honey! More where that came from!' He started his own drink, and continued until his glass was empty. Some of the liquid ran down his chin and into his shirt. He wiped his chops with a grand gesture.

She clutched his arm. 'Andy, let's get out of here. I can see my husband over by the bar, and he can be real mean.'

'Leave it to me. I'll take care of that bastard! Where is he? Which one's him?' He stared pugnaciously at the throng of people by the bar.

'I'm not having any fighting. I thought he was a thousand miles away. Let's get out of here fast and back home, if you're sober enough to drive.'

'Balls, go and tell him to join us. Let's buy him a drink.'

She put her face closer to him and said, 'Andy, if you don't come out to the car this instant, I swear to you that everything is over between us from this moment on, and I will never speak to you again. I know my husband better than you do, and I'm telling you to come on out.'

'All right, all right, I heard, relax! He won't kill us!'

'You'd be surprised!' She put her arm round Angsteed and dragged him through the crowd and out of the saloon, keeping her face away from the bar. Angsteed tried to determine whom they were avoiding but, as far as he could see, none of the people at the bar was taking any notice of them.

Outside, they made their way through the parking lot to Angsteed's car. Angsteed was argumentative and wanted to return to give Dempson a going over; Rose-Jean had some difficulty in getting him into the driving seat.

'Please drive carefully, Andy! Oh, you look so wild!'

He steered a way slowly through the lot and towards the main entrance. As they came under the fake carriage lights at the gate, Rose-Jean cried that she could see Dempson, head down, walking towards the exit.

With a roar, Angsteed threw the vehicle forward. Rose-Jean screamed. A man in their path turned and jumped to one side, and the off-wing of the vehicle rammed a brick pillar. Sounds of falling glass as one of the headlights went out. Automobiles behind began hooting. Both Angsteed and Rose-Jean jumped out to inspect the damage.

'You were going to run him over, you madman!'

'No, I wasn't. I only meant to give him a scare.'

'When I got a proper look at him I saw it wasn't Allan anyway.'

In her arms later, the drink still in him, he cried in self-hatred, 'What sort of a man am I? Is there a curse on me, something I can't get free from? How wretched, how circumscribed, my goddamned life is!'

'Don't talk so loud, Andy! You'll give me a bad reputation.'

'I love you, Rose-Jean, you're marvellous, you're natural, in a way I could never be. I want to please you, yet all I do works against our relationship. A repetitive event, like Alice says. Anything I love, it dies on me. Even now, even saying what I am saying, I'm conscious that I may be driving us further apart.'

'I love having you in my bed, Andy. It gets lonely. Did you ever make love to Alice?'

'What the hell kind of question is that? What's that got to do with what we're talking about?'

'What are we talking about? I don't know. I'm not really intellectual, as you seem to think. I mean, people are what they are, aren't they?' She started to stroke him. Finally, her hands and her kisses had their proper effect, and they filled her narrow bed with loving.

She fell asleep before he did. Angsteed lay huddled against her, claustrophobic in her narrow room, yet relishing the experience of having his head on the same pillow as that other head, which contained – or projected – a world he regarded as much more splendid than reality.

Gradually, eyes still open, he built up, in his dream cartography, a misty globe not unlike a celestial globe, with quadrants, sectors, figures, and mythological figures scrawled over it, every one with its own intense magic. This was Rose-Jean's personal globe. What puzzled him was how it related to her personally, how far it was beyond her or even antithetical to her, how far it was on a completely other plane from her own limited consciousness. That puzzlement faded as he lowered himself into the unlimited globe; his own reactions were dimmed out under the kaleidoscope of emotions in which he found himself moving.

At first, it was as if he were running amid a herd of reindeer in a storm – either a snow blizzard or a sand storm. Glittering particles obscured almost everything. Shaggy things stood to one side, fir trees of which neither boles nor crowns were visible. The eyes of the reindeer were yellow in their melancholy faces.

The colours blended perfectly. He was moving nearer the source. Currents of heat served as compass-bearings. Somewhere ahead were the mountainous Heartlands, living under different times, different suns. People and animals were transformed there.

Already, the process was happening about him. As he bent his head to climb, the reindeer were going into people, the people going into animals, coming out, going in again, eating and being eaten, diving into what appeared to be the ground, springing up again like divers, their movements beautiful and horrific. He tried to look into the faces of the people, which somehow eluded him. He could tell that some were unaffected by the majestic process and walked with sunshades or in flowing robes.

Someone was running beside him, matching him stride for stride. Under the jogging hair, eyes, lambent. A hint about the mouth of – what? Joy, lust, laughter, despair? Together, they came to a narrowing way, where windows loomed above them like the luminiferous eyes of fish.

He felt his heart hammering as darkness, heat, walls confined him. Now he was in a house, and someone was explaining – or attempting to explain – that this house was all there was, anywhere, that it was coextensive with the universe. The being beside him was denying the explanation.

'It's the other way about – the universe is in the house.'

They sat down, on furniture scarcely indicated, and a woman entered the room. She was tall, she came towards them bearing a precious gift, something that changed shape so that they hardly comprehended it. The woman's motion also set in being other shape changes. The room itself responded to her, began to grow tremendously tall and the walls to become soft, so that he clenched his hands and felt the pulse in them like a spring.

She came and looked him in the face. The other had gone. The room was more like the hollow trunk of a tree – and more and more, until her eyes and face seemed like leaves and he became part of her and they were both merely patterns on the sinuous green growth.

'Just a minute,' Alice mumbled. 'Who is it? What time is it?'

She threw on a gown and padded over to her outer door. Rose-Jean was standing there. Night lay behind her in the corridor.

'Rose-Jean? What's the matter. I feel such a mess. What time is it?'

The girl was near to tears.

'Oh, Alice, I'm in such trouble! It's Andrew, please help me. He's unconscious or something and I can't wake him up. Maybe he's dying. I've tried pouring water on his face and everything.'

'Jesus Christ, child, try whisky, try the college quack, or the shrink, or the fire department – just don't try me. Andy's not my responsibility!'

'But he may be dying. People do die!'

'You don't have to wake me in the small hours to tell me that. I know people die. That's never been news!'

She backed into her room and started to search for cigarettes. Rose-Jean followed her round. Darkness lay outside the windows.

'The trouble is, Alice – I had to come to you. I'm in trouble. Andrew's blacked out in my bed.' She laughed feebly, in apology.

Alice looked at her. Still looking at her, she lit a cigarette, sucked in the smoke, began to laugh and cough. Finally she managed to speak.

'Gee, that's sweet, that's just sweet! Oh, Rosie, you kill me! Poor Andy was never too much of a lover, and I guess you just wore him out. He's catching up on his beauty-sleep, that's all. Now you trot along back to him and leave me to my beauty-sleep – if that's the phrase I'm looking for any longer.'

'Alice, please – there's something really wrong with Andy. I know it.'

'There's something wrong with him all right,' Alice said, as she stared down at Angsteed, a few minutes later. She lifted one of his eyelids and watched it fall back into place. 'Did you hit him?'

'Of course not. At least he's not dead. Is he dying, do you imagine? How are we going to get him over to his room without anyone seeing us?'

'Can't be done. I'll phone Dr Norris for you. He's a nice discreet guy.'

Angsteed lay curled in Rose-Jean's bed, his face colourless, his lips slightly parted, hardly seeming to breathe.

'Catatonia if I ever saw it,' Dr Norris said, when he arrived. He rolled Angsteed over on to his back. Angsteed lay awkwardly in the new position, unmoving.

'What happened to him?' Rose-Jean asked.

'Can't say yet. We'll have to get him to hospital.'

'Seems a pity,' Alice said. 'Must be something two women could do here with an absolutely helpless man. I'm sure we'd think of something.'

Three Interviews

Interview A. Mrs Rose-Jean Dempson

INTERVIEWER. Mrs Dempson, Andrew Angsteed has now been in a condition of schizophrenic withdrawal for forty-one days. On occasions, he shows some awareness of his surroundings, but he will not communicate. We hope by talking to some people who know him well that we may be able to help him. Did you at any time hear him say anything which led you to suspect that he was suffering from mental stress?

ROSE-JEAN. Why, no, he was perfectly fine, I mean he was so intellectual that I doubt if I – well, he could be violent, I suppose. But what's violent? It's a violent world, isn't it?

INTERVIEWER. In what way was he violent? Did he hit you?

ROSE-JEAN. Hit me? What makes you say that? I don't give anyone cause to hit me. Besides, Andy was pretty gentle, I guess. Too gentle, really; he was sort of withdrawn, now I come to think of it – not in any nasty way, of course. But I wouldn't call him violent. He ran his automobile into a gatepost, that I do know. Broke the headlights on the driver's side.

INTERVIEWER. Was that an accident?

ROSE-JEAN. No, that was deliberate! (*Laughs*) You see, he was drunk that night. We were driving out of a night club and he thought he saw my husband – did I tell you I was married? My husband and I live apart. I told Andy it wasn't Allan. I said, "Allan's in Detroit, you loon!" but he was drunk, and he drove the car at the man. The man jumped clear and Andy ran into the gatepost. Just an accident, of course.

INTERVIEWER. Was Angsteed often drunk?

ROSE-JEAN. Not to my knowledge. He was too wrapped up in the dream project. I don't drink at all myself. He was on the verge of a breakthrough when – when *this* happened. He was on the verge of a breakthrough that was about to change the world, so he said.

INTERVIEWER. Do you know what he imagined this breakthrough to be?

ROSE-JEAN. It was going to be something entirely new. I think he said he wanted to alter the essence of things. Could a new thing alter the essence of things? I seem to remember someone telling me that human life was cyclic. (*Pause*) Anyhow, about this breakdown, this *breakthrough*, I mean, of Andy's, he had some new idea about timing people's dreams in relation to their circadian mechanisms. That was somehow going to show that we have all sorts of different times going on in our heads at once. I forget the details, but that was it in general.

INTERVIEWER. Did you regard this as a feasible idea?

ROSE-JEAN. I used to contribute my dreams. I was one of his guinea-pigs. That was how we met, really.

INTERVIEWER. Did you believe in Andrew's theories or did you think they might be illusions?

ROSE-JEAN. Oh, he didn't know that himself. He was just working along a scientific hypothesis. I guess a lot of things sound nutty before they're proved, don't they? Like people didn't used to believe in acupuncture, except for the Chinese, I mean, until modern science showed how it all worked. But Andy's ideas weren't way out to me. I went to Europe for vacation once, and got most terrible jet lag, so I know there are different times in the body. Maybe Andy found a time he liked best and settled for that. Maybe we shouldn't disturb him.

INTERVIEWER. You think he is happy as he is?

ROSE-JEAN. Golly, who's ever happy? I just meant – well, I don't know what I meant. I mean, maybe Andy isn't sick – maybe he made his breakthrough. You people at the mental hospital ought to see how his brain-waves register. But just don't fool around with him. I'd say – I know you don't want my advice – but I'd say let him be as he is. He could be happy, who knows, properly looked after. Gosh, *I'm* happy, don't think I'm not, but – well, it's nice to be looked after, isn't it?

Interview B. Miss Alice Butley

INTERVIEWER. It's good of you to see me in your lunch hour, Miss Butley.

ALICE. Who wants to hang around this place? What can I tell you about Andrew Angsteed? He's real sick, is he?

INTERVIEWER. We are curious to know why he went into a state of complete withdrawal just when he was excited by new things he was discovering.

ALICE. New's a relative term. As a philosopher, I distrust it. Everyone's hot for the new, the novel. I'll tell you what my old man used to say – I've got a great admiration for my old man, and I don't care who hears me say it – he used to say 'Boffers' (that was his nickname for me, kind of a baby-name), 'Boffers, if it's new, it won't last, and if it's lasted, then it's not new.' Andy wanted to find something new, something to weary people's minds with. I told him, nothing new is going to alter the essence of things.

INTERVIEWER. I believe that Angsteed claimed his discoveries could affect the essence of things.

ALICE. Don't make the mistake he made. Say what you will, the essence of the human experience is cyclic. It's largely a matter of repetition, with every generation suffering the same basic joys and sorrows.

INTERVIEWER. You're not suggesting that Angsteed has suffered from this sort of withdrawal before?

ALICE. How do I know? I haven't known him all that long or all that well.

INTERVIEWER. But you were lovers at one time?

ALICE. Be your age! Does that have to mean I know him well? He was always a closed guy. He never knew me, never took any interest in me as a person. Yet I was prepared to love him – my mother died when I was just a girl, so I was always stock full of love to give to the right person, don't believe otherwise. And we did have a bond in common ... oh well ...

INTERVIEWER. You were going to say?

ALICE. Things sound silly in daylight to strangers that seem important whispered in bed at night. The idea of philosophy is to knock the silliness out of things. But why not say it? Andy had an older sister die when he was eight years old. She drowned in a lake at a summer camp. He always said it marked him for good. He really loved that sister. Still – not quite so much drama in that as losing your dear old Ma, even if she did tan your hide, is there? (*Pause*) I guess we'd all like to withdraw at times – on full pay, of course. Was Andy's trouble sexual or to do with his work? Or both?

INTERVIEWER. We hoped you'd tell us.

ALICE. Well, I don't know. Is that thing switched off? Maybe I shouldn't suggest this, but all this business with dreams, it could have become obsessive with Andy. Who knows, maybe he vanished into the recesses of his own mind. Maybe he's *happy* where he is! (*Laughs*)

INTERVIEWER. Mrs Dempson suggested the same thing.

ALICE. Did she? She's hardly the person to know about such things. A little immature for such speculations, wouldn't you say?

Interview C. The Author

INTERVIEWER. Mr Aldiss, the interviews with Miss Butley and Mrs Dempson didn't get us very far. Don't you feel both ladies could have been more revealing?

AUTHOR. No. I thought they were very revealing about themselves. I agree they produced no astounding revelations about Angsteed, but then that's the way life goes.

INTERVIEWER. This is a story, not life. Do you intend to finish the story without telling the reader what happened to Angsteed? Did he have some sort of personality collapse, or did he actually find his way into a dream world?

AUTHOR. It's a good question. You are asking me, in effect, whether this is a sad story or a happy one. I believe you are also asking me whether it is a science fiction story or not.

INTERVIEWER. I wasn't aware of so doing. Like Miss Butley and Mrs Dempson, you wish to talk about yourself?

AUTHOR. Not at all. Unlike those ladies, I am intensely interested in Angsteed as a person. You see, I know him. He is an actual person, although I have changed a few details to protect the parties involved, as they say. And I have a particular reason for ending the story here and now: because the real Angsteed is still in his state of schizophrenic withdrawal, or however you care to label it. So the resolution has yet to come.

INTERVIEWER. May I say on behalf of the readers that I think it might have been a better story if you had waited till the resolution came?

AUTHOR. Ah, but then the quality of my interest would change and you would get a different story. A science fiction writer is like a journalist in that respect – he gets hooked on something that is still happening. The mystery intrigues him just as much as the solution. However, I have no wish to cheat. Far from it. Let me give you not one but two possible endings, just briefly. Okay?

INTERVIEWER. Go ahead.

AUTHOR. Right, first the sad ending, the non-sf ending.

Eventually, Angsteed is brought out of his withdrawal. He seems not quite as he was before, and is reluctant to return to the university. He is kept on at the mental institution for some while, but shows little interest in the outside world. His prognosis was not favourable. As for the diagnosis, while it was couched in abstruse and precise-sounding terms, it actually revealed little.

Angsteed, it said, had suffered a mental collapse caused primarily by overwork. Rose-Jean had inadvertently brought about the crisis-point. Angsteed wanted her love, while realizing that he and she were nevertheless incompatible.

His 'case history', slowly compiled from various sources, revealed a number of affairs over the years with older women, Alice Butley being his most recent involvement. Rose-Jean, a younger woman, was identified in his mind with his dead sister. The terms 'incest-fixation' and 'guilt association' were bandied about.

INTERVIEWER. And Angsteed's promising line of dream research?

AUTHOR. There was no promising line. The dream research was getting nowhere; Angsteed's fantasies of imminent revolutionary discoveries were to protect himself from knowledge of yet another failure. The unit was closed down shortly after his breakdown and its appropriations reassigned.

INTERVIEWER. There had been other failures in his life?

AUTHOR. The essence of human experience is cyclic, you know.

INTERVIEWER. Do things work out better in the alternative ending?

AUTHOR. Oh, much better. The first story, you see, is just a little downbeat study of character. Whereas the science fiction story, the story with the happy ending, is an upbeat study of ideas. Whereas Angsteed's theories prove, in the first story, to be just a paranoid fixation, in the sf story they are proved to be true.

INTERVIEWER. True?

AUTHOR. Yes, true – part of the external world. A whole range of sf stories operate like that: the screwy ideas, instead of being certifiable, turn out to mirror true reality. The hero is proved right and everyone else is proved wrong, from Aristotle onwards. Paranoia triumphs, logic is defeated. That's one of the reasons why outsiders believe sf to be a load of nonsense. Why did Angsteed so enjoy Rose-Jean's dreams? Because they strengthened his growing conviction that the 'cold sane', as he called them, were deluded and that the mad were the really sane.

INTERVIEWER. Yes, but that was just his interpretation of her dreams.

AUTHOR. That's what I'm trying to say. To my mind, interpretation is everything – and not merely in my story. However, here's how the second version goes.

Angsteed comes out of his withdrawal in a few weeks. He remains quiet and reserved, but is again in control of himself. Since his post remains open for him, he returns to the university.

He is as convinced as ever that he has – no, I'd better phrase this with care – he is aware that his consciousness penetrated into Dream Time. Dream Time is his phrase for it. Dream Time is obviously akin to Jung's Collective Unconscious.

The place he went to was no particular place – not in Rose-Jean's mind, not his own mind, although her dreams gave him the key he needed. He regards that as important: that he was in some impersonal place.

He feels sure that many other people have been there, often maybe in one form or another of madness, where time-displacement is a familiar phenomenon; but those people were unable to recognize where they had been.

'My conception of a dream globe enabled me to navigate, and to control my consciousness, deeper into the Heartland than anyone else had ever been,' he says. 'I return, just as out of madness, as a person reborn. I feel older, wiser, replenished at source, as people do after sleep and dreams.'

'You're a real pioneer, Andy,' says Rose-Jean. 'An astronaut, no less!'

'In a sense I've discovered nothing new,' he says. 'Yet I know that when I come to publish my findings, a slow revolution in human thought will be set in motion, a unifying revolution that will make us revise our ideas about the unity of human life, not only in waking and sleep, in madness and sanity, but one with another. Eventually, everyone will be able to visit the Heartland and replenish themselves.'

'The problem with the human race is that it needs to wake up, not go further asleep,' says Alice. ' "Sing heigh-ho, the wind and the roses, This life damn soon closes!" … '

'It won't be like that, Alice. We will no longer be cut off from our inner beings. It's nearer immortality than death, believe me! Maybe madness and psychosis and neurosis and the rest will fade away in a couple of generations. Why the human race was barred from its own Heartland for a million years, we don't know. Maybe we'll find out now. Maybe it was necessary for growing purposes – like an adolescent's quarrel with his family. Now we're back, back to an entirely new vision of reality. At last we're going to be able to change the essence of things.'

'It sounds marvellous,' says Rose-Jean. She hugs him.

'Sounds too good to be true,' says Alice. She laughs.

She pours them drinks. Martinis for her and Angsteed, a Coke for Rose-Jean.